A Game of Love

"You bested me!" Gideon cried.

"You are smiling," Elizabeth said accusingly. "You did not let me win, did you?"

"In chess? No indeed, madam. There is no 'letting someone win' in chess. You took the game all on your own. If I am smiling, it is to hide my agony at losing."

"Liar," she said, but she did not mean it. "My sister Lorraine likes to play chess." It was only when he looked up once more, a startled light in his eyes, that she realized she had revealed something personal by naming her sister.

Gideon did not say anything. He did not build on the moment, did not push her for an explanation or for more information.

In that very instant when he granted Elizabeth her privacy and asked nothing of her, she knew she loved him.

The Misfit Marquess

Teresa DesJardien

A SIGNET BOOK

SIGNET
Published by New American Library, a division of
Penguin Putnam Inc., 375 Hudson Street,
New York, New York 10014, U.S.A.
Penguin Books Ltd, 27 Wrights Lane,
London W8 5TZ, England
Penguin Books Australia Ltd,
Ringwood, Victoria, Australia
Penguin Books Canada Ltd, 10 Alcorn Avenue,
Toronto, Ontario, Canada M4V 3B2
Penguin Books (N.Z.) Ltd, 182–190 Wairau Road,
Auckland 10, New Zealand

Penguin Books Ltd, Registered Offices:
Harmondsworth, Middlesex, England

First published by Signet,
an imprint of New American Library,
a division of Penguin Putnam Inc.

First Printing, September 1999
10 9 8 7 6 5 4 3 2

 REGISTERED TRADEMARK—MARCA REGISTRADA

Printed in the United States of America

To: Ann, Paul, Meg,
and Don's memory.
Thanks for the years and tears,
babies and birthdays, and for
sharing this munificent last name of ours!

Author's Note

In Regency England there were four classes of "doctors": the barber, the apothecary, the surgeon, and the physician. Most small towns (such as the fictional one of Severn's Well) did not have a university-trained physician available to them. Either the patient would travel to a larger city, or else make do with home remedies or those acquired from the local barber or apothecary. A village would feel fortunate to have a surgeon living among them and offering his services.

While a physician would make minor physical examinations, his real duties consisted mainly of diagnosing and distributing prescribed medicines. The surgeon, however, was the real workhorse of the vocation, being the one to actually cleanse a wound, saw off a limb, or otherwise physically handle the patient.

Please note that the medical man in this story is a surgeon, and does not bear the title of "Doctor." He is properly referred to as "Mr." Clifton.

Chapter 1

I will not cry," Elizabeth told herself fiercely, her voice echoing back from the night-darkened trees that lined the public lane on which she rode. "Since I chose to play the fool, I cannot cry because I have been treated like one."

The truth of her own statement, however, only caused her to blink all the harder, for there was no denying that the situation in which she found herself was directly her own fault.

Her difficulties were too plentiful to be counted on one hand, but they all added up to one enormous reality: she was alone, friendless, penniless, and without a doubt ruined.

Surely there was an inn *somewhere* along this dark, deserted road? Her stomach rumbled with hunger. All she wanted at this particular moment was an inn, with a warm fire on the grate and a hot plate of food, no matter the lateness of the hour. Why had she not fully eaten the supper offered her at nightfall, some eight or nine hours ago? It could be hours yet until she had a chance for a meal. What would an innkeeper make of a demand for food, it now being almost dawn? He would find it most peculiar, almost as peculiar as the sight of a lone woman, lacking any baggage, riding an unsaddled horse astride like a man.

That is, if Elizabeth were to discover that the building that just now loomed ahead was the inn she so fervently hoped it was. She had ridden as far as she could tonight; she simply had to eat, to rest, just for a short spell.

But, no, she realized with a sigh, the building was not an inn or a tavern. As the horse plodded forward, Elizabeth saw that the building was surely too large to be a simple country inn. It must be a manor house for some local gentry, or perhaps a poorhouse with one wing for men and another for women. No welcome there.

However, the place was certainly lit up with a welcoming glow, at least at first glance. A lavish amount of light shone brightly on the oval of grass before the building, especially given the extreme lateness of the hour. Golden light streamed from most of the upstairs windows. In fact, the light was very odd, swaying. . . .

Elizabeth's horse put back its ears and stopped suddenly upon the road. Elizabeth lifted her heels from where they hung inelegantly on either side of the animal and urged her mount forward. The animal whickered and sidled forward, clearly reluctant to continue down the road. Elizabeth might have had more control over the beast had she a saddle, but speed and secrecy had been more important than the proper tack. She had managed to get a bridle on the animal; a saddle had been too much to ask in the still of the night.

Something landed on Elizabeth's nose. From the feathery tickle, the dark color, gray against the predawn sky, from the scent in the breeze that had carried it to her nose, she knew it for what it was: ash.

Comprehension swept through Elizabeth as she realized that the night air was warmer than it ought to be: the house was afire. It was not welcoming lamps that shone from the windows, but darting, devouring flames that filled the sills. She saw that the front door was gone, or standing open, and from the large house's dark mouth billowed a curling, twisting cloud of smoke.

As Elizabeth stared in horror, a woman stumbled out through the doorway, and even from this distance Elizabeth could see where smoke had stained the woman's garments, hands, and face with sooty residue. She heard a horrible screaming sound—but it did not come from the woman, who collapsed mutely just outside the doorway. It came from somewhere inside the building.

Other sounds intruded, horrible sounds: horses' screams; men's shouts; the crash of wooden beams that could no longer bear their load. Most of all, she heard the fire, a terrible whispery sound that belied its hungry, destructive thrust.

Her horse danced nervously beneath her, and for a moment she let the animal retreat. This was too much for Elizabeth to bear. Her own difficulties were too awful, life-altering, all-consuming. These people, one of whom she could see fleeing into the night, this was their problem, not hers. She should ride on, should do all that she could to put distance between her and Mr. Radford Barnes, the man she had escaped from this night. She had her own cares, more than one person should have to bear. She should ride on.

She should—but the woman still lay unconscious, too near the fire that burned inside that darkened doorway. It was but another moment's thought before Elizabeth grimly conceded that she would be truly lost, truly ruined, if she turned her back on someone so patently in need of help.

She urged her reluctant horse forward toward the still woman until the beast simply refused to go any nearer. Elizabeth slid from the horse's back in an unrefined dismount and firmly secured the reins to a tree limb that had grown long enough to stretch over a ditch at the side of the road. A glistening in the ditch revealed itself as fire reflecting off of water. It was too little, though, too tiny a stream to make any difference with the fire. Great barrels of water were needed, and buckets, and men; many men to throw bucket-loads of water at the raging fire. Elizabeth patted the horse's neck, as if the action would somehow work to soothe the wild-eyed creature. The gesture certainly did nothing to calm the knocking of her own knees as she turned and ran toward where the woman lay.

It took only moments to run across the road and the oval of grass to the unconscious woman. The acrid taste of smoke filled Elizabeth's nose and mouth. She tried to breathe shallowly. As she dropped to her knees beside the woman, the poor creature remained limp and unmoving, even when Elizabeth rolled her over to press an ear to the woman's chest. She heard nothing, but then again the fire was roaring higher and crueler, a rumble rather than a whisper now.

Sparks rained down of a sudden from on high, and Elizabeth could smell the fabric of her own cloak where the sparks singed it. With a cry, she batted at her own hair, scattering pins, hoping no sparks smoldered there, and knew she must move away quickly. She took the woman by both arms and dragged her from the doorway, fear lending her the strength to move beyond the hot fingers of heat and flame that radiated from the burning building.

She knelt anew, to listen once more to the woman's lungs. Nothing. Neither did the woman's chest rise and fall. The woman was dressed in naught but a night rail, lacking even shoes or stockings, but still coming through smoke and fire could not fully explain the unkempt nature of her dirty, un-combed hair. Her nostrils were ringed black with soot, and her eyes remained opened and fixed. With a shudder of a sigh, Elizabeth realized the woman, someone obviously arisen from a sickbed or worse, was dead. The woman's last lunge toward escape had been too late to save her.

Elizabeth rose to her feet, gazing about, searching for . . . for what? Someone to report this death to? Someone else to help?

A black horse, presumably broken free from its stable, ran by, but aside from that the only moving thing to be seen was the flames. She was alone.

Elizabeth let the tears flow then, but even as they rolled down her face, she rose to her feet. She was too angry to kneel and wallow in grief. She was too furious with fate, ill luck, and random cruelties to sit and mourn. In the space of one day, her life had become harsh and empty.

"No," she vowed aloud, as she strode purposefully back toward her horse, hot tears tracking down her cheeks. "Not empty," she challenged the soot-filled air. Altered, yes. Frozen perhaps, for now. But not empty.

Patience was all it would take for her to start anew—even if "anew" would be unfortunately fettered by the past.

"Endurance," she told herself, knowing a battle cry even as it crossed her lips. "And no men," she added from between gritted teeth—as if the words needed to be said. Men only brought complications. They must not, could not, be a part of her life. Elizabeth had but two goals now: to rebuild a life for herself, and to assure her sister's happiness. Her sister, Lorraine, was why she had eloped with Radford in the first place. Whatever else happened, Lorraine's happiness must be secured. Elizabeth could not, dare not be involved in any further scandals, especially any that involved a man. She must, in fact, become invisible.

Besides, who would want a woman who had orchestrated her own ruination? Never mind that Radford Barnes had lied to her, had played at love and played Elizabeth for a fool. The bare and awful truth was that Elizabeth had shared a bed with a man not her husband.

No matter that she had believed herself married to Radford. Ruination cared not whom it touched, the blameless being as susceptible as the culpable. There was no compassionate word for "un-virgin"; Elizabeth knew the world would assign her epithets to match those of the villain who had deceived her, no matter her ignorance of her "husband's" true nature.

A fat tear rolled down onto Elizabeth's bodice as she reached to untie her skitterish horse, but she ignored the tear as thoroughly as the world would ignore her protestations of ignorance and deceit. What was done was done, and although her body sought release in tears, weeping could not wash away the stain her reputation now bore. So she cried. She would cry again, she knew, but the tears came from her heart, not her head. Her head had more important worries—such as where her next meal might be coming from.

The horse bucked as Elizabeth worked the knotted leather free, and for a moment she was confused by the animal's increasing excitability, for the fire burned still, but was no more a threat than it had been all along. Then something large loomed next to her, and a sharp, stinging pain presaged a sticky warmth along her jawline.

"Get back!" a man growled near her ear. "I'm taking the horse."

Elizabeth stared up at the face too near her own, belatedly realizing that a man had seized hold of the horse's reins, and that he held the knife that had cut her poised between her face and his own. Its silver length glittered, reflecting the glow of the raging fire behind them. Out of pure instinct she reached up and touched the sting on her jaw, and her hand came away red with blood.

"You cut me," Elizabeth said, hearing the astonishment in

her own voice even as a trickle of warm blood formed a single track down her neck.

"Cut!" the man repeated. "Cut, cut cut!" His voice rose with every repetition. "I'll cut you again. Why'd you take my money? I want my money!"

"I do not have your money," Elizabeth said. She stepped back as far as she could, but she did not release the reins despite her fear of the man's looming presence, of the knife gripped tightly in his hand. She saw now that he was strangely dressed in a faded night rail, a pair of boots, and a long frock coat that had seen better days.

The man waved the knife, staring directly into her eyes. "I said you'd perish in flames, Mitch, you son of a whore! Didn't I? And now you will."

"Mitch?" Elizabeth repeated. Whom was he talking to? Who did he think she was? God help her, the man was surely mad.

His eyes narrowed, and he waved the knife again. "Horse!" he shouted.

Despite her fear, Elizabeth hesitated, keeping her grip on the reins. The horse, even though it did not belong to her, was virtually all she had left. Without it, she would be stranded. She could not just give the animal up.

"The *horse*!" the man screamed, causing both Elizabeth and the horse to start. Belatedly, she released the reins.

"It is yours. Take it," she said, truly alarmed now. She stepped away.

His hand sprang forward, the knife a silver flash in his hand as it came toward her face. Elizabeth cried out, then stepped back and stumbled to her knees, her hands instinctively reaching to catch the man's coat, to break her fall. A sharp pain ran along her forearm, but before she could fully take in that the man had cut her again, a blow to her temple sent her sprawling in the dirt.

She struggled to her elbows and then into a half-sitting position, blinking and shaking her head. Her ears were ringing, and her eyes did not quite want to focus equally.

"You won't lock me in again, I swear by all that's holy!" the man took a step closer to scream at her. Still dazed and a little dizzy, Elizabeth put up her hands in a hopeless gesture meant to shield her from his next attack. But it was a cry of astonished relief she uttered instead, for he turned abruptly away from her.

She tried to rise to her feet, but got no farther than her bruised knees when she saw the man had vaulted onto the horse's bare back. She wished he would just go and leave her in peace to sort through this latest disaster.

He issued the command, "Ha!" to the wild-eyed horse and slapped its withers with the reins. The animal startled forward. In an oddly prolonged moment of comprehension, Elizabeth knew there was no time, no opportunity to avoid being knocked to the ground. The horse whinnied in protest, but no amount of equine grace could avert the sudden collision of woman and beast. All the breath left Elizabeth's body as she was shoved backward, against soil. One shoed hoof made a glancing blow across her brow, and another came down on her foot. She felt something tear and thought it was her slipper, but then the pain hit, and she knew she would see blood and a terrible wound if ever the horse untangled from her and if she were left alive to look. She tried to curl into a ball.

Just as suddenly as it had begun, all at once the horse was free of their entanglement. Elizabeth lay still, listening to the retreating hoofbeats, willing the animal and its rider to leave, to hurt her no more.

When the hoofbeats had been swallowed by the night, Elizabeth moaned and forced herself to roll to her knees. The action assaulted her mangled heel, and some violated muscle in her right shoulder protested with a wrench. Her vision swam, and she was aware of warmth on her forehead—blood, no doubt. She knelt, gasping at the multiple pains, unable to move, unable to resume her former position, until that wave of agony passed, replaced by a less acute torment. She lifted her face from the dust of the road and looked at the smoldering ruins of the building, toward light and heat. She tried to crawl toward it.

But the pain was too much, her shock too deep. Her last conscious thought was that she was falling, although she could not imagine why or how, but then her vision and her mind both went mercifully blank.

Chapter 2

Gideon Whitbury, the fourth Marquess of Greyleigh, stood up from his kneeling position at the side of the prostrate body and announced in a quiet tone, "The woman is dead."

Talbot Wallace, Alderman of the small village of Severn's Well, nodded in sad agreement. "Like the others we've found." He kicked at the grass with one booted foot. "This makes nineteen bodies." His voice, too, was little more than a whisper, out of respect for the dead, and because he was just a little afraid of the man who had awakened him in the predawn hours.

They might as well have waited until clear morning's light, Talbot reflected, for the alarm that the asylum was burning had been raised too late to be of any help. All they could do now was recover bodies and keep the smoldering ruins from leaping back into active flame and setting the surrounding woods afire.

Talbot wondered how it was that Lord Greyleigh had been awake at such a godforsaken hour, to have even spotted the fire . . . but Greyleigh's household was a strange one, and odd hours were only in keeping. The master of Greyleigh did as he pleased, and apparently this night it had pleased him to remain awake and clothed all night long.

Talbot Wallace knew what Mrs. Wallace would say to that, and her with a knowing look: "'Tis the devil who dances at night."

Talbot cleared his throat and shook his head, as though to drive out such superstitious thinking. He scented the air, a grim mix of burnt wood and other things he did not like to think about. "Do you suppose every last one of 'em in the asylum perished?" he asked.

The already grim set to Lord Greyleigh's mouth grew even

more taut, and for a moment a dark shadow crossed his features. "What else is to be expected, given that half the inmates were no doubt strapped or chained to their beds?"

Talbot nodded solemnly. "They found the warder and the two night keepers, they're fairly certain. All three dead."

Lord Greyleigh lifted his gaze to glance around, but if he sought for signs of life amongst the smoldering embers, he sought in vain.

Talbot, too, glanced toward the ruined, still smoking remains of the building, and shuddered. The nearness of dawn did naught to relieve the pall that flame and misfortune had brought to the place, and in fact only lent a ghoulish gray shroud of melancholy. A half-dozen of Lord Greyleigh's servants mixed with as many townsfolk roamed over the property, searching for someone or something to rescue. They searched in silence, with no shouts to summon help or raise hopes.

In half an hour the lanterns carried by the would-be rescuers would not be necessary, for dawn would light the scene, but for now the weave and bob of their light was the only sign of life among the ruins.

Talbot turned back to the body at his feet: it was obvious from her simple homespun night rail and her unkempt hair that she had resided here, had been one of the "lucky" asylum patients who had not been constrained within her room. Poor thing, he thought, to have lived and died in such a place.

"I wonder if there's anyone left alive to tell us the names of these poor souls," he murmured aloud, worrying his lower lip between thumb and forefinger. And who was to pay for the interments—the village council over which Talbot sat would be wanting to know that. There were so many dead, nineteen at least, so many to bury.

Talbot looked to Lord Greyleigh, but declined to ask the most powerful and richest of Severn's Well's inhabitants to donate the funds for a mass funeral. It was not so much that Talbot feared the master of Greyleigh . . . well, truth be told, that *was* it. But unlike others, it was not Lord Greyleigh's physical appearance that troubled Talbot—although Greyleigh was the oddest-looking bird to have ever resided in Greyleigh Manor. The man's hair was so blond it was nearly white, and worn long and often in a queue, in the fashion of twenty and more years past, an odd style for a young man closer to twenty than thirty. At first glance one could be excused for thinking he powdered his hair, which no young buck of fashion did these days, but at second glance one discovered the pale color was all Greyleigh's own. Yet, if that warlock's mane were trimmed away, the man would appear normal enough—except for his eyes.

The man's eyes were penetratingly clear; they were color-less . . . but, no, that wasn't true. In bright summer's light they were seen to be a very pale blue. However, in any other light they were the palest of greys, making the pupil stand out—some said like a black well that swallowed all light. In candle-light, all hint of softer color was gone from the irises, and one felt as if one stared at a kind of silver sheen, a hint of color that made one think of steel just below a layer of water. They were ghostly eyes—there was no better way to describe them. And there was no denying that when Lord Greyleigh leveled his gaze upon a person, it made that person want to look away in discomfort, as if the man held up a looking glass to one's very soul. Others less kind said it was like looking into a bottomless well, one that led straight to Hades, and who could blame them for turning away from such a view?

Yet, despite the townspeople's inclination otherwise, it was not Lord Greyleigh's appearance that took the steel from Talbot Wallace's spine at the thought of asking Greyleigh to pay ex-penses. It was that the last few times Talbot had approached their village's grandest resident, Lord Greyleigh had icily de-nied his simple request. There had been something like frosty rage just underlying the calm tone Lord Greyleigh was usually so adept at maintaining, some boiling pot of emotion barely held in check that Talbot was loathe to disturb further. That rage had been out of all proportion to Talbot's request that Greyleigh cease employing itinerants for completing his pet tasks about the village and his own property.

The request had been hardly unreasonable, given that two murders had occurred this year, and both of them had been sus-pected—if not proven—to have been executed by one of the wanderers whom Lord Greyleigh employed. A hiatus from the constant influx of strangers to their community, that was all the council had wanted—but Greyleigh had coldly replied he would hire whom he liked, and when, and the devil take the council.

No one even dared to say aloud what all of them half feared—that the violence that had come into their little village was not from an outsider at all, but from within their own ranks. No one dared to voice the opinion that Lord Greyleigh, he of the white-blond mane of hair and the ghostly eyes, might have inherited a terrible sickness from his mama. Certainly there was no proof of such a thing—only fear and old rumors and an increasingly stern visage that Greyleigh displayed to the world. That is, when he bothered to be social at all.

And now there was this terrible affair of a fire, and all these bodies to be buried, and records to be found if they hadn't burnt up.

Greyleigh would certainly not lend one penny to rebuild the asylum, that was a certainty. He had long since made it clear that he wished the place closed and abandoned. It was well known that he had detested the structure ever since the tender age of eight or so, when he had visited his own poor deranged mama there. He would be glad, no doubt, to see the few remaining scorched walls torn down and never replaced, even though his mama was dead and buried these two months past.

The asylum burning was a shame, say what you would, for not even a quarter of the patients had been in the "difficult-to-manage" wing. Most of them had been mild enough, certainly harmless even if they needed to be confined to keep them from wandering away.

Truth is, the community would feel the loss of income the asylum had engendered, for there had been jobs to be had there, as warder, as keepers, as stable lads, and groundskeepers. Also, the asylum had provided custom, for the inmates had needed to be fed and clothed, however humbly. A lucky few had family who had called upon them occasionally, and those good people had brought coin to the local inns and taverns and craftspeople. Yes, the loss of the asylum would be felt, in one form or another, by the entire community.

So if Lord Greyleigh opposed the rebuilding of the asylum, could perhaps the place be rebuilt in another function? Not a hospital, with its attendant diseases and death—but a guild-house perhaps. The Needlemakers were said to desire a larger hall for their growing concerns. . . .

"Mr. Wallace." Lord Greyleigh interrupted Talbot's municipal thoughts for the future.

"My lord?" Talbot answered at once, responding to the tone of authority.

Lord Greyleigh indicated the oval of grass upon which they stood. "I said, this is as good a place as any to bring all the bodies, that we might perhaps begin to determine who is who—" he said, only to suddenly go very still.

He did not move, except for his eyes, which cast about in the darkness, searching. Talbot turned to gaze in the same direction, until he saw what caused Greyleigh to make a small, angry sound from between his teeth.

There, through the gloom, was the outline of a man appearing oddly stooped, until Talbot realized that the man stood in a ditch. The man, his face lost to shadows, held an arm pinned between his knees. Obviously a body must lie at his feet in the ditch, only a portion of its arm visible over the grassy edge. The man worked frantically at something—Talbot realized the man struggled to remove a ring from an ungloved hand—but the stranger was not so intent that he forgot to glance suspiciously about.

When he did, Talbot did not know the man but recognized raw panic as it crossed the man's features, especially since the man gave a cry of alarm, dropped the inert hand he held, and turned and ran.

Lord Greyleigh growled again, the sound instantly catapulting Talbot into action, and both men sprang forward in pursuit.

It was too late, however, for the man plunged into the trees that surrounded the asylum property. Talbot thrashed into the woods after the man, as Lord Greyleigh did without evident consideration for his grey silk waistcoat or polished boots—but there was no light. Within five steps into the snagging brush it was impossible to make out any trail or obvious sign of the man's passing. The would-be thief was gone from sight, and within seconds from hearing as well, the sounds of his twig-snapping retreat swallowed by the night.

"He was raiding one of the bodies," Greyleigh declared, his tone incensed despite puffing a bit from his exertions.

"The scoundrel!" Talbot acknowledged with feeling. His own breathing was more labored, but then he did not cut so fine a figure as did Lord Greyleigh.

Both men worked their way free of the woods, brushing at their coats and trousers to remove leaves and debris.

"As soon as it's light, I'll have members of the Watch out after him," Talbot stated.

Lord Greyleigh nodded, even if he did not appear particularly hopeful that any lawmen would actually apprehend the villain. He moved back to the ditch, looking down at the body there. "A woman. We may as well move this body—" he began, but he was interrupted by a moan.

"Good gad," Lord Greyleigh cried, stepping down at once into the muck of the ditch. "This woman. She lives yet."

"She's alive?" Talbot echoed, moving to stare down at a pale white face half covered with a splattered dark pattern that even in the dim light looked ominous. He felt stunned, having given up any hope of finding any of the inmates alive.

Greyleigh pointed at the woman's head. "You take her shoulders, I will take her legs. We must get her out of this gutter."

The words galvanized Talbot into action. He reached down, as did Lord Greyleigh, and with hands under her arms and legs, they awkwardly brought her up from the ditch to gently lay her on the thin grass lane that ran between the dirt of the road and the ditch.

Lord Greyleigh went down on one knee and put a hand to her throat. "I feel a heartbeat, and it is fairly strong. And she is breathing. Wallace, fetch one of those lanterns."

Talbot did as he was told, quickly returning with lantern in hand, its golden glow making no difference in the coloration of the woman's hair, which was as inky a black in the light as it had been in shadow. "She's filthy," Talbot noted, meaning the mud from the ditch, but now also seeing that blood spotted her face, her cloak, her arm, the bodice of her gown. "Is she still bleeding?"

"No. I think the cuts look worse than they are. Look here, these wounds were not had from the fire," Lord Greyleigh pronounced. "See this bruise by her eye? And these cuts were made with some manner of blade, unless I miss my guess."

Greyleigh stood, removing his coat. His look was tight, even harsh, and Talbot thought, as he had more than once before, that this was not a man in whom one would seek to provoke ire. What was my lord thinking? He appeared angry—but, then, he often appeared angry, especially of late. "Hold my coat," he ordered now, giving no hint of what thoughts formed behind his strange, light eyes.

Talbot took the proffered coat, and then watched in some surprise as Lord Greyleigh stooped to take the woman up in his arms. "Put my coat over her, for warmth," Greyleigh instructed, his steady gaze brooking no questions or comments.

"Are you taking her to your home, my lord?" Talbot dared to ask anyway, because it was his duty as senior alderman to see to the well-being of those who resided within the confines of Severn's Well, including the inmates from the asylum as well.

"Of course," Lord Greyleigh replied, his jaw tight.

Talbot started to remind Lord Greyleigh that the council did not wish his lordship to take in any more strays, as people were wont to call the strangers and itinerants who seemed to gravitate to Greyleigh Manor. But the look on Greyleigh's stony visage forced Talbot to choke back the comment.

"Very good, sir. I'll have Mr. Clifton come to the manor immediately, to see to the woman," he said instead, naming the local surgeon.

Greyleigh replied merely with one firm nod, then turned in the direction of his home, calling loudly for a servant to run at once and fetch a horse.

Talbot stood and stared after Lord Greyleigh for a long moment. He watched as Greyleigh seemed to effortlessly carry the woman toward where several servants hurried to assist him. Talbot watched as another servant broke away, no doubt sent after a horse, up the long, graveled lane that inclined to where Greyleigh Manor resided upon a rise overlooking the village.

Greyleigh Manor was a rambling pile of an edifice that might more appropriately be named a castle by those who took a fanciful view of the world. It was built of bricks that had once been red, but now with age had taken on the color of an old bloodstain. Talbot looked to the large manor that Lord Greyleigh called home, and shivered, and wondered if to live in such a place was to be affected by its somber appearance. Certainly it was whispered by more than a few of the locals that Lord Greyleigh was not in his right head.

And there was no denying that Greyleigh's mama had been mad. Besides her time in the asylum, there were plenty of other village tales about the now deceased Lady Greyleigh's bizarre behavior. It would be easy to believe that Greyleigh Manor and its inhabitants were all cursed—even by a modern, moderately educated man like Talbot Wallace.

"God bless you," Talbot whispered toward the woman Lord Greyleigh carried away in his arms, and meant the words literally. Then he hurried to fetch the surgeon, the better to treat the injured woman . . . and by the surgeon's attendance keep her as safe as possible within the walls of Greyleigh Manor.

Pain rippled through Elizabeth, and she tried to stir, only to find she could not move as she wished. Her right arm was pinned against something solid, and her legs were held as though in a vise. She felt a sense of motion, and she was only belatedly able to put all her impressions together and realize she was being carried in a pair of arms, by someone riding a horse.

She opened her eyes, and was for a moment too dizzy to make sense of anything. Then her befuddled sight was caught by the sight of a lock of pale hair. Grandfather? But Grandfather was dead these five years and more.

She blinked, and moaned, and then the face above her own turned downward to glance at her briefly. In that moment she recognized the man carrying her, even though the sight of him was as unexpected as would be Grandpapa. She did not know this man except by sight, having never been introduced to him, but it was impossible not to recognize Lord Greyleigh. It was a strand of his peculiarly light hair, far too long for fashion and escaping from a queue, that had puzzled her.

"A surgeon is coming to see to your injuries," Lord Greyleigh told her, not bothering to look down at her again. His words were clipped, no doubt from the effort of supporting her.

How had she come to be in his arms? Where did they ride to? Was she ill? Fevered? Her foot ached abominably with every stride the horse took.

The pale sunlight disappeared, and Elizabeth opened her eyes to find the newly rising sun had been blocked by a large, looming brick edifice, the imposing façade of a weather-aged manor house.

"What is . . . this place?" she managed to whisper.

Lord Greyleigh glanced down at her again. "Greyleigh Manor."

She tilted her head to glance upward at the man who spoke, amazed that Greyleigh was not part of some dream she had been having, but real and warm and holding her steady between his arms.

"Not *your* house!" she said, the words pathetically small and thin.

"What? Afraid to enter the madman's house? I cannot say I blame you, my dear lady." His voice did not sound annoyed, as she might have expected—if anything, he sounded amused. Darkly amused, no doubt, even if she judged from only half of the rumors attached to his name—rumors that circulated every parlor, even so far away as London.

Even though Lord Greyleigh spent little time in London— preferring his rural estate near Bristol—rumors about him traveled into the City all the same. The kinder gossipmongers called him eccentric, and the less kind dubbed him lunatic.

She wanted to say any other circumstances would suit: a farmer's holding, or the local squire's home might provide her a temporary shelter, perhaps—anyplace other than the home of Lord Greyleigh the madman. She wanted to insist he release her, that she was well enough, that she did not wish to be any bother to him. . . . But the shadows grew darker, and were inviting and far less horrible than reality, and Elizabeth gave in to their gentle summoning, until she knew nothing more of being cradled in Lord Greyleigh's arms.

Chapter 3

Elizabeth's heel ached dully, but in the end it was her inability to flex it that finally dragged her out of an already fitful slumber. She blinked her eyes open, finding the room inadequately lit by a single branch of candles. She was absolutely at a loss to explain how it had become night again, for the last moment she remembered was the faint grey of early morning showing just beyond the shoulder of a crazed man . . . a man who struck her, who presumably took her horse.

Still, it was now clearly night again, as if time had been wound backward. How she could be so sure it was evening, she did not know, but there was a stillness around her that spoke of nighttime.

She was alive, and she was in an unfamiliar, white damask-covered bed with its curtains tied back. Her own bed at home sported neither posts nor white damask. Her next thought was to ponder how she'd come to this bed, one wholly foreign to her, and into a night rail she knew was not her own. She could not imagine how she had come to be here.

The mystery was beyond the cloudy reasoning that seemed to have taken the place of rational thought, and so she allowed her attention to shift entirely to the condition of her right foot. She struggled up to a sitting position, and a flick of the light coverlet revealed a heavy bandage encasing her heel. It was secured by a length of torn linen cloth that looped several times over the bandage and around her ankle.

She knew at once that the damage her foot had suffered was not trivial, although a twinge in her shoulder revealed a less severe injury. There were other parts of her that stung, and then she remembered a horse coming at her. She recalled she had received cuts to her jawline, her arm, and where the horse's hoof had struck her head. She reached to feel for a sticking plaster on her forehead, and was not disappointed.

The clouds in her head dissipated rapidly, as though to keep pace with the return of sharp and painful sensation to her body. Feeling faint, she almost wished she had not looked at her foot, had not reminded herself of her injuries.

"My heel!" she said aloud, hearing the amazement in her own croaky words as she remembered the wound that had left her gasping in the premorning dark.

She was answered by nothing more than a nod, but the nod was enough movement to catch Elizabeth's eye. The hair stood up on her nape, although she had no reason to think why it should, other than the lateness of the hour. Her gaze slowly lifted from her injured foot to the space beyond the bed. Despite knowing someone was there, she was still a little shocked to discover the viewer was Lord Greyleigh, not a maid as one might have supposed. Unmoving and unblinking, he sat in a chair opposite the bed, watching her every movement.

Ah. Yes, she thought. Lord Greyleigh. There had been a horse, other than the one taken from her. . . . Lord Greyleigh's horse. This man had held her as he had ridden. He must have found her, must have brought her here. . . . It all came flooding back at once, and she understood that she had to be within Greyleigh Manor.

Their gazes locked, and the moment grew long. Elizabeth felt slow heat fill her cheeks—not embarrassment, not anger, but something wholly new, outside her previous experience. It was a kind of self-awareness, she thought, or perhaps it was a shared awareness of one another. This was the look that two tigers surely exchanged upon meeting in the jungle, a wary ac-knowledgment of the other's existence, a fiery curiosity only just banked by primal caution.

She shook her head once, as though to cast off such fanciful notions, and the moment was broken. Lord Greyleigh blinked, Elizabeth's flush grew deeper, and she felt social order replace uncivilized stares.

"Why are you in my room?" She spoke in a soft, confused tone, less croaky this time.

"Not your room," he answered, his words coolly polite if not cordial. "The room belongs to me. I am Lord Greyleigh. Your . . . home has been destroyed by fire. We are searching for records, but are afraid they are destroyed. Do you know your name?"

What a curious question. And what did he mean, her home had been destroyed by fire? And why that hesitation when he said the word "home"?

"Come, surely you know your own name," he pressed.

"Elizabeth."

"Your surname, girl. I need your surname."

Elizabeth put her head on one side, as much from vexation as from a curious exhaustion, the latter no doubt owing to having been dosed with laudanum, at least to judge from a spreading headache and queasy sensation that had begun to grow in the pit of her belly.

Despite any lingering fuzziness, however, she realized in a flash that she could not tell him her name. If he had no notion of her identity, better that she remain anonymous. But how not to answer his question?

He sighed, a soft sound that was somehow still ripe with meaning—frustration perhaps. But why frustration? That emotion seemed disproportionate to the circumstances.

He reached with a small show of irritation to the queue that was no longer quite securing his hair, and pulled it free. The pale strands of his hair fell to his shoulders. While she had never talked to this man the few times she had seen him in London, she'd had eyes to see that in a well-lit room his hair was palest spun gold. In this dim candlelight, it was a ghostly white, not too dissimilar from his eyes, dark pupils surrounded by a nearly colorless sheen that made her think of a highly polished silver tray.

What a curious fellow this Lord Greyleigh was, as peculiar to meet in person as she had ever thought he must be. Not for the first time, she wondered why he wore his hair long, so unfashionably. If he had meant the style to be off-putting, he had been correct in that, for it was one of the things about him that had kept Elizabeth from seeking out a mutual acquaintance to introduce them. It was rumored he was mad as a March hare, and his lack of fashion sense certainly did nothing to gainsay the tale. He had no wife to request an improvement in his mode of dress and style. He was rich, and so might be called eccentric, but it was the disparity between his words and his actions that unnerved her and made her think of darker, less kind words to describe this man.

"You have nothing to fear, my girl," he said, almost as if he could read her thoughts. "You have been rescued from the fire. We brought you here to tend to your needs. A surgeon has seen to your heel and your cuts. He tells me the cut to your foot runs very deep, but fortunately does not involve any tendons. Once healed, you should be able to walk normally."

He paused, as if assessing her responses. Whatever he saw, he chose to go on. "What you must understand is this—there is no place for you here, not beyond a day or two it takes to find your people. We must return you to your family. So you must see that I require your surname, and the direction of your people, that I may tell them to come and fetch you home." He spoke slowly, deliberately, as if she were a child.

Again, what a curious choice of words: "There is no place for you here." Had she, in delirium, been asking for employment, for sanctuary?

He rose from the chair, as deliberate in movement as he had been in speech, and she thought perhaps he was at some pains not to startle her. He was tall, taller than most men. That hair, those eyes, that height—he was intimidating despite his cool and level tone.

"Why is there no maid in this room?" she asked, because the lack disturbed her. "Why are we alone together?"

If he had meant to pace, he instead abruptly came to a halt. "I never thought it should prove a difficulty." He scowled. "I am used to sickrooms—to females in sickrooms." His scowl grew deeper, giving him a rather fearsome appearance. "I suppose I should have considered otherwise."

"Indeed."

He stared at her, then gave a very brief, reluctant snort, not a laugh. "My butler was not sure you came from the asylum." He pointed at her. "Your clothes . . . your soft hands. Were you newly arrived there?"

She understood everything all at once. *Asylum. Fire.* The building that had burned had indeed been no inn, but instead an asylum. To judge by the curious questions he asked and the guarded looks he threw her way, it had been an asylum for the impaired and deranged rather than the merely lame or ill. He thought she was one of its inhabitants, that she was so lost to reality or so deluded that she could not even recall her own name.

He had given her a perfect cloak, a perfect way to hide her name from him, from all of Society. That was all she had left, the ability to keep her name out of the news sheets, to keep from tainting her family's hopes for the future any further. All she need do was tell a lie, a very small lie—that she could not recall her surname—and she could keep her sister's dream of happiness alive. She could even tell herself it was a noble lie, used toward a righteous purpose . . . no matter that it stuck in her throat and would not be uttered.

He stared at her, as though willing her to speak.

She tried. She shaped her lips to the task, but this lie did not feel so small at all, but more like a sin, a serious sin, to tell a lie to a man who had rescued her from . . . from what?

"Where did you find me? Was I unconscious?" she asked instead.

"In a ditch. Outside the asylum. And, yes, you were unconscious. Someone was trying to steal your ring—the one on your left hand," he said pointedly.

Elizabeth gasped, and she clutched her hands together, her gaze fixed on the ring. It was a signet ring, with a B carved into its flat gold surface. Radford had worn it, until he had given it to her at their supposed wedding ceremony.

"Are you married?" he asked.

"No!" she cried, for it was only the truth. She had thought the ceremony with Radford Barnes was a real one, but knew to her everlasting regret now it had not been real at all. That the marriage had been false was at the very heart of her difficulties.

"Why is the band on your left-hand ring finger then?" He took a step toward her, putting out his palm, silently demanding she place her hand in his.

She held her hands clutched together, meeting his stoic gaze, refusing his silent order. "I wanted to appear as though I were married," she said, because that also was the truth. A married woman had a few protections that an unmarried woman did not, and she had meant to pass herself off as one. She still meant to, after a fashion, for her true intent was to pretend to be a widow.

"Why?" He reached out and took her hand, not forcibly, but with a strength of purpose it would have been churlish, if not impossible, to resist. He examined the ring, and then her face. "Tell me why, Elizabeth B."

"Because," she took a deep breath, then plunged straight into the thickest lie she'd ever told—"because married women get to wear a veil, and a pretty dress, and I could dance and dance and dance at my wedding breakfast. I like to dance. Do you like to dance?" She had made her voice go singsongy, and hoped her expression was at least lax if not downright childish.

For a moment she thought she had gone too far, had performed too poorly. Something flamed in the back of his eyes, and he quickly released her hand, as though in disgust. "Tell me straight," he said in clipped tones, "do you know your surname or not?"

A tear formed on the lashes of her left eye, and although she had not planned it, although it had been a spontaneous reaction to his tone and to her playacting and to the horror of the past four-and-twenty hours, she saw that the little tear instantly took all the fire out of his gaze. The transformation was almost as disconcerting as his appearance.

"Ah well," he said, half reaching for her for a moment, perhaps to cup her chin, but then letting his hand fall idly to his side. "Well then, Miss Elizabeth B., it is no matter if you cannot recall your last name. There are times I wish I could not recall my own. We shall find a way to let your family know of your change in circumstances. Until then, rest easy."

He said no more, turning with an abruptness he had not hitherto shown, and left the room. However, when he closed the door, it was with the gentlest of clicks.

Elizabeth became aware that her bosom rose and fell rapidly, as though she had been running. She took several deep breaths to steady herself, and considered that Lord Greyleigh was a man of conflicts, of unexpected pairings of words and actions. Lord Greyleigh was, with no gloss upon it, a peculiar man.

It was easy to believe him mad, easy to know she had to leave his house as soon as possible. There was no record of her for him to find, of course, not in the smoldering remains of the asylum. She could not let him know her family's name, could not involve them in the scandalous ruin of her "marriage." She would have to find another way, some manner of excuse to leave on her own.

The people of this community would be reluctant to allow a supposed madwoman to roam the countryside, of course, even if Elizabeth still had her stolen horse to ride away on. Not that she could ride with her foot so badly injured anyway, even if she had the gall to steal one of Lord Greyleigh's horses.

How to leave here was a problem, a huge problem. Admittedly, too big a problem for a head made weary by the effects of laudanum. She would have to sleep first, to presume on her strange host's hospitality a while longer. There was naught else for it.

Even as she lay back and allowed the drug's shadows to reclaim her, she found it odd that she could so easily give in to slumber, here in a madman's home. But there was something about Greyleigh's demeanor that had, oddly, reassured her. He was not a violent man, she thought, secure in that groundless conclusion. It was an instinct . . . not that she ought to trust her instinct when it came to men. Radford had proven that. But Lord Greyleigh had made it clear he wanted her gone . . . and there was reassurance in that realization, because it meant they both wanted exactly the same thing.

That was not logical . . . but it was growing difficult to care about logic, let alone escape this place. . . . Elizabeth let dreams claim her once more.

Gideon stepped back from the closed door, and let his chin fall to his chest as he cast the weariest of all sighs. He had fought his own nature too long, that was the problem.

Along comes trouble and, sure enough, he had not remembered his own vow, very recently pledged, on how to deal in the future with all strangers, with outcasts, with the unfortunate.

His heart was gone, eaten away. It was all used up. It did not exist within him any longer. He had nothing, no part left of it to give away, not even in simple courtesy.

And yet . . . and yet he had acted, just as he always had. Out of habit—long, weary habit, and nothing more—he told himself this, and he believed it as truth.

It was too late to change his very nature—he sensed that, understood that. But the only alternative was never to change at all, and that was impossible in this world. Change came regardless. It did not matter that Gideon was hollow; outwardly he must continue to make a good show of it. What else was there? Nothing. Weary, terrible nothingness. People said Gideon was mad—and was not this nothingness, this hollow feeling, the very essence of madness? If he could believe it of himself, how could he blame anyone else, even his brothers, for suspecting him of having inherited his mother's lunacy?

Life went on, however, whether he was mad or not, he thought with a low, dark, humorless chuckle. He turned from the door, blindly seeking the stairs, to go down to the comforting isolation of his library.

He must rid himself of the chains he had placed on his own wrists, he reminded himself as he moved through dark corridors. He must start somewhere, sometime—and so he would start with this peculiar creature who had worn a silk gown in her asylum cell, who suddenly became childlike and claimed she wished to dance at an imaginary wedding.

He would send her away as soon as possible, even if he had to pay another asylum to accept her.

At the thought, his hands formed fists and a touch of guilt lashed him. But guilt was an old, familiar companion, and he would not be swayed by its whispers and innuendoes. His course was clear. The others who had survived the fire, three of them, would be easy, for they had all supplied names and directions. He would very soon rid this house of their tainting presence. However, the wounded woman-child just beyond this door would be harder to cast out—but she most certainly would be cast out.

Madness or the devil might as well take him now if he did not do this thing, did not make a change. But he *would* make it so. It was his due. It was the only choice left for him to make. He would not care a whit for the woman's future—and thereby perhaps, just perhaps, preserve whatever he had that could be called sanity.

Chapter 4

When next Elizabeth roused, a glance at an ormolu clock she spied on the mantel over the fireplace told her twelve hours had passed since she had awakened last. It had been the heart of the night then. Now birds sang outside a partially open window with the particular gusto they reserved for mornings; a maid had presumably opened the window to let in some air for the good of the "patient." Logic had returned, for Elizabeth found that her now unmuddled mind was able to discern that, from the time of the attack, she had slept through two dawns.

Imagine, more than a whole day abed, in a virtual stranger's home. Well, if there was any good to be had from a day lost, perhaps it was that Radford Barnes could not approach Elizabeth, not here in a private home. That was something for which to be grateful.

That is, if he had ever come after her at all. Perhaps he was just as happy to let her go. He could always buy another horse to match the pair she had broken by taking one of his team. More important, and harder to believe, perhaps he had not realized that she yet wore his ring, that distinctive signet ring of his.

Elizabeth sat up, aware the twinge in her shoulder was nearly gone, assuring her the injury had been but a bruise. Not so her heel—she was well aware of the throbbing there.

The effort of sitting up had been a major one, leaving her feeling shaky. She was not sure she had the strength to do what she must, which was to sketch out her immediate future. Still, strength or no, she *must* plan, and the sooner the better.

First, of course, she must learn the extent of her injuries, for that would determine how quickly she might be up and about.

Second, she must find new lodgings. And there was the rub, for she had absolutely no destination in mind.

Well then, best to approach the problem from a different direction: where must she *not* go? Not to Papa's, of course, nor any other place in London. There were too many knowing eyes in London. The same must be said of Bath, and Brighton, and Bristol. In fact, no large city would do at all. It must be a reclusive place, a place where no one could know Miss Elizabeth Hatton by sight.

Very well then. A remote location would be easy enough to come by. Any place would do so long as it was neither a spa nor any kind of fashionable place where Society might gather. The real problem, of course, was how to get there. Radford's horse was long since gone, and Elizabeth had no coin by which to hire a coach or ride the Mails. . . . At the thought of coins, her hand flew down to her waist, quickly discovering that the purse she had tied to her shift was missing.

Her shift—where was it? It flashed through her mind to wonder who had removed her garments and replaced them with this night rail, but her modesty held a decided second place to her financial alarm.

"No!" she cried aloud, for the only thing that stood between her and utter poverty was the contents of that purse. The little leather drawstring bag held her share of her deceased mother's jewels—not a lavish inheritance by any means, but still fine enough to be bartered for a sum of ready cash. Elizabeth thought perhaps the value of the pieces might draw as much as a hundred pounds, and a hundred pounds was enough for rent, food, coal, and the other necessities of life in some remote village. It could last as long as six months, or perhaps even a year if she was very prudent and rather lucky.

Although, she counseled herself bitterly, it would be best not to rely on luck—not if the recent past was anything by which to judge.

She swung her legs over the side of the bed, grunting in pain and ignoring the shooting spots of light that flared before her eyes. She had to get up and search the room, the drawers and cupboards. She had to find the purse, no matter if she injured her heel further. She stood, balancing precariously on her unin-jured foot.

Next to the bed stood a table topped by a bowl, a ewer filled with water, and a towel neatly folded to one side. The table had two drawers. It was just close enough so that Elizabeth was able to lean forward, balancing on the one foot, and grasp the pull on the nearest drawer. It slid open, revealing a set of silver-backed combs, brushes, and a hand-held looking glass. Eliza-beth did not bother to shut the drawer, but with a groan levered herself fully upright. She took a small hop that jarred her in-jured heel so much that her teeth itched and her eyes watered, but she just managed to reach the other pull. The drawer slid open, and Elizabeth almost fell to the floor in a mix of relief and exhaustion, for her leather purse lay within.

She pulled the drawer out farther and stretched her fingers, and managed to snag the purse before she sagged back against the bed, half on and half off, but feeling triumphant nonethe-less. The weight of the purse felt right, and a quick inspection proved the original contents remained.

A sense of cheer flooded through her, followed immediately by a doubling of the pain in her foot. That which could be ig-nored when she was desperate now became painfully insistent the moment her greatest fear—abject poverty—was relieved. She slumped back, practically prone, but could not find enough purchase with one foot to lever herself back atop the rather tall bed.

"Great heavens," she said aloud in disgust and not some little pain. "I am quite stuck where I am!"

There was nothing for it. She was going to have to hop one-legged around the bed to where the bellpull dangled, to sum-mon assistance. The very idea made her brow break out in beads of perspiration.

Before she could hop one step, however, there was a knock at the chamber door. "Come in," Elizabeth called in relief.

A youthful maid poked her mob-capped head around the door, peering within. Elizabeth had just enough time to note that the girl sported a black eyepatch over her right eye, before the maid turned away to murmur something to someone on the other side of the door.

The door was thrust open, and the maid stepped in, admitting Lord Greyleigh.

Elizabeth felt a dark flush fill her cheeks, to be caught out of bed so, with naught but a night rail on, and by none other than the master of the house.

He stopped short, not quite staring but looking directly at her all the same. He carried a sheet of paper, a quill, and an inkpot.

"You should not be out of bed," he said in a level, serene voice, the type used in the presence of simpletons. Although his tone was undoubtedly appropriate in his mind, it was inordinately annoying to Elizabeth all the same. But this was no time to object to being patronized, because she must remain an unnamed stranger, and the only way to do that was to play the idiot. She had chosen this path, and it was a choice that still made the best sense for her future—and for Lorraine and Papa's future as well.

She offered Lord Greyleigh a wobbly, one-footed curtsy. "Have you come to dance at my wedding?" she said, wondering if she looked as guileless as she tried to sound.

"It is time to be abed, not dancing time," he said as evenly as before. He turned to the maid, handing her the items he'd brought. Without ado, he took the ten steps to cross to Elizabeth's side, scooped her up in his arms, and deposited her in a half-reclining position on the bed. Her heel protested the movement with sharp twinges, and a small moan escaped her lips. Lord Greyleigh seemed to take little notice, however. His hands were unhurried yet efficient as they pulled the hem of her night rail down around her ankles, adjusted the coverlet over her length, and tucked the cover's edges around her. If he noticed that Elizabeth tightly clutched a purse in her hand, and that it disappeared beneath the covers immediately once she was atop the bed again, his expression did not show it.

"Do you think we should tie her down to the bed, to keep her—" the maid began.

"No," Lord Greyleigh said calmly, but there was such steel underlying the word that the little maid lowered her chin as if she had been disciplined.

Apparently Lord Greyleigh saw no reason to offer comfort, however, for he took the writing implements from her and then waved her away. The maid bobbed a curtsy, gave a quick glance back from her one good eye, and when she quit the room, she left the door wide open.

"Now then," Lord Greyleigh said, snagging a chair with his foot. He dragged it in awkward jerks away from where some-one had placed it before the fireplace, and when he was satis-fied it was near enough to the bed, sat. "I will write. You will talk. We will find out something about you, and thereby be able to find your family. Or guardian, or whoever sent you to the asylum."

He uncorked the inkpot and reached to place it on the nearby washing table, only to hesitate in mid-motion to stare at the half-open drawers. "You have been snooping," he said seem-ingly without censure, even as he slid the two drawers closed.

He obviously did not expect a response, for he paused only long enough to inspect the tip of the quill, and then he turned his face to meet hers once more. "Do you know where you were born?"

"No."

He did not sigh or shake his head, but there was exasperation in the set of his shoulders.

"Do you know why you were sent to the asylum?"

It would be foolish to refuse all knowledge. "For my nerves," Elizabeth said. She left the purse under the covers, drawing out her hands to fold them atop the white damask. It was easier to look at her hands as she told lies than to look this man in the face. And she probably ought to be ranting, or chattering, or in-appropriately ebullient. She ought to be putting on a show . . . but she was no actress. Such foolishness would soon pale. Bet-ter to be silent and act moody, whenever possible . . . not unlike her host.

"Why do you wear your hair long?" she asked of a sudden. There, that was a peculiar thing to blurt out. Elizabeth thought it fit the moment, but, too, she asked in part because she truly wished to know.

"When you were found, outside the asylum, you were wear-ing a fine silk gown. Why?" he countered.

He was not one to be easily led off the scent, she saw that now, if she had not gathered as much before.

"Because 'tis my wedding day," Elizabeth replied calmly.

"Ah. So you have said before."

She frowned, trying to remember if she had said anything contradictory, anything that might make him think she was fabricating her replies. She couldn't think of anything, but the pain and medication of yesterday might have erased memory of prior claims. But any such contradictions might serve to make her appear all the more unsound of mind anyway. She parted her lips to answer him, but he spoke before she could.

"Never mind," he said, and despite his perpetual cool politeness she got the feeling her frown had somehow chipped away at his patience. "I wear my hair long," he said in the resolute tone she was coming to know too well, "because I have not had a valet in six months, and I have not trusted anyone else to do the task properly."

"Why have you not had a valet?"

"We are speaking of your concerns now, Miss B, not myself."

"Did you kill your previous valet?" There, he would think her truly mad now. It didn't signify that she could half-believe in her own ghastly question; it was easy to believe violence swirled through this oversized house with its brick walls stained the color of blood.

"No," he answered her simply. She expected him to sigh, but instead he merely reached to dip the quill's tip in the ink. The simple reply ought to have been reassuring, but the blank, cold manner in which he had responded only served to chase a chill down her spine. "He left my employ over a dispute, that is all."

"What manner of dispute?"

"It does not matter. Now, tell me, Miss B—" Now he did sigh. "'Miss B' does not suit," he said. "Would you object to being called simply Elizabeth?"

She shook her head no. It made sense and was certainly less awkward, even if there was an unwarranted intimacy in the use of her Christian name.

He nodded his approval, then dipped the drying tip of the quill again in the ink. "Do you recall where you last lived before the asylum?"

Elizabeth hesitated one long moment, in which she decided

misdirection was the quickest way to satisfy him for the time being and to end these questioning sessions. "Nottingham."

His gaze narrowed. "So far as that?"

"I remember . . ." She squinted her eyes and tried to look as though her memory were being vexed. "We lived on a street that was not very pretty. It had a big oak tree out front, though. We picnicked in Sherwood Forest. I wanted to live there, where it was pretty, but Papa said no."

He leaned forward, as though in interest. "And what is Papa's name?"

"Papa?" Ah, she had almost lied herself into a tangle! She had disobeyed her own rule, to be as silent as she could—and the lies were beginning to grate in her own ears. "Why, 'Papa,' of course."

"I meant his surname, or his title. I'm sure you've heard servants call him something."

"Servants?"

He compressed his lips. "Well, perhaps you did not have any, but to judge by the softness of your hands, I have difficulty believing that."

"Papa's name was Papa," Elizabeth repeated with a toss of her head. She added a pout, a childlike one she hoped.

"Humph." Lord Greyleigh sat back again. "Do you recall what any doctors have said about your condition? Why your nerves brought you to Severn's Well?"

"I came because there was nowhere else to go," Elizabeth said, and it was easy to sound sad because in this regard she spoke the truth. "I could not be with my family anymore."

His gaze met hers squarely, and to her surprise she saw a muscle jump in his cheek, and she thought he must be angered. What had she said? Did he suspect her of dissimulating the truth?

"Were you violent?"

"Oh, no," she said at once, without thinking, but then she was glad she had said it for it was not in her nature to act violently, not even to keep her secret.

Whatever his thoughts, he did not share them. Instead he stood, and quickly gathered up his writing tools. "I shall write to the mayor of Nottingham at once. Someone is bound to recognize a description of you, especially coupled with the name Elizabeth B. I will send one of my own servants on horseback, so we should hear in as soon as a week or perhaps a fortnight." He spoke brusquely, and his gaze did not meet hers anymore. He turned to leave.

"Lord Greyleigh." Her call stopped him at the door. He turned back to face her, and she thought he did so with reluctance. "What dispute did you have with your valet?"

The look he cast her was enough to set her cheeks to flaming and to raise the hairs on her nape. It was a darkly sardonic look, one that transformed his face by removing all coolness and replacing cold logic with something warmer but far more disturbing. "If you must know, Elizabeth, he left because he claimed there was a ghost living here at Greyleigh Hall."

He did not persist with more of the tale, but merely stared at her, as though daring her to goad him into further explanation. It was impossible to know if he wished it of her or not, but he waited, and the hairs on her nape rose once more.

"I do not believe in ghosts," she said, lifting her chin in a strangely defiant fashion.

"Truly? Not what I would have expected from someone who suffers from nerves." Underneath that now restored cool politeness, was he laughing at her?

"Nerves and sense are two different things," she pointed out.

"So I've been told before," he said. "By my valet, in fact."

Now he grinned, and Elizabeth felt both rebuffed and drawn at the same time, for his grin was not kind, but devastatingly attractive.

"You fought with your valet, because he believed in a ghost and you did not?" she said, as if the skeptical words would make her feel more bold, less troubled by this man's disturbing and yet still oddly engaging smile.

"We fought because I insisted he not mention ghosts in front of the other servants, but he could not seem to help himself. He was alarming everyone, especially the chambermaids."

"So you think he did not actually see anything ghostly?"

"I did not wish him to speak of such things, Elizabeth, but not because I did not believe in the ghost myself. In fact," Lord Greyleigh said calmly, "I do believe some manner of creature has been haunting this house for the better part of the last four or five months."

So saying, he turned and left the room, leaving Elizabeth to frown at the closed door even as a shiver coursed up her spine.

Chapter 5

Unfortunately, after a day of sleep, Elizabeth was not the least bit drowsy. She sat alone in the bed, aching all over despite the warm touch of the morning sunlight. Only slowly did it occur to her that events had been so all-consuming that she'd given no thought to being grateful she was alive. And she had failed to thank her host for saving her from the ditch and the thief.

The ditch. She remembered a sensation of falling, and that must have been when she'd tried to crawl away from her pain. She recalled the narrowing black tunnels that had formed before her eyes, the pain she had tried to escape—she had surely put herself in that ditch when she had crawled blindly forward.

And who had first found her there and been trying to steal her ring? The obvious answer was Radford. She must be sure to ask Lord Greyleigh if the thief had been finely dressed, a dandy even, and then she would know for a certainty that it had not been some mere common cutpurse.

Radford. Did he think so little of her that he would leave her for dead in a ditch? If the would-be thief had been Radford, he could have taken the ring and at least called for help. While she had lain there unconscious, it would have been simple to see that she was cared for. He could have brought attention to her condition, and could have denied knowing anything about her, at least until he'd seen to it that she did not bleed to death. Instead, all he had done was to attempt to take back his ring, a distinctive ring that he'd said had been given to him by his father. Of course, even that might have been a lie. Unfortunately for her, were the thief Radford, he had left her unconscious and bleeding at the side of the road.

Elizabeth covered her face with her hands and gave a body-rattling shudder in place of tears. She would not cry. She had wept all the tears she ever would because of Radford Barnes, and there was no point in sobbing over her own folly.

It was time to take stock of her situation, as it stood this day.

She knew the cut on her heel was deep, which would make travel difficult. The thought of a carriage bumping and jolting over the public roads and what it would do to a bandaged foot made Elizabeth feel ill. But nothing else about her person would prevent travel, even if her wrenched shoulder and various cuts and bruises would make for an uncomfortable journey.

But where to go? A small, secluded village—but which? Every place that came to mind was wrong. She knew people in Chichester, and Tilbury, and Marlboro.

She would need a map to find a place in a far county she had heard little of, and whose populace presumably had heard nothing of her or any of the Hattons of London. Surely Lord Greyleigh would have a map or two in his library? Or did he even have a library? Did she dare ask a maid to bring a map to her, provided Greyleigh had one?

For that matter, she could start out upon the road without direction and simply find her way as she went. She could stop when she came to a place she'd never heard of, traveling by Post perhaps.

And how to pay her fare? There was that worry again. Did Severn's Well—that was presumably the name of this village, for Lord Greyleigh had called the asylum by that name—did it have a shop where jewelry might be pawned? How would she get to it? Leaning on a crutch? Would Greyleigh obtain a crutch or perhaps canes for her, if she asked?

He might, if she went to him and told him the truth and stopped pretending to be a scatterwit. But in telling the truth she would have to reveal all—and that only brought Elizabeth back to the realization that she could not protect her sister, Lorraine, if her folly became public fodder for the gossipmongers.

Lorraine deserved better.

Lorraine and Papa—and even Papa's new wife, Francine. Francine might be all that put one in mind of the epithet "shrew," but that did not mean she deserved to be dragged down by coarse gossip, especially not when anything that touched Francine touched them all.

But it was really Lorraine's happiness that had prompted Elizabeth to flee her home, to agree to elope with Radford Barnes even though Elizabeth had known him but two weeks.

Two weeks! Elizabeth shook her head at the shortage of time, at the madcap pace she had agreed to. She had allowed herself to be persuaded that all would be well, even though a moment's clear thinking would have shown that such haste was far beyond unseemly. But she had not wanted to think clearly; she had wanted to flee from shrewish Francine, who was so unlike the gentle, quiet woman Mama had been. And Elizabeth had wanted to clear the way for Lorraine.

Would Lorraine's marriage go forward? The betrothal had all but been announced—but sweet, soft-spoken Lorraine could be persuaded to cry off if others felt the marriage unseemly, if enough pressure was applied.

Her beau, the Honorable Broderick Mainworthy, one day to inherit the title of viscount from his father, was clearly smitten with Lorraine, but her advanced age of five-and-twenty had made his family look askance at the heir's choice. Lorraine's lack of fortune had also worked against her. That was the final reason Elizabeth had allowed herself to be persuaded to elope, because then her half of the dowry allotments would go to Lorraine. Papa could hardly be expected to support a vulgar elopement by awarding any income to the man who had carried his daughter away in the night. Everyone knew it took at least four days to reach Gretna Green—and everyone knew a girl's reputation was gone the minute a carriage rolled out of her yard with that location in mind.

That was why Elizabeth had written in her parting note that she understood her share would not be forthcoming and must go to Lorraine, and why she had surrendered all chance of a dowry except for the few jewels she carried with her. Broderick Mainworthy's family would be pleased to learn Lorraine's portion had doubled. It was still no great sum, but any additional honey would only serve to sweeten the pot, surely?

Of course, giving her dowry portion to Lorraine had made

perfect sense when Elizabeth had thought she was marrying a wealthy man. She had been mistaken on more than one account.

Eloping with Radford had been a gamble, of course. A foolish one, Elizabeth saw that now. But it had all seemed so logical, so neat and tidy, at the time.

And unless Elizabeth stayed hidden, discreetly missing—so that some taradiddle about her going to visit an aunt or godmother or cousin could be got about, as she had instructed in her note—it would all be for naught. She could not let that happen. She had to be invisible. She had to smother any hints of scandal.

That was that, then, Elizabeth thought. Her path was clear: she must play the part of addled inmate until such time as she was able to exchange her bits of jewelry for money to hire a carriage to carry her anonymously away. She must do all she could to become mobile once more, and if possible consult a map for the sake of finding an out-of-the-way hamlet in which to pass the next few months, or however long it was before Lorraine was safely married.

Elizabeth frowned, not liking the duplicitous slant of her plans, but there was nothing for it.

Her frown deepened, for it occurred to her that it was odd that Lord Greyleigh had not mentioned her small purse filled with jewelry. Surely it had been reported to him that she had it. Someone had placed the purse in the drawer. He would not be unjustified in thinking she had stolen the pieces, but perhaps he had already seen their worth was not great, and had dismissed them as of no consequence regardless of why she had them.

A sharp knock at the chamber door caused her to startle and flush guiltily. It was one thing to be a liar, but another to feel at ease with the charade. "Come in," she called, her voice not quite even.

The maid with the eyepatch curtsied her way in and announced, "Mister Clifton to see you, miss."

The surgeon, a heavyset man somewhere in his fifth decade and with kind eyes, entered and bowed at the waist. "I see my patient is awake at last."

"You must be the one who bandaged my heel," Elizabeth said, resettling on the bed in a more upright position. She flushed scarlet again, realizing she had forgot to seem vague or disjointed. This was a rocky path she had chosen, this playacting.

"I am." The surgeon nodded, crossing to the bedside, his black bag in hand. "A wicked cut that was. I would like to see if there is seepage, if I may?"

Elizabeth surrendered her foot, and grimaced when he said the bandage must come off and be replaced.

"Can it be left off altogether?" she asked, trying once again for a singsongy, rather childlike tone. "Please?"

"No, indeed not, my girl! This wound is very deep. Do you understand me? The bandage serves as much to hold the sides of the wound together as it does to stop any bleeding. You must have it on for several weeks, or else the damage will only worsen." He stared into her eyes, as if looking for comprehension.

What could she say, or do? This was unbearable, this role playing. Better to retreat into silence . . . indeed, had she not heard of people so disturbed that they never spoke again? Better silence than lies, for silence could not trip her up.

She pursed her lips, and looked away.

The surgeon clucked his tongue, then proceeded to bandage her wound. When he was done, he took her chin in his hand and turned her face up to where sunlight could illuminate it. He stared into her eyes, then asked to see her tongue, which she obligingly thrust out for his inspection. He clucked his tongue again, and met her gaze squarely.

"I am going to see that Lord Greyleigh understands you are not to travel soon, not even if your family should be quickly discovered. It would do this wound great damage. We will have to see what level of putrefaction occurs. Although I do not favor leeches in all circumstances, this might also be required. If not properly cared for and left to mend, this wound might even affect your ability to walk with this foot later. Do you understand me?"

She must have gone pale, for he nodded, and said, "I can see that you do. Do not remove this bandage, miss, and avoid putting any weight on the foot. It is very important it be left to mend, unmolested, for at least two weeks."

Two weeks? she cried out in her mind. There went all her plans to leave promptly! How could she ever keep up a charade of insanity for two weeks? It was impossible. She simply would have to ignore this man's advice.

"At worst, you could be crippled," the doctor warned, apparently not liking something he saw in her expression.

She lowered her eyes. "I understand."

He seemed satisfied with that, nodding his head and gathering his supplies once more into his black bag. "I will speak with Lord Greyleigh," he repeated just before he left the room.

Elizabeth sighed and settled back into the pillows. Two weeks? So which was the greater: the need for quick removal from this place, or the risk of permanently injuring her foot? Logic said the latter, but a kind of deliberate logic had led her to elope with Radford—and what a disaster that had proved.

Either way she chose, risky speed or impatient lingering, there was only one way to get on with things. She withdrew her purse from under the covers and loosened the knotted drawstrings. She up-ended the contents on to her lap: one ivory cameo; three pairs of earbobs, two of precious gems and one of pearls; one diamond and amethyst choker; two gold hair combs studded with diamond chips; and five rings of varying decoration.

It was a fair feminine inheritance, in the normal sense of things, but in terms of purchasing a half year's existence, it was precious little. She hated to sell them, these last gifts from her mama, but there was no use in feeling regret that they must go. A girl had to eat and pay her keep. All the same, she sighed heavily as she replaced the jewelry in the purse.

Things about this atypical household put a body on edge— for even as Elizabeth pulled the pursestrings into a knot, she jerked up her head at a glimmer of movement that had caught the corner of her eye. A flash of red, but then it was gone, and it was at that moment Elizabeth realized she stared at an angled looking glass placed over a dresser. Her own reflection did not reside in that angle—she turned abruptly to face the area mirrored in the silvered surface.

A tapestry hung there, its bottom edge just touching the floor. It stirred ever so slightly.

"You there, come out!" Elizabeth ordered, her voice roughened by alarm.

There was no response, and the tapestry settled once more.

"I shan't be perturbed with you, but I would like you to come out," Elizabeth insisted. She studied the far wall. Where would someone hide, for the surface was flat. Was there a door behind the tapestry? Or perhaps a window to echo the open one to her left?

No one came forth.

What had she seen? A flash of red—a cloak? But, no. For a heartbeat she had thought she had looked at her own reflection. . . . Had she seen a face? Gooseflesh raced up Elizabeth's arms at the thought.

She threw back her coverlet, only to catch her breath and go utterly still. Her movement had caused intense pain to radiate all the way up from her heel to her knee.

Gasping and moving gingerly, and with an eye on the tapestry, Elizabeth reached across the width of the bed, her fingers just managing to grasp the bellpull.

A sharp tug brought a knock at her door in short order. "Come in," she called at once.

A maid entered, one Elizabeth had certainly not seen before, for this one was undeniably in the family way. The woman's high, rounded belly thrust forward, tightly covered by a white apron.

"Miss?" the maid inquired on a curtsy.

Elizabeth stared, realizing she had never before seen an expectant maid, at least not one clearly engaged in service. Most maids were unmarried girls, in service until such time as they attracted a husband, whose house they then went to and where they spent their confinements. "I . . ." Elizabeth floundered for a moment as this newest shock displaced her previous alarm. She shook her head, as though to clear it of cobwebs, and uttered, "The tapestry. Please pull it aside."

The maid glanced between Elizabeth and the tapestry, open puzzlement etched on her features, but she moved to do as she was bid.

Behind the tapestry there rose a flock-papered wall. No window, no door.

"But," Elizabeth said on something near a gasp. "Is there not some manner of door there?"

"No, miss," the maid said, and now it was her tone that implied puzzlement.

"There must be a . . . what are they called? A secret passage, used by monks, to escape persecution."

The maid just stared, still holding back the edge of the tapestry.

"Well, then, don't just stand there, knock on it, on the wall," Elizabeth instructed, pointing at the width of the tapestry.

The maid obliged with a series of raps down the wall, atop the tapestry, all of which made a solid thunk as she knocked. "It's just a wall, miss," she said.

Elizabeth gazed at the wallpaper, pale yellow and white, and then back at the looking glass. Maybe she had considered the angle wrong? But a quick glance proved nothing in the room was red, and no matter how one considered it, the flash of red that the looking glass had shown had to have been in the vicinity of the tapestry.

"Did you want luncheon, or perhaps tea and biscuits, miss?" the maid asked, releasing the tapestry to come back around to the bedside.

"No," Elizabeth said, only to instantly reconsider. Perhaps that blow to her forehead had done more harm than she had thought? Or perhaps she was faint from lack of nourishment, and she was seeing things. "Rather, yes," she said, causing the maid to ever so slightly raise her eyebrows. "I would care for luncheon after all, please."

The maid nodded, then left, a decided waddle to her step, betraying yet again her enceinte state.

Left on her own, Elizabeth glared at the tapestried wall—she was unquestionably being affected by this house, with its curious selection of maids, its somber walls made of brick like a prison, and its master who was rumored to be unsteady in his mind.

Two weeks. Things could not go on as they stood.

Elizabeth reached once more for the bellpull, and this time it was the maid with the eyepatch who answered. "Miss?" she asked, a tinge of exasperation in her voice. "Luncheon is coming."

"Very good. What is your name?"

"Polly, if it please you, miss." The pronouncement was accompanied by a small curtsy.

"Polly, I rang again because I need to see Lord Greyleigh."

"Before luncheon?"

"Yes, if he is at home."

A mutter of reluctant assent was all Elizabeth got before the maid retreated once more into the hall. At least, Elizabeth thought to herself, if the maid found it odd that Elizabeth wished to receive the master of the house here in her sickbed, she did not say as much. That, for once, was a happy reaction in this peculiar household.

"Has the doctor reported my condition to you?" Elizabeth asked of Lord Greyleigh twenty minutes later. He stood three large strides from her bedside. Really, one might think from his remote stance that she was contagious—although three strides' distance was preferable to his usual seated pose nearly at her elbow.

"Mister Clifton did confide in me, yes."

"It was made clear to me that I ought not travel for a week."

"Two weeks."

Elizabeth compressed her lips together, then had to concede the point. "Yes well, I suppose the surgeon did say two weeks. I hope this length of time is not an inconvenience for you."

Lord Greyleigh cocked his head ever so slightly to one side, and Elizabeth could almost read his mind: he must be wondering why she was suddenly sounding so rational.

She would explain to him in a moment, but first she wanted no other misunderstandings. "I do want to be clear, very clear," she rushed on, "that I will not impose on your hospitality beyond the two weeks."

He nodded in acceptance, and it seemed his countenance cleared as though in relief. "You recall where your family resides?"

"That is something I cannot share," she stated, sounding prim even to herself. "But I wish you to understand something, Lord Greyleigh." Elizabeth took a deep breath and plunged into one final lie. "I came to this place to . . . to restore my nerves. Such a cure has been effected. I may have been of a nervous disposition, but I was not then nor am I now mad, my lord."

She glanced up at Greyleigh to judge how her words struck him, but she might as well have been looking at carved marble.

His regard was marked only by its usual banal aspect of half-interested attention.

Elizabeth pursed her lips again, and decided the man was decidedly lacking in social aptitude. "I have reasons for not wanting to return to my family, and therefore have made other plans," she said firmly.

"Plans?" he echoed casually, as if she talked of going on a mere jaunt to view the ocean.

"These plans need not concern you, my lord, other than to make you aware that I shall leave promptly after two weeks have passed." She folded her hands together, a gesture of finality.

"What if your wound remains unfit for travel?"

"Even so, I will go. All I require from you is information as to when the Post runs through Severn's Well."

"The Post, Elizabeth? I think not, not with a foot that requires coddling. You will make use of one of my coaches. I insist."

"You are very kind," Elizabeth said, trying to sound sincere, but it was difficult to be grateful when the look that suddenly crossed his face was strained. He looked . . . distressed, but Elizabeth could not think why he should.

Still, this offer of a private coach was a boon, for heaven only knew how dreadful travel, while nursing an injury, would be on a Post coach.

Lord Greyleigh took a dismissing step backward. "Very good," he said crisply, still with an edge of agitation in his manner. "Good day, Elizabeth," he said over a swift bow.

The abrupt end of the conversation caught Elizabeth off-guard, but she managed a nod and a smile. "By the by, I do thank you, Lord Greyleigh, for rescuing me." It felt good to speak without reservation, without pretense. "I am aware I might have perished in that ditch had you not found me."

"From pneumonia perhaps, but otherwise your injuries would not have proven fatal, I think," he said in answer.

What curious light eyes he had. Although calm and seemingly benign in all his manners, those eyes seemed to place peculiar emphasis on any words he spoke. Elizabeth found herself searching for hidden meaning in the mildest of terms and for sinister meaning in such phrases as "proven fatal." This man made shivers course up her spine at unexpected moments; when she looked into those exotic eyes, it was easy to wonder if nature had whitewashed his eyes to match an emptiness in his soul.

"Yes, well," she said with a disconcerted little laugh. "Even so, I thank you, sir."

He inclined his head again, as he might in casual recognition of a common courtesy, and although nothing changed in his demeanor, it was at that moment that Elizabeth was convinced she had not been believed. Her thanks, yes, but not her claims as to a cure, as to having full possession of her wits.

There was something in Lord Greyleigh's aspect that she had seen before, in him, in herself, in Papa. It was a kind of genteel doubt, evinced usually through an avuncular laugh or a slide of the eyes or a nervous shrug. In Lord Greyleigh it was something to do with his eternally even tone, with the way he held his shoulders.

So he yet chose to believe she was not in her right mind—it mattered not. She was once again comfortable in her own truths, and she would be gone in two weeks—sooner if she thought it possible to travel safely before then. He had no reason to hold her here. No one in the village would blame him for letting her go, particularly now that she had no intention of maintaining a pretense of insanity. Even if he chose to continue to believe she was bewildered or even incoherent, the maids would see that she was neither mad nor dangerous. Once she was mended enough, she could be happily sent on her way, no threat to the community, no longer a burden to Lord Greyleigh's household. Greyleigh could believe her demented if he wished, but it would change nothing.

Still, when he bowed his way out of the room, Elizabeth was left with a sense of disappointment that he had not accepted her word that there was nothing wrong with her. Or perhaps disgruntlement was the better word. Either way, she was glad for the distraction of the one-eyed maid, Polly, arriving just then with a luncheon tray.

Chapter 6

Five minutes later, Gideon stood behind his library desk, staring down at the list he had been compiling. It was wasted work now—a list of places to inquire after an inmate's relations.

Though perhaps not wasted after all. Just because the girl claimed she "could not share" the name or locale of her family, it did not necessarily follow that he must not find such information for himself.

But why make the effort? She would be gone, escorted away by his own coach-and-four within a fortnight. It would be empty effort to pursue her name and lineage simply for the sake of possessing it. But there was something about this girl, this young woman, something that nagged at one's sense of right and wrong.

Where could she mean to go, if not home? What thoughts tumbled in her pretty, dark-haired head? He could not doubt "tumbled" was the proper term—for had not his own mother many times declared herself cured? But such cures had never been true, never a reality except in her own befuddled mind.

Gideon could not trust a woman who blithely claimed that all was well. He supposed there were women for whom such assertions were true—but he had yet to meet such a one. In his experience women held secrets, and they held them close, sometimes even closer than they allowed *themselves* to know.

This woman had done nothing to change Gideon's first impression. One moment the female had been preparing to dance at her imaginary wedding, and the next stating in a clear and sane-sounding manner that she would be going away without first identifying herself, her origins, or her destination. In

Gideon's world this vacillation, this altering of manner, meant there was little doubt the woman's nerves were unsteady.

So Gideon would do as he'd planned; he would pay Clyde Arbuckle, an investigator from Bristol, to learn what the man could of Miss Elizabeth B. Too bad they were far from London and its celebrated Bow Street Runners, but Mr. Arbuckle would serve well enough, as he had in the past, to find out something about this female who chose to remain lost. Mr. Arbuckle had done other "quiet" work for Gideon, and would not demur at finding out a name and direction.

In the meanwhile, Gideon would avoid his guest, as much as good manners and conscience would allow. He'd be happy enough to see the back of the coach bearing Elizabeth away—one less burden among an already overwhelming mountain of burdens. But through Mr. Arbuckle he would know something of the stranger in his guest room before she went. Knowing was how he protected himself. It was what he did, what he was good at. Never mind for now his own weariness at juggling a dozen problems, to say nothing of a dozen desires.

Desire—a strange word, all but foreign to Gideon. No, that was not correct; he was used to desire.

Now, desire's *fruit* . . . ! *That* was something of which he had too infrequently tasted.

He had a normal man's appetites, those of the flesh, and there had been the occasional and accommodating females in the village for the last eight of Gideon's six-and-twenty years, so he had not lacked for sexual congress. In the three years just past, there had been one particular farmer's widow who had fancied having Gideon call upon her of an evening, a situation that had proved satisfactory for both. The fact that the Widow Denbarry was barren had been part of her charm, for Gideon was not anxious to leave by-blows about the countryside, not least because there was a part of him that feared he might pass on his mother's lunacy.

The Widow Denbarry was married and moved away now though, going on four months, and Gideon had not found suit-' able company since. He had yet to summon the time—or was it the energy?—to find another outlet for dalliance. Had he become too accustomed to desiring a thing without being able to achieve it? That was an appalling thought.

So while his sexual appetite went neglected, another hunger in him grew even stronger, even more fierce, that often left him pacing late into the night: he longed to be free. He longed for a life that included "more."

But "more" must wait.

I am used to waiting, he thought to himself.

But it grows more difficult each day, came an answering whisper in his head, and there was no argument to be made in return.

With an effort, he forced himself to sit down at his desk. He wearily reached for a quill and looked again at his list, a piece of foolscap marked with many lines of writing, some of which had been scratched out by a stroke of the quill. He uncapped the ink in the stand before him, dipped the point, and wrote below the other lines: "Asylum/four living patients. Three males, all identified or awaiting family contact. One female, unidentified." Below this he wrote: "Hire Arbuckle."

He glanced down the entire sheet, realizing how many items remained on the list, waiting to be crossed out upon completion. There was so much to do, always so much more.

And why did he even try? Once upon a time, when he was younger and full of the energy of hope, it had been his plan to create a paradise, to turn what had been a hell into a haven. He had meant to remake this house into a refuge—only to make it into a prison. A prison whose walls were built of duty and yet more duty, each stroke of his pen adding another brick to the battlements of his bondage.

He could walk away. The physical leaving would be simple, even easy. But there were bonds that tied a man to a certain patch of soil, bonds far stronger, far more taxing than a chain or a moat could ever form. There was no peace beyond these walls, not for Gideon, not if he simply left his obligations behind.

His dream was an impossible one. Had his mother's madness taught him nothing? Did he not know that some things were simply fated to fail forever? That Dame Fortune played tricks as neatly as she granted treats? He must go to find his peace of

mind—but to leave everything as it was, was to know no peace.
He was eldest. He was obliged. He was doomed. His dream
could never succeed.

In one thing he would succeed, he thought to himself with a
toss of the head that would have belied his turmoil to an ob-
server, had there been one about to witness his dogged return to
the matter at hand. He *would* set Mr. Arbuckle to the task of
finding out more about the mysterious female inmate. He
would learn more of the woman who had brought from her asylum cell those soft hands, satin slippers, a fine wool cloak, and
a silk gown. Something was decidedly not right here, and
Gideon would know what it was, because knowing was what
kept him feeling some measure of control.

"What is your name again?" Elizabeth asked the maid with
the black eyepatch when the girl came to retrieve the dinner
dishes that night. The maid who was in a family way, Jeannie,
knelt before the fireplace, stoking the fire for the night.

"Polly," the one-eyed girl answered as she rearranged the
used dishes on the tray so that they would not teeter and fall off
when she lifted it.

"Polly, might I be so bold . . ." Elizabeth began, only to bite
her lip in consternation.

The maid looked up from her task, a hint of amusement
gleaming from her one good eye if not quite on her lips. "You
mean to ask what happened to my eye," she stated.

"Yes," Elizabeth agreed, relaxing her shoulders and giving a
tentative smile in return. "Do you mind?"

"No. Everyone always asks, miss. I got cinders in it when I
was stirring up a banked fire one night, oh, maybe five years
ago now. It festered, and before you could so much as whistle,
I'd lost the eye, miss."

"How dreadful! I am sorry to hear it."

The maid nodded as she gathered up the tray. "Thank you,
miss. Will this be all? Would you be wanting more blankets
tonight, d'you think?"

"No, thank you. And ought I thank you as well for the use of
this night rail I wear?"

"No, miss. It was a found garment."

"Found?" Elizabeth gave a tiny frown of confusion.

The maid shrugged, noncommittal. "Things get found around this house. And things go missing, too."

Ah, the ghost, Elizabeth thought. Well, the servants would gossip about such a rumor, would they not? It was only to be expected. Anything found out of place would be blamed on "the ghost" of course. Elizabeth refrained from glancing toward the tapestry, not wanting to give credence to a rumor, not even one that made her wonder what she had seen after all.

Polly left with the tray, leaving Jeannie, who now sat back on her heels, her hand pressed to her spine as she gave a tired sigh. Elizabeth felt sorry for the girl, so far along in her pregnancy and still having to work at such physical labor, but the reason seemed obvious. The girl sported no wedding ring. It could be that she and her fellow could not afford a ring, but Elizabeth suspected she knew the truer story here: that the baby must be that of the master of the house. Why else would a bachelor tolerate the girl's employment despite her obvious state?

There was nothing extraordinary in a man having his way with a chambermaid—it happened all the time—but drawing attention to the evidence . . . ! Well, that was just another sign of how bizarre this household was.

Elizabeth shook her head, and the gesture caused the sticking plaster on her forehead to pull a bit. She reached up, finding it was coming loose. She worked the edges off, making a few small noises of discomfort until it came loose and she could place it on the table next to the bed. The maid rose and left the room.

What to do with the rest of her day? Elizabeth settled back against the pillows, frowning at the lump under her covers that was her bandaged foot. If not for it, she could be on her way, establishing a new life, a new way of going on until such time as she read the announcement of Lorraine's wedding in the papers.

In the way sound sometimes does, Elizabeth realized that a noise had tiptoed into her conscious understanding. She held her breath until she was assured that, yes indeed, she had heard something. Was it . . . humming? But if it was, it was a strange, muffled humming. She slowly turned her head toward the ta-

pestry, gooseflesh lifting the hair on her nape as she realized the
sound came from behind the tapestry, from behind the wall the
maid had shown her.

It was too much. Elizabeth could not remain sitting in the
bed, transfixed by an uncomfortable mix of dread and consternation. She must touch the wall for herself.

She slid from the side of the bed nearest the tapestry, grimacing at pain and a nervous tightening in her stomach that
made her breathing rapid and shallow, and balanced on her
good foot. Working her way along the mattress, she took small
hops down the bed's length, until she could grasp the post at its
nether end. She swallowed hard, her ears still tuned to that dis-
embodied, vaguely harmonious humming, and let go of the
post. Spreading her arms wide for balance, she hopped once toward the tapestry. She nearly put down her injured foot as she
teetered dangerously, but balance was restored, and she dared
attempt another hop. The exercise made the heel wound scream
with pain, but pain could be overridden by fear.

Completing four hops away from the bed brought her within
reach of a high chair back, which she grasped with relief and a
labored sigh. A few more hops forward brought her to the tapestry, which she pulled back from its left side, same as the maid
had done.

Nothing—no window, no door, just as before. There was a
line where two strips of wallpaper met, but one slightly lifted
edge proved there was nothing but wall behind them.

Elizabeth shrugged the tapestry over her shoulder, splaying
her now free hands against the wall. She inched along the wall's
length, scarcely able to see except where combined light from
a branch of candles and the fire on the grate barely crept past
the edges of the tapestry, but feeling with her fingertips.

"Ah!" she cried as her fingers found an edge, a crack perhaps, halfway along the wall's length.

She needed more light by which to see, so she gathered up
the heavy tapestry, folding it in her arms, atop her shoulders,
piling it on her head. She scrambled to make it stay in place, but
it kept insisting on falling from her grasp, its weight and awkward size nearly unmanageable. Perspiration dewed her upper
lip and forehead, and a trickle of moisture ran down her back,

but the humming just on the other side of the wall persuaded her to try again and again.

At last she realized she need not hold up the tapestry, but instead turned and pushed against it, hopping forward until she had it extended so far out into the room, nearly to the bed, that light could flood around the edges. She awkwardly reversed her position, the tapestry pushing heavily against her head and shoulders, but it was enough to let her see the dim outline of a kind of door. It was covered with the same yellow-and-white paper as the rest of the wall, the pattern expertly matched to aid in the door's blending out of casual sight, especially in the half-light of evening. The oblong shape sported no knob, hinges, or decoration, but it was the shape of a door all the same. Elizabeth realized in amazement that, without the humming to prompt her, she could have lived in this room for a dozen years without ever discovering the door's presence behind the tapestry.

Her heart in her throat, she hopped forward, only belatedly becoming aware the humming had stopped. The tapestry's weight pushed her insistently forward until she was once more touching the wall, running her fingers along the door edges she now knew existed. She pushed, with no result. She tried to find purchase by which to lever the door toward herself, but her nails proved ineffective. A hairpin missed by the maids who had taken down her hair proved useless as a lever with which to pry open the door.

Wearily, Elizabeth worked her way free of the tapestry. She spent a long time clutching the chair, trembling from fatigue. How quickly one lost one's strength from lying abed, she thought to herself, even as she wished she had thought to exit at the other end of the tapestry, nearer the head of her bed. This way, she must not only achieve the bed's surface, but then push her way up toward the headboard, a feat that seemed increasingly infeasible to muscles gone shaky with pained fatigue.

Should she manage to get to the bed without first collapsing, she thought wryly, at least she would be able to sleep there in peace. She had proven to herself that there was no mystery, no ghost—only a servant, surely, using a long-forgot hiding place or passage. There was no threat here, nothing that could not be

banished by some simple investigation and a refusal to be
cowed by tall tales.

She hopped forward, each movement now a torturous re-
minder that she ought to have stayed abed, but feeling a glow
of reasoned triumph all the same.

The next morning Gideon quietly opened the door to Elizabeth's room, deliberately without knocking. He quickly and
boldly made a circuit of the room with his gaze, although he
was prepared to retreat quickly if needed. When no feminine
cry of outrage met his action, he narrowed his gaze on the bed,
quickly ascertaining that Elizabeth was not there.

No, that was not true, she was there, but oddly splayed across
the foot of it, only the top coverlet serving as a blanket to her.

With a frown Gideon quietly closed the door, then turned his
back to it and stared across the room toward the bed. An old
emotion swelled in his chest for a moment, but it was not an
emotion such as to raise tears. Anguish, yes, but never tears.
Only cold, frosty glares and imperious, demanding words had
ever got him what he wanted—tears had been rewarded with
scorn and denial, and he had long since forsaken their release.

All the same, it took tremendous effort to push away from
the door and softly step across to the bedside. He looked down
at the prostrate being, some fanciful corner of his mind half
fearing to see his mother's face there, but Mama's pale blond
curls were absent.

Elizabeth was so dark of hair, as if designed to be the perfect
foil against his own white-blond mane. Her inky tresses had
been left unplaited to fall to hip level, where the loose, natural
ringlets tangled, crying out for a good brushing. Hers was not
the kind of hair that was easily managed, but must be disciplined into patterns, and best when the air was not humid. In
her sleep, several wisps had formed around her face, making
delicate ringlets that made her appear more childlike in sleep
than she was presumably in age.

She must be, what, nineteen, twenty? If her mind had been
whole, she most likely would have married by now. She might
have no dowry, for all he knew, but her face was pretty, and that
could serve well enough as a girl's dowry to a man who liked

what he saw. No, pretty was not the correct word—striking, or unique was perhaps the better word. She was apple-cheeked without appearing heavy, perhaps because her nose was a tad thin, making a balance. Her mouth was well shaped, the lips of even size and not too wide, and she had good teeth. She was fortunate enough not to be terribly pale, even though that was all that was fashionable, because with her dark hair it would have made her appear sickly rather than genteel.

What a waste, Gideon thought, that this charming package should contain a befuddled mind. She claimed otherwise, but then the afflicted always did.

In her slumber, all was innocence, and even her strange positioning at the foot of the bed seemed innocuous. But how many times had Gideon looked upon the seemingly innocuous only to later recognize a symptom of disordered thinking? Disorder, disease, mania—they were cruel, unforgiving of even the most blameless of victims. Mama had been blameless. Mama, curled on her bed, an unearthly keening accompanying endless tears. . . .

He reached down and touched Elizabeth's shoulder, shaking her lightly. "Elizabeth," he spoke quietly, knowing that the dreams of the disturbed ought not be intruded upon abruptly.

Elizabeth blinked once, then appeared for two heartbeats to slip back into slumber, only to open her eyes and focus with instant clarity upon his face. For a moment, disappointment crossed her features, and he knew she had dreamed she was someplace other than here in his home. He could hardly begrudge her that, since it was his own dream to escape this house, but something in the vulnerability on her face tugged at him, making the lump reform in his chest, making him feel unbefittingly angry.

"I have come to inform you that callers have arrived," he said, and at least his voice remained gentle even if he was not so at his core.

"Callers?" she murmured, her brow wrinkling in bewilderment. "For me?"

"Local women, from the parish. St. Bartholomew's. They were told that you could not recall your family name. They are concerned, and wished to meet with you."

"I am nobody," she said, and the anger in him flared and danced, then died out, becoming nothing more than a dim pain between his temples. Mama had claimed the same, had been made to feel useless and worthless, a nobody. Echoes—this house had too many echoes.

"You are somebody," he said firmly. He extended his hand to her, and felt a tiny measure of victory when she placed her fingers there. He helped her sit up, the coverlet and her hair both falling to pool around her hips. The fabric of the night rail she wore was well used and thinning, and in the morning light it was possible to see where the fabric ended and her form began. The cool morning air had brought her nipples erect, and a dusty pink shadow showed through the material as well. Gideon forgot for a moment to avert his gaze, struck by the sight of a luscious form surrounded by dark tresses, but then he recalled himself. He had seen many a night rail over the years. He knew how to work without letting his mind take in what the eyes must see.

"Your own clothes were ruined beyond repair, except for your slippers," he told her, "but I will have a dressing gown sent in for your use, for modesty's sake. Would you mind if a maid put your hair up? Or at least plaited it? It would be more seemly."

"Must I see them? These callers?" Elizabeth asked, her distress clear to read in her gaze.

"Yes," he answered simply, with gentle firmness, as one would to a frightened child. "They only wish to be sure you are well cared for here." At her continued anxious stare, he added, "It is good of them to come."

"Just tell them I am well."

He shook his head, and before she could say anything more, he scooped her into his arms. She gave a small squeal of surprise and glanced at him with approbation. "What do you think you are doing?" she asked with a briskness that betokened more affront than aggravation.

"Carrying you to this stool, where your hair may be combed out."

At least she made no further protests, instead turning to the looking glass set before the vanity stool on which he had perched her.

"Oh! I *do* look a fright," she admitted at once, reaching up to comb her fingers through her tangled locks.

Gideon was not so stupid as to reply to such a comment from a female, so instead he made her a bow. "I shall send a maid to you at once. Is ten minutes a long enough time in which to make yourself ready, do you think?"

She stopped raking her fingers through her hair, and looked up at his reflection, their gazes meeting in the silvered surface of the looking glass. "You want these people gone as soon as possible," she stated.

He was faintly intrigued by the way Elizabeth tilted her head, an obvious sign of comprehension. Mama had often not heard his questions, living as she had in a world of her own making, but then again she had also had a habit of blurting out sudden comments or observations just as this lady did. "It is as obvious as that?" he murmured.

"Why is that?" she asked. "Why do you not want the ladies to call upon you?"

He was not concerned for what the church ladies would make of him, or even of Elizabeth. If the fates were kind, the ladies would find something to make them whisk the dark-haired lovely from his home. No, what interested him was the clarity with which Elizabeth spoke, the flash of sanity she seemed to exhibit. She was having a "good day," as Mama used to call those days when she appeared alert and aware of the people and situations around her.

He shrugged in answer to her question. "I am not a social man."

"Why not?"

Ah, now there was a question more in keeping with his experience, a question such as a childlike mind would pose, wanting to understand subtleties that could never be explained with mere words.

Instead of answering her, he repeated his earlier question, "Is ten minutes sufficient time to be readied?"

"Yes," she said, turning back to her reflection in the looking glass.

Gideon knew he should turn and leave, but there was something in the set of her shoulders that made him linger a moment, that made him glance once more into the reflection in the looking glass. Their gazes met there, and locked for a moment. How tempting it was to search for sanity and reason there, to hope the clarity of her unblinking gaze meant clarity of mind, but he knew better. God save him from old memories, he knew far better.

He bowed then, annoyed at himself for the stiffness in the gesture, and strode from the room and down the stairs. He went at once to summon a maid to bring a dressing gown—one of Mama's old ones—for Elizabeth. For she surely required something to cover her charms.

Although, he thought with a spike of dark humor, the church ladies might be all the more likely to whisk Elizabeth away from his evil influence were they to see her in the dishabille he had witnessed.

Chapter 7

Blushing, Elizabeth gratefully received the dressing gown from Polly's hands. Lord Greyleigh must have seen what Elizabeth had eventually noticed in the looking glass—the diaphanous nature of her night rail. What must he think of her, stretching and sitting up in a gown that revealed too much?

On the other hand, what was *she* to think of *him*? How had he come to be at her bedside, awakening her? Had she been so lost to dreams that she had never heard his knock? Why had a maid not been sent to awaken her?

And what had been that look on his face? For the first time she had caught an expression there other than annoyance or cool indifference. He had appeared almost . . . pained, as if looking upon her had caused him some injury. The thought made her flush with embarrassment, but it was an awkward embarrassment that did not quite make sense.

She knew she was not ugly—only a few days ago she had believed Radford when he had whispered in her ear that she was beautiful. Love had made her beautiful, or so she had thought at the time. But even if she had not believed his words, her own looking glass told her that the face there was not the sort to make a man blanch. Men had never fallen at her feet in adoration, but neither had any male called her ugly since she had achieved the changing age of thirteen.

What injury, other than repulsion, could she represent to Lord Greyleigh? What had made his cool demeanor crack for that brief moment and reveal pain, or upset, or some other emotion at which she could only guess?

But there was no time for questions now, for a bevy of presumably keenly interested local ladies waited to meet with her.

And what was she to tell them, the truth? Of course not, for the
truth did no one any good, least of all Lorraine and Papa. Then
the half truths she had told Lord Greyleigh? Or the truth as he
so obviously believed it to be, the lie she had first allowed him
to believe—that she had come from the asylum?

Two footmen carried her down to the front parlor, insisting
they could not put their hands about her person, and so she was
made to ride upon a chair the two men carried between them. It
made for an ignominious entry, and made the ladies of the local
parish lift their eyebrows in mild disapproval that dissipated
once they saw her bandaged heel.

In the end, Elizabeth found it was easiest to remain largely
mum, to gaze blankly when to answer was to jeopardize her
anonymity.

When they asked her name, she answered "Elizabeth," and at
the insistence that she had a surname, she merely stared sto-
ically.

When they asked where she was from, she shook her head
and allowed her gaze to wander from face to face. It was Lord
Greyleigh, sitting in a chair in the corner, deliberately apart
from the circle of chairs in which the ladies resided, who answered. "She says she spent her childhood in Nottingham."

"I knew the inhabitants of the hospital came from all directions," Mrs. Fitzhamm declared, "but Nottingham? My word,
such a distance!" The woman's daughter and niece nodded in
agreement with her.

"But, my dear girl," Lady Sees said down her nose, "surely
you have of recent been to London? Or at least Bristol or Bath.
I mean to say, why else would one arrive at Severn's Well,
which is such a distance from Nottingham?"

Elizabeth just gazed back, neither smiling nor frowning. Naturally, such a lack of response, such vagueness, could only play
into the very farce that had first been put in place. Within ten
minutes, certainty as to her want of wits bloomed across their
faces as clearly as if they had pronounced it aloud.

It was ironic that she had once hoped to convince her host of
her unstable mind, and now she had no choice but to allow
these ladies to underscore that impression. She glanced toward
the chair where he reclined, one leg crossed over the other, his

head half turned away as though he could scarcely be bothered to attend the conversation. Well, she had told him as much of the truth as she could, and she could not help the wrongful impression these ladies underscored. She could not think why it even mattered to her, other than it seemed churlish to repay his hospitality with lies.

When more impossible-to-answer questions—all echoes of those already pressed upon her by Lord Greyleigh—drew only more silences or shrugs, Lady Sees rose, a signal that brought the other ladies to their feet as well.

"Poor thing," Elizabeth heard one lady mutter to Lord Greyleigh as they made their adieux in the outer hall, and another said, "'Tis a tragedy."

Well, and what other judgment could my performance garner, Elizabeth thought to herself, although her pique was tinged with amusement. How easy it was to mislead people, to give the wrong impression, to let them think what they would. In their place, she had no doubt she would have done the same, would have chosen not to think well of a mute and vague creature.

For who would suspect pretense? What was to be gained by it? Freedom, of course . . . but the ladies could not know Elizabeth sought escape rather than protection.

It was the way of a lone woman to seek protection—Elizabeth would have done so herself, were there any place to turn to gain it. But, no, her protection lay in an anonymity that could buy her escape—from this house, from the hospitality that did her cause more harm than good, from gossip's wicked tongue. She sighed, regretting the afternoon's encounter, in fact regretting everything from the moment she had agreed to "elope" with Radford Barnes.

Lord Greyleigh returned to the parlor, his hands crossed behind his back, his expression in its usual polite but neutral arrangement.

"That was not too terrible," he said, not quite looking directly at her.

"No," she agreed.

"You did not remember anything new?" He phrased it as a

question, but his tone implied he already knew the answer would be negative.

"Nothing," she said honestly enough, for there was a difference between remembering and sharing.

"How is your foot?"

The question surprised her, for it was the first thing he had asked her that went beyond mere politeness, however minutely. He had not needed to inquire after her health, not really. Perhaps he merely sought to make idle conversation while they waited for the footmen to return and carry her up the stairs.

"I wish it might heal more quickly," she said, a kind of apology for lingering in his house.

He made a noise in his throat that might have been an agreement or a dismissal, but nothing about his demeanor told her which. He unfolded his hands from behind his back and crossed to her side. Without asking her permission, he scooped her up into his arms.

"My lord!" she squeaked in surprise, her arms slipping around his neck in order to help support her position in his arms. "I am content to wait upon the footmen."

"Why, when I am standing about doing nothing?" he said, his tone almost bitter, or perhaps more accurately, a bit self-mocking.

He carried her from the room and to the stairs, plainly exhibiting good health and strength, for he did not even begin to breathe with effort until halfway up the stairs. She was neither tiny nor slight, and many a man would have labored to carry her the distance required.

So, Elizabeth thought, he was not an idle man, and indeed the fit of his coat suggested arms and chest that were forged by physical labor. When he saved his footmen from the task of carrying her, it was because he himself must be used to doing what needed doing. Her grandpapa had been such a man, a man to labor in the fields beside his steward, a man who liked to ride and fish and swim, and toss granddaughters in the air and catch them as they fell giggling back into his strong hands.

This man had twice now made her think of Grandpapa, but where one had possessed open arms and a lap upon which to reside, this man's physical nearness filled Elizabeth with an odd tingling awareness of maleness that had nothing to do with childhood games.

Being carried by a man, a stranger, was a curious, enforced intimacy, out of keeping with most of Society's rules. She must cling to him, her arms about his neck as though he were a lover, their bodies meeting in ways that would be severely frowned upon were they dancing. She could smell his scent, some manner of shaving soap no doubt, and the warmth from his arms penetrated her senses, warming her skin.

She felt a ripple of attraction, which shocked her. How inappropriate! Had she not learned her lesson from Radford Barnes about the dangers of mere attraction? She would not allow her mind to venture down that path, not with this man.

Still, she was too aware of where Lord Greyleigh's arms held her, despite liking the feel even as she rejected it—what an intolerable position in which to be! Her own fluster made conversation insipid and silence impossible.

"My lord," she said, to fill the void, "I would ask you a question."

He grunted and nodded once, saving his breath as he achieved the top step and began down the hall toward the room she had been given.

"I must ask . . ." She hesitated, but in the end decided he already thought her mad, so what did it matter if she was blunt and forthright? "Why did you come into my room earlier today? Did you knock? Why did you not send up a maid to waken me?"

He gave her a quick glance, and for a moment she thought she read a sheepish guilt in his gaze.

He did not answer at once, instead kicking open her door and striding in. He set her in a chair, then took two large steps back. He breathed deeply for several moments, and she could not help but think everything he did was designed to put her ill at ease, with overlarge gestures that spoke of resistance.

"In my own home, I go where I will, when I will, Elizabeth," he said, and his tone broached no arguments.

"Even a lady's chamber?" Elizabeth protested, matching her tone to his.

He narrowed his eyes for a moment, but she had the odd impression it was more from surprise than anger. "Yes," he said, but now there was no hint of surprise in his succinct words. "Even a lady's chamber."

"Perhaps the ladies from the church were wise to call upon me," she threw at him.

"They would have been wise to take you away from here."

Elizabeth's lips parted in shock. "Do you threaten me, my lord?"

"No," he said at once, and now he did appear angry. "I only tell you the truth, that I go where I wish to go, and I'll not be gainsaid in my own home, not even by a guest."

He was as mad as everyone had always whispered him to be—he must be, to be so indifferent to common courtesy. Elizabeth stared up at him, wishing she could stand, that she need not look up at him from the inferior angle of a chair. There was something of an obstinate boy in the way he stood, although the hard light in his eyes and the rapid rise and fall of his muscular chest beneath his cravat proved him to be anything but a boy. He was a man, and an angry one at that, although she could not imagine what had occurred to anger him so.

The hard light slowly receded from his gaze, and Elizabeth stared in fascination, much as she would have stared at an ice floe breaking apart. What wrought this change? What took the wrath from his eyes? What did he see when he stared so contemptuously at her that would cause ire one moment and a strange appearance of softness—call it even vulnerability—the next?

"I will, however"—it was clear the words were dragged with utter reluctance to his lips—"knock before I enter."

"Thank you for that at least!" she said, forcing her tone to remain arch. Instinct told her that to appear weak or uncertain would only invite more unseemliness from this man of contrasts. It was too ironic, really, had she the nerve to laugh internally at the strange moment, for he thought her mad and yet it was he who exhibited the oddest behavior, he whom gossip had labeled insane. He was certainly eccentric. She vowed on the moment that there would be a chair barring her door from now on, until she could be free of this place, this man and his odd behavior.

He made no reply other than to bow his way out, leaving Elizabeth to ponder sourly if he knew how to bow in any fashion other than stiffly. It was only then that she realized he had more or less stranded her by placing her in the chair, but she would sooner bite her tongue than call out to him to come back and remedy the situation. She glanced toward the bed, and sighed to find it so far away. Of course the bellpull, to summon a servant, was next to the bed.

"You can do it," she told herself, but the thought of the resulting pain to her heel kept her seated. Instead, she reached toward the fireplace, toward a log piled to one side awaiting its turn on the grate. She upended it and thumped it against the floor. Inelegant, but the pounding might eventually cause a servant to come investigate.

Just as she'd hoped, her door swung open. It was only then that she realized the servant had not knocked first, and she parted her lips to offer a scold, but stopped as she realized the woman before her was dressed all in white, wearing a night rail in the middle of the day. The being had flowing, long red hair, rather unkempt.

They stared at one another in silence. Elizabeth felt a chill climb her spine when she realized the woman looked in her direction but her eyes had a blank, unfocused quality, as though the woman saw right through Elizabeth. The creature was young, very young, perhaps not even yet out of the schoolroom, and a wistful cast to her mouth was made tragic by the furrowed brow above her pretty face.

"Who are you?" Elizabeth said, her voice little more than a whisper.

The creature never focused her gaze, but only turned and left the doorway. Elizabeth listened breathlessly for retreating footsteps, but heard none.

"Come back!" she called, only half meaning the words, only half wanting the strange creature to come back into her line of sight.

Grasping the chair arms tightly, Elizabeth stood, and for a moment her courage failed her. Had she seen the ghost, the spirit the servants whispered about?

Chapter 8

The being had seemed solid enough, but her white night rail, her unfocused stare . . . Elizabeth shuddered.

With reluctance she hopped her way to the doorjamb, but a quick perusal up and down the hallway revealed the being had disappeared from sight.

Elizabeth closed the door, longing for a bolt she could run home. She hopped across to the bed, where she sat for a long time, her teeth gritted in pain, her heel throbbing as though to echo the rapid pulse that had begun at the sight of that strange, silent, staring woman-child.

Eventually, Elizabeth slid across the bed's surface, grasping the bellpull. She needed a servant, someone to answer a question or two.

To her chagrin, when she called, "Come in," following a brief knock, it was Lord Greyleigh who entered. He had added a greatcoat and beaver hat to his ensemble, with gloves in his coat pocket and a riding crop tucked under one arm. Clearly he was on his way out, and she wondered fleetingly if he went to attend a club, the theater, or perhaps to dance attendance on some woman of his acquaintance.

"Yes?" he demanded without polite ceremony.

Elizabeth could not quite keep exasperation from crossing her features. "I rang for a servant."

"If you recall, I do not have an excess of servants, Elizabeth."

"Because of the ghost," she stated, doing her best to ignore the shiver that coursed across her shoulders.

"In part, yes."

In part because of you, Elizabeth thought, for wouldn't she too be gone from his presence if she were able to leave?

"What did you require?" he asked impatiently as he reached for his gloves.

She put up her chin. "I wanted to ask a servant about the ghost."

"For pity's sake, why?" He pulled on a glove, sparing her only the briefest of exasperated glances.

"Because I just saw her."

His head snapped up sharply at that. "Rubbish," he said, and she thought he must surely have used that same word to put down any servants' whispers that had dared to be breathed in his presence.

"I assure you, I saw a red-haired woman in a white night rail," Elizabeth said firmly. "Or does the ghost have a different appearance from that?"

He pursed his lips. "Was she young?" he demanded.

"Very young. A child almost."

He frowned as he pulled on his other glove, and remained silent for three long beats. He looked up then, and pronounced once again, "Rubbish. You should not listen to servants' gossip, because it obviously gives you fancies. I have no doubt you merely saw a servant."

"With long, unbound red hair?" Elizabeth countered, both puzzled and intrigued by his denial. He had seen the ghost himself, or at least had come to believe there was something to the tales—he had said as much himself. Besides, he had betrayed himself, his denial, by knowing the creature was young in appearance. Yet now he was obviously intent on disallowing her claim. Why?

"I do not believe the woman was a ghost," she said, because it was true and because she meant to entice him into a revelation by one of her own.

Instead of being either annoyed or relieved by her comment, however, he cast her another narrowed-eyed glance. "You do not believe the dead come back to haunt us?"

"I did not say that. I think perhaps I do believe haunting is possible. What I meant was that I thought this woman was very real, not a ghost at all."

He crossed his hands behind his back abruptly, the riding crop still tucked beneath his arm. "Really? And why is that?"

"Because she looked very real. She did not float, she walked. I felt I could reach out and touch her. She *appeared* real."

He compressed his lips for a moment again, then nodded. "At least you make sensible observations."

That was an odd thing to say, but Elizabeth chose to point out the meaning behind his words. "So you do not believe she is a ghost either? But earlier you said you believed a spirit had been haunting this house for some time."

He gave a small sniff. "A poor choice of words perhaps."

"Or deliberate."

He frowned quickly, and yet he quirked his head as if in assent. "You say the oddest things," he said quietly. "You ever surprise me."

"*I* surprise *you?*" She could have laughed. *She* said the oddest things? No, that shoe belonged on *his* foot. And yet there was something about him, this man both peculiar in look and deed, that made her feel almost compelled to tell all, to unburden her soul, to step out of the shadows of the lies she let him go on believing.

"Is that all?" he asked, sounding exasperated.

"Yes. I thought a ghost sufficient reason to summon someone," she answered tartly.

He snorted, a significantly disrespectful sound, and turned without bidding her good day.

"My lord." Her call stopped him from crossing the threshold. "Since it was you who came and not a servant, I do now have a question for you specifically."

"And that is?" There it was again, that patient tone that ought to be soothing, but which struck her as anything but.

"The man," she said, also with exaggerated patience, "the man who was attempting to steal the ring from my finger. How did he appear? Young? Old?"

He turned back to face her, and perhaps that was curiosity underneath his composed demeanor. "My age. Six-and-twenty. Perhaps thirty," he said promptly. "He had dark hair, I believe, although I only saw him in shadow."

"How was he dressed?"

"Quality clothing, I should say, with a good fit. I cannot tell you colors. It was not quite dawn when I saw him. Although I did think he would look more in place stumbling half drunk down a pub street in London, frankly, than on the road in our sleepy little village. He looked decidedly out of place."

She peered into Lord Greyleigh's face, striving to read between the stoic lines that made up the set of his features, unsuccessfully. "You did not know him?"

"No."

"Thank you." She nodded, dismissing the topic.

Lord Greyleigh was not done with it however. "Do you know who the man might be?" he asked. "Shall I have a warrant sworn out against him?"

Elizabeth shook her head at once, denying any desire for official intervention. "Even if I could say who it was, I would have to guess he believes me dead. You thought so, at first, or so the maid tells the story."

"Hmmm," was all he said. He studied her a moment, then gave her a quick parting bow and exited.

She ought to feel relieved that he had gone, taking his skepticism with him, but instead she felt as deflated as one of those newfangled balloons when its supply of hot air was denied. She had wanted to tell him more about her situation, she realized. She had wanted him to look at her with something other than doubt, something other than a suspicion as to her want of wits.

It would be folly if he had, if she had spoken of her past, of course. No one must know her identity. She must fade away. She must await a happier day, a day when she could return to a version of the life she had once known. To tell this man of her invalid marriage was to invite censure, and impediments to the only path she had left to her. No matter how uncomfortable she must become to do so, she *would* protect Lorraine's happiness.

Lorraine—how Elizabeth missed seeing her sister! It would be weeks if not months before they saw one another again. Elizabeth lay back against the bed's pillow and remembered the day Lorraine had first spoken of her beloved. . . .

"Broderick has asked me to marry him!" Lorraine had said, delight dancing in her eyes.

"Oh, Lorraine, I am so happy for you!" Elizabeth had said in reply, her hands seeking and holding her sister's, to physically share in the exciting revelation. They stood in their bedchamber, hiding their excited girlish whispers behind a closed door. Papa was newly remarried, but despite the passage of only two short weeks since the wedding, the girls had already learned their new stepmama would not tolerate what she called "giggling and gossiping."

"Has he asked Papa for your hand?" Elizabeth asked.

"Well, no," Lorraine blushed. "He has yet to speak of his intentions with his own family, and he wishes to do that first, you know."

Elizabeth tried to hide her disapproval behind a wrinkling of her nose. "*His* family?" She tried to make it sound like a gentle reproof.

"You know they are very aware of consequence."

Elizabeth began to reply, but Lorraine forestalled her.

"I know you care little for matters of prestige, Elizabeth, but Broderick's family does. You must agree I am hardly the catch of the Season, even though you love me and think otherwise. I am almost five-and-twenty, and I am sure his family cannot help but wonder what is wrong with me that I have not yet married! And you know the sad state of our dowry portions, and Papa is a mere knight whereas Broderick stands to become the next Viscount Mulland. And our new stepmama,"—Lorraine lowered her voice even further, for fear the lady in question would overhear—"well, she is not of the best *ton,* is she? If he did not care for me, Broderick could look well above my station for a wife. We must be sensitive to his family's tolerance of the connection. He needs to bring them to acceptance slowly, and then he will feel free to speak with Papa." Lorraine spoke with a quiet confidence that took some of the bite from her words.

Still, Elizabeth grumbled, "I should think he would expect them to love the woman he chose, regardless."

"And so he does. But there is no need for haste."

"I suppose not," Elizabeth had grudgingly agreed, because the joy that had radiated from her sister's face was all the further persuasion she had required to believe in a happy future for her sister.

It had been, after a fashion, Broderick Mainworthy, one day to be the Viscount Mulland, who had created Elizabeth's woes. He had done so by moving forward in his courtship of Lorraine with achingly slow discretion. While three-quarters of a year drained away, he had held Lorraine's hand in secret, and whispered words of devotion that made Elizabeth's sister float upon a cloud of bliss. But it had been his inability to publicly commit to the socially inferior Lorraine that had finally driven Elizabeth into her grandly foolish debacle.

Her debacle—little more than a moment's decision, now turned into a lifetime's regret.

Elizabeth could not look back on her decision without wincing. She supposed some part of her had known, even then, that things had moved far too quickly for good judgment to be any part of the matter.

The night Radford Barnes had proposed an elopement, she had known him but fourteen days—two weeks. It was folly, utter folly to believe anything he had said after so short an acquaintance! Yet, although the logical part of her mind had known better, Elizabeth had listened to Radford's declaration of undying affection, and one day later had consented to elope with him. Three nights later she had sneaked out her papa's front door to Radford's waiting carriage, and there had been no turning back from that moment on.

Had she believed herself in love? Looking back, it was difficult to conceive she might have been capable of such determined blindness—or name it what it really was, stupidity. How could anyone love another after a mere fortnight's acquaintance? Attraction had existed. Oh yes, she had been attracted to the darkly handsome, slightly dissipated-appearing façade of Radford Barnes. But which young, single female of her acquaintance was not? His presence in a room had eclipsed all others. There was something dangerous about him, something exciting and headstrong and enticing—or had that only been true for Elizabeth? Had she willed it to be true?

The truth was, she had required a beau. No, a husband. Marriage had been an escape, she saw that now.

So she'd had to delude herself into believing she loved Mr. Barnes—Radford—and what of that? Most people did not marry for love, but for security and the mutual exchange of advantages. She had done no more than most of the females she knew.

But, no, she could not lie to herself, not anymore. Unlike her counterparts, she had been decisive, hasty, and doggedly determined to plunge into obvious folly—marriage to a stranger. Marriage without guarantees, without an investigation into facts, marriage without any safeguards. If she had fallen, she had deserved to, for it had been through her own actions that she had come to stand upon the precipice.

In her own defense, it had all seemed so clear. If she eloped she would no longer have to live under the disapproving eye of her father's new wife, Francine. Her stepmama would certainly *not* approve of an elopement, even if she would be keenly happy to have at least one of her stepdaughters out of the house. It was not that Francine was an evil woman . . . but she was not Mama, two years dead. And Francine did not love her husband's children, nor graciously share "her" home with them.

More important, if Elizabeth eloped, there was the matter of her dowry, for no self-respecting father would award a dowry to the scoundrel who eloped with his daughter. That Elizabeth would deliberately make the choice to surrender her dowry seemed opposed to basic logic, until one considered that her portion then could be transferred to the remaining daughter, to Lorraine. Mr. Broderick Mainworthy's family could only look upon a doubled dowry with an approving eye. They were of the kind of wealth that did not question sudden discreet increases in value; only the increase itself, not its origin, would concern them.

And Elizabeth had blithely believed she would not need her dowry. Radford was wealthy, or so Elizabeth had judged from his up-to-the-rig equipage, clothing, and gentleman's apartment at Albany in Piccadilly. She had heard the odd grumble or two about Mr. Radford Barnes, yes. Nothing of consequence, nothing that she couldn't blame upon jealousy on the part of other gentlemen, those not quite so gifted with that essence called flash, nor so glib of tongue, as her soon-to-be-spouse.

Yes, an elopement had seemed the very thing to create happiness all the way around, and Elizabeth had thought herself daring and clever.

If only it had turned out to *be* an elopement in fact and not just a fiction!

But no, she did not really wish for that either, not truthfully. To be legally bonded to Radford Barnes was a fate she could not wish upon the foulest harridan London ever produced, let alone on herself. Not even to save her reputation.

Of course, she had to admit to herself, Radford had not offered to marry her in truth once it was revealed the ceremony had been a false one, so the point was moot.

She had already determined her reputation was irredeemable, and that she must disappear from sight, so there was no value in looking back, except to know to avoid a similar stupidity in the future. Yes, she must learn from her grievous mistake.

No man, she vowed to herself yet once more, would ever again find Elizabeth Hatton susceptible to sweet words or honeyed promises.

Not that she was in danger of any man coming near enough to offer such sweet nothings, she thought wryly as she settled back upon the bed Lord Greyleigh had provided her. Only look at her situation: there was no man in sight, for one certainly could not count Lord Greyleigh, her scarcely tolerant host, as a potential suitor. Even if she wanted a suitor, which was impossible in the situation, Greyleigh would not be the man to fill those shoes. Even though, a quiet and unwelcome little interior voice whispered, Lord Greyleigh was handsome enough to make a girl's heart turn somersaults.

"He is odd-looking," Elizabeth said aloud, as though to deny her own traitorous thoughts. Then she scowled, because someone's appearance, she now knew to her sorrow, was a very hollow reason for accepting or rejecting that person. "He is just plain odd, period," she next said, but even though she spoke the truth, the words did not sit well on her tongue.

Had she learned anything from her mistakes? Her judgment

of men had proven to be atrocious. She would be a fool to trust ever again to her intuition, for look how far afield it had led her already! If she were to feel guilty for maligning Lord Greyleigh's character, she would have to feel guilty for maligning all men. Papa had married a shrew; Lorraine's beau might never kick over the traces in which his family held him in check; and Radford had been especially appalling—and she had once made herself believe she could love him. If that was not proof of her lack of perception, what was?

She leaned back against the headboard and closed her eyes. She tried to empty her mind of all distressing thoughts, but truth was she had little else to think on. She recounted every distress that had come her way—only to have her eyes snap open when she realized, in sudden clarity, that all of them had taken place *before* she had entered Lord Greyleigh's home.

Other than seeing a strange woman who might or might not be a ghost, her situation had done nothing but improve since she had been brought into this house. Her foot was under a doctor's care, Radford had presumably given up pursuing her because he believed she had perished, and she had decided upon how to direct her future. That anonymous future she needed looked not only possible, but entirely obtainable.

It was coincidence, of course, this sudden turning up of her luck. But she could not quite escape a nagging sensation that, for all his oddities, Lord Greyleigh had not quite proven himself of the mold from which Elizabeth considered all men must be made.

But Lord Greyleigh was considered to be at least an eccentric, if not a madman. Given his reputation, it was not odd that he stepped outside the realm of normal behavior. She must keep that in mind. She must remember that because he was different did not mean she ought to forget the lesson already learned: she did not understand men, and she could not trust them to do what was best for *her.*

Chapter 9

Late that afternoon, Gideon looked across his desk to where Elizabeth was ensconced in one of his large library chairs. She wore a gown that had been his mother's, stored these two months past. Mama's gown had proven too voluminous for Elizabeth, so that she had been obliged to pin a fichu at the neckline for modesty's sake.

His mama had been as fair as Gideon was himself. He remembered the gown Elizabeth now wore, because he had never thought it suited Mama's coloring. It was a vibrant green silk, a rich emerald. It was most unsuitable for Elizabeth's place in life, a young unmarried woman presumably only a few years out of the schoolroom. It was, however, eminently suitable for her coloring, setting off her dark hair and flattering her brown eyes in the same way that in summer leaves flatter a forest. Although the fichu somewhat detracted from the lie of the gown, Elizabeth still managed to look quite fetching.

Gideon frowned at the word "fetching" and turned his attention back to the estate books before him on his desk.

Only to look up at her again two minutes later when she gave a small laugh.

"Oh, yes, I know that one well," she said, holding a book aloft. *"An Appointed Meeting,"* she stated, reading the title. "The meeting being between Sir Francis Drake and Queen Elizabeth, I recall. My sister first read it aloud to me, and I adored it. I have read it many times since. I might do so again if I cannot find a book that I have not yet read."

Gideon turned back to his account books and tried to focus on the columns of numbers there despite sudden distracting thoughts of ships full of gold sailing back to England and her queen, also named Elizabeth.

Scattered around his guest were stacks of books taken from Gideon's shelves by two attentive footmen, Biggins and Simons by name. Biggins did the fetching, while Simons helped the lady sort the books into piles of "no" and "possibly." The latter was the better job for Simons, since he had lost the two primary fingers on his left hand from a firearm explosion while he was fighting as a common soldier against Napoleon. He was strong of arm, for lifting and hauling, but naturally not as dextrous of hand as was Biggins. Elizabeth had made no comment about Simons' loss, but she had either accidentally—or deftly—given him the job better suited to his abilities.

Gideon played with the feathered end of the quill, contemplating the thought that Elizabeth's mental state seemed less fragile than Mama's had been—but then again it was difficult to remember Mama as a younger, less disturbed woman. Age had not wrought any kind changes with Mama, only taking her deeper and deeper into her delusions. Perhaps she had once also seemed as composed as this woman seemed at times.

The footmen consulted again with the lady, seeking her opinion, and then Biggins went to retrieve yet more volumes for her review.

"I have read that one before, too," Elizabeth said of the binding Simons showed her. She accepted the book, saving him from having to transfer it to his marred left hand, and put the rejected book on a growing pile near her knee. With her other hand she reached for the next book the footman handed her. "Oh yes, that one, too."

She had read quite a few of them, Gideon noted—or so she said. She was either a bit of a bluestocking or else she was simply making wild claims.

He suspected the latter.

Curious, that. There were not many females of his acquaintances who not only liked to read, but who would readily admit to that scholarly pursuit. Granted, his shelves did not offer much in the way of Greek or Latin tomes. Most of Gideon's inherited library consisted of dreadfully dry religious tracts, tales of travel almost as dusty, and a daunting profusion of Minerva

Press novels. Mama had cared for the latter in her younger days, and Papa had cared for books only as decoration of his library. Still, there was the occasional volume of poems, treatises on farming practices, and recent popular reading that Gideon had added to the collection, and most of those presented to Elizabeth she claimed to have already read.

"Collection of the Essential Works of John Gay." She read another title aloud, and Gideon noted she placed it in her "no" pile.

"Am I to take it you have read John Gay?" Gideon scoffed.

"I have." She gave him a curious look, one that suggested she bordered on being insulted.

"Quote me something by him then. Anything at all that you recall," Gideon said, not bothering to hide his skepticism.

She gave him an arch look. *"'If the heart of a man is deprest with cares,'"* she recited with the slow dawning of a superior little smile in her eyes, *"'The mist is dispell'd when a woman appears.'* That is from *The Beggar's Opera."*

"So it is," Gideon agreed, blinking away his surprise. "Thank you," he murmured, and ungraciously turned his attention back to his account books.

"Now here is something I have not seen before," she said, and Gideon had to credit her for not sounding smug. He glanced up from his work once more, despite an interior command not to keep allowing her activities to distract him, and saw she had a Minerva Press volume in her hands.

"The Serpent's Tooth." Elizabeth read the title aloud. "It is surely about ungrateful children, do you not think?" she asked the room in general.

Gideon frowned at the pages before him, realizing he had yet again lost his place. He would have to start the sums all over again.

He took a deep breath, and let it out in an audible sigh as he wondered for the hundredth time why he did not simply hire a secretary to do this tedious estate work for him. Other men left estate affairs to their men of business—but other men ended in bankruptcy or debtor's prison. Not Gideon. Not with a houseful of dependents relying on him and his ability to remain solvent. That was why he watched over his own books.

If only some of those dependents were not immediately in this room and disturbing his thinking, Gideon thought sourly.

He was almost relieved when his butler, Frick, stepped in at that moment, interrupting the resumption of his calculations. "The post, my lord," Frick informed him, bringing the same into the room on a silver salver.

Gideon removed the single missive, and Frick bowed himself out, but not before inquiring if Miss Elizabeth required anything for her comfort and nodding to a request for tea. Gideon looked up at that, disgruntled by the obvious indication that she meant to linger here a while longer. Maybe he should leave, for he certainly was not getting much accomplished with Elizabeth in the room. She was a dratted distraction.

"Is your letter from someone you care to hear from?" The distraction spoke yet again.

Gideon glanced at the handwriting in which his name had been penned on the outside of the folded missive. "Benjamin," he answered curtly.

"Benjamin?" Elizabeth echoed, quite evidently content to make idle conversation.

Gideon sighed, but in all fairness he could hardly blame her; time could be a heavy weight on the shoulders of an invalid. In some minds time was a flexible thing, not a straight line ruthlessly ticked away second by second. In some minds, one day could go on and on, revisited, relived for years, or never ending. Mama, in her later days, had returned in her mind to her youth, so far lost to reality that she could not even think how to don the clothes in her wardrobe, for they no longer had the shape or purpose of the clothing she had worn as a girl forty years earlier.

Elizabeth continued to look at Gideon with a question in her gaze.

"Benjamin is my brother," he explained. "I have two. Benjamin is younger by two years, and Sebastian by five."

"You have no sisters?"

"None. And you?" He gave her a level gaze, and hoped he had not allowed his interest to visibly sharpen.

She parted her lips, then closed them deliberately. He would swear she was perfectly aware he had meant to trap her into a confession of her past. She might be of the nervous sort, but she was not stupid.

"I cannot say," was her reply.

"You do not know?" he queried sharply, now not bothering to hide his keen interest. "Or you will not say?"

"I cannot say," she reported. She turned her gaze down to the book she cracked open in her lap, her mouth set in a firm line.

"*Could* you say, if I promised to do nothing to find your family?"

She glanced up sharply. "Do you promise that?"

It would be easy to lie, but some sense of honor or correctness held his tongue. "Of course not. Your family has a right to know where you are—"

Putting the book under her arm, Elizabeth turned her attention to the nearest footman. "I would like to be returned to my room, please. At once."

"You are running away," Gideon said with surprise, and wondered if he meant from their conversation or from her past.

"No," Elizabeth said, nodding as Simons brought the usual chair for her to transfer into. "I am running *toward* something, Lord Greyleigh." She hesitated, then looked back at him. She squared her shoulders. "I do wish you would not ask me questions. If you will insist on doing so, I will have to leave this house at once, no matter what the doctor cautions."

He stared at her, not so much angered as shocked. It wasn't her apparent lucidity that shocked him, nor her demands to remain unquestioned, but the stark anguish sitting in the back of her eyes. She tried to hide it, tried to stare him down haughtily, but Gideon had looked too many times into despondent eyes not to recognize the agony he saw now.

The footmen glanced between the lady and their master, clearly at a loss as to whether or not they should proceed. Elizabeth did not signal them, her attention wholly fixed on Gideon.

She had been through some terrible ordeal—he could see that as clearly as he could see by the rapid rise and fall of her bosom that her breath had quickened in agitation. Or perhaps the ordeal was something that lived in her brain, torturing her, making her unable to cope with the world around her.

It did not really matter which. Sane or mad, she was a soul in pain—lost, wandering, afraid.

She surely feared that her refusals to speak would cause him to cast her out, before her enfeebled body was able to withstand the risk. She feared her future swung on this moment, and she waited with bated breath to learn her fate. He knew it as clearly as if she had spoken. He had looked into fear-filled eyes a hundred, a thousand times, and despite his strictest intentions to safeguard his own soul, found himself succumbing to the plea he sensed now from her.

"Come back in a few minutes," Gideon said in a rough voice to the footmen, who withdrew at once. When they had gone, Gideon turned back to Elizabeth.

"My dear lady, if it distresses you so, I promise I will not ask you any more questions," he found himself saying, wanting to do what he had always done, wanting to make that despondency recede from her eyes.

"Thank you," she said on a breathy sigh, manifestly relieved. "Perhaps, one day. . . . My lord, I would like to repay your kindnesses in some way—one day, if it is in my power to do so."

"To tell me the truth?"

"To explain everything. Yes."

"You could write to me," he said, indicating his brother's letter with a forced half smile, an attempt to lighten the moment, to make her relief complete.

She responded with a half smile of her own, and he experienced a physical thrill when he saw that the fear had retreated from her gaze. "Yes," she went on. "I would like to tell you all. When I can."

"When you can," he repeated, and the words made some manner of pact between them, as firmly as if they had shaken hands over a bargain. How had this happened? How had they come to a moment where words were not necessary, but the force of her will, her intent gaze, the anxiety there, had been enough to communicate silently with him?

She smiled again, a tremulous twist of the lips.

"Do you still wish to return to your room?" Gideon asked for something to say while he frantically tried to sort through their conversation, tried to see how it was that he had been made to shape this odd agreement with her.

She smiled again, this time a yes to his question, and he stood to summon the footmen once more into the room.

He remained standing until she was clear of the room, and then he slowly regained his seat. He put one hand to his forehead and planted his elbow atop his desk. His other hand slowly rose to join the first, and he cradled his head in growing exasperation, wondering what manner of fool promises not to ask questions of an addled stranger who has invaded his home.

"A gullible fool," he responded to his own question.

Mama had sometimes manipulated him this way . . . and despite having dealt with her moods and fits for years on end, he had still been easily gulled. He had not only let this Elizabeth with-no-surname lead him by the nose, but it seemed to him he had done so willingly.

The absurd part of his eager capitulation to her demand was that he'd had every intention of asking her why she had recognized his description of the dandy, the one who had been trying to remove her ring in that ditch. But now he could not.

"Deftly done," he murmured aloud, and wondered if Elizabeth's face, could he but see it at this moment, would be wreathed in a smug smile. Oh no, she was not stupid, not this stranger who refused to tolerate any more of his questions.

Elizabeth made an awkward transfer from the chair to her bed, dismissed the footmen, and for once felt she deserved the stinging pain in her heel.

It was not that she felt bad for Simons, even though he had explained to her how he had come to lose his fingers, and even though she knew his injury had much longer lasting repercussions than her own.

It was not the promise she'd extracted from Lord Greyleigh that made her feel deserving of discomfort, even though she suspected he had never wanted to promise any such thing.

No, it was the way she had reacted to his presence, to his steady regard when he had fixed his attention on her, that made her now concentrate on her heel's pain, as if to do penance.

His steady regard. She had been keenly aware of his presence in the library, even though he sat across the room from her, even though he spent most of the time with his head down, hard at work. When she had first glimpsed him there, she had begun to order the footmen to carry her elsewhere, but Lord Greyleigh had looked up and seen her, and waved her in. It had seemed churlish to decline once she had already disturbed his peace, and she had wanted a book to read, after all.

It was his appearance, of course, that made him difficult to ignore. His hair had become lightly kissed by gold in the slanting afternoon sunlight, reminding Elizabeth of the luminous painted halos in religious art. And when he glanced up at her, she was shocked as ever by his pale blue eyes, eyes to rival any painted saint's—and a few devil's eyes she'd seen painted as well.

As she moved her leg onto a pillow, hoisting her injured heel, she considered that one thing about the afternoon had been gratifying: Lord Greyleigh had promised not to question her further. It would be good to be done with that particular tension between them. Now she could just be a guest, lingering awhile, until she was gone—no complications, no ties, no worrying constantly about what clue to her past he might wring from her.

He could be lying about questioning her no more, of course, or ranting despite sounding rational. Yet, without evidence to the contrary, Elizabeth did not think so. Whatever else he was, Lord Greyleigh was not a man who spoke for the sake of hearing his own words; what he said, he meant. His thinking might be muddled—how else had he gained the singular reputation he bore?—but he was consistent within his own thinking at least.

No, it was not his word she doubted, but her own nature.

Damn Radford Barnes to Hades, Elizabeth thought, shocking herself with the blasphemy, but even more with the knowledge that she really would condemn Radford to the flames if she could. She detested him for all he had done to her, but what she hated him for the most, what shamed her to the core, was that the man had awakened in her a carnal longing.

All the passages in the Bible, the ones she used to think she understood, but had not really, now made humiliating sense to Elizabeth. *Abstain from fleshly lusts, which war against the soul. . . . Can a man take fire in his bosom, and his clothes not be burned? Can one go on hot coals, and his feet not be burned?* She could have written one herself: *Can a woman know physical love and not be changed?*

When she had believed herself married to Radford, she had tried to love him, tried to be all that a wife is to her husband. She'd had no thought that the special license he'd presented was worthless, a forgery, that the man who had "married" them was but a hired accomplice, no more real than the marriage bond she'd thought she'd entered.

She had learned from Radford the pleasure of physical love. God help her, she had enjoyed the intimacy. Up until the night he had revealed his perfidy, she had been content enough in her decision to wed the man, and to take this stranger nightly into her bed. No, not just content, she had been eager.

God had been merciful in one regard at least: she was not breeding. It was in fact her womanly cycle that had finally brought out the dark side in Radford, had finally set him to telling her the truth. Denied her bed four days running, he had resorted to the bottle for entertainment instead. The drink had loosened his tongue and had brought out his true nature. Eyes that had gazed upon Elizabeth with loverlike zeal had then turned dark with a malicious kind of glee. He had shown her the special license and revealed its worthlessness.

"No, 'scuse me, that's not quite true, it's not worthless," he had slurred. "It has quite a bit o' worth. Your papa will pay dearly to have me hand it, and you, back to him."

"Radford?" Elizabeth remembered asking with a quivering voice, but even then, even at that first moment of revelation she had believed him. Even in their brief time together, there had been something missing between them, something that even the pleasure of the marriage bed could not cloak. They were on their bridal journey, granted, but all mention of returning home had been deftly turned aside by him . . . but it was more than just his vagueness about their future together. It had been the occasional look she'd surprised in his eyes, or the way he had phrased a comment, a small hurtful way of saying something to her. She had already begun to wonder if her husband always spoke the truth . . . and, most important, if he spoke it when he said he loved her.

"Now don't you worry, m'dear," he had gone on in a growing sneer. "I'll reward your papa for payin' me for your return
by keeping m'mouth shut." He had put a finger to his lips in a
shushing motion. "Shhh! No one tells nothin', once m'pockets
are full. Everythin' goes back to normal, and everyone is happy.
You'll see."

"I shall take you to court," she had declared, wishing she
sounded fierce, but even to her own ears she had only sounded
devastated.

"No, you will not. Courts bring scandal. Trust me, m'dove,
no one's ever taken me to court. It's all 'pay up and hush up,'
and your Papa will want it just the same. How else will he ever
pawn you off on some unsuspecting half-wit if it gets about
you've been diddled with? Just be glad I'll take the money and
leave it at that."

Tears had slid down her cheeks, as much from comprehension of her changed circumstances as from the pain he dealt her.
She had eloped with him in order to increase Lorraine's chance
of wedding her beloved Broderick—and now Elizabeth would
have to return home, ruined, bringing scandal to the family
name. It was the very kind of scandal that would put paid to
Lorraine's acceptance by Broderick Mainworthy's family. Elizabeth did not want to weep in front of this monster who had
pretended to marry her, but the thought of the pain that lay
ahead for her entire family was too overwhelming.

"Oh, stop that blubberin', you silly cow. Did you think I actually loved you?" he had slurred with a drunken laugh.

She had stifled her tears until he had fallen asleep, intoxi-
cated and snoring on the inn's bed, and then she had gathered
her jewelry, stolen one of his carriage horses, and ridden out of
his life.

But some things could not be ridden away from—and one of
them was her schooling in the ways of the flesh. Once that gate
had been opened, there was no shutting it again.

When she looked at Lord Greyleigh, admittedly a strange
man of peculiar look and even more peculiar ways, still she saw
the man beneath the trappings. She knew what existed under a
man's waistcoat, under his unmentionables, and, Heaven help

her, men were no longer the sexless creatures they had been to her once innocent eyes.

She saw now wide shoulders where a woman's were more narrow, and narrow hips where a woman's were wide. She saw tone of muscle under a well-cut coat; she saw the way an Adam's apple pushed at a man's cravat; she saw a difference in the way a man balanced on his feet. Where men had once been "un-women" to her sinless mind, now she saw them as "males," and Radford had been of a male beauty such as to make her lips part and her breath catch.

Lord Greyleigh was such a male, although Elizabeth would have been hard-pressed to explain why. He was handsome in his own extraordinary way, but it was more than that. There was some quality to his voice, as well, the deep timbre of it, yes, but also what he said. She supposed it was that she could not always guess what he might say, and not knowing was interesting, even stimulating.

It did not matter, of course, and her awareness of him as a male was wholly inappropriate.

She had known he was exasperated with her in the library, that her presence had disturbed his work, but she had not wanted to leave. It was interesting, fascinating even, to watch a man at work, to see him bite a lip in consternation at something in his logbooks, to see him stand and stretch and be heedlessly male in his movements.

Elizabeth had begun to study men in this new way, with these newly opened eyes, almost from the moment Radford had first taken her in his arms after their hasty "marriage" in a little village chapel. No man was outside her circle of regard: footmen, innkeepers, hawkers calling their wares in the street—all of them were intensely fascinating. Some for their muscles, their "foreignness"; some for their speech, the pitch of their voices or the amusement of their banter; some for a certain *savoir-faire* that was difficult to define but now easy for Elizabeth to see. She felt as if she had been living in a fog, near these fascinating creatures called men, but yet removed from actually seeing them fully.

Some were coarse, some profane, some polished, and others

too effeminate, but all engaged Elizabeth's senses in a way they never had only a few weeks earlier.

Which, sadly, just went to prove her utter lack of judgment. Men could harm her, control her, forbid her what she wanted, and thwart her.

To be fascinated by men was like being fascinated by one of the lions in the Menagerie at the Tower: they were a marvel to behold from afar, but a woman would be a fool to ever climb into the cage with them. One knew it, one understood it, one feared the creature's power . . . but something made one want to open the trapdoor and reach out to the very thing that could destroy one.

Elizabeth could not even say it was all Radford's fault, for he had only awakened in her a desire that was already there, lying dormant. She could not blame the lion for having its allure. She could only blame herself for responding so avidly to it.

And, God save her, she feared her impulses, feared they could lead her to an even darker future.

In simple, honest terms, she was ruined. She would be removed from Society for six months, maybe more, dependent on Lorraine's situation. During that six months, people would wonder where Elizabeth had gone. People would whisper. Once she did come home again, Elizabeth knew that, as a matrimonial prospect, she could not look high—if she married at all.

Oh, someone might want her to wife despite the whispers. An older man whose wife had perished, leaving him with a half dozen children, perhaps. Or a Cit, possibly, looking to align his lack of a good surname with that of a knight's daughter.

For that matter, Elizabeth did not fear being alone, for Papa would see that she had a home and a small income. Indeed, she could live with Papa and Francine, even though there would be little enough happiness there.

No, what she feared was that any path she took, alone, or with Papa, or with a man she married for convenience, she would never know love.

No matter how brief it had been, for a very short while she had been happy, and had meant to be a loving wife. The physical act had been wonderful, because she had believed it was meant to be wonderful, had believed that she was married to a man who loved her so much he had needed to marry her in haste or die from wanting her.

Silly, foolish thoughts—impossible dreams—she saw that now. She thought she'd loved once, so fleetingly, but long enough to know what love ought to be. And she feared she would never know such a thing for even the briefest moment. How could she lie abed with a man and not love him? It seemed impossible, horrible—but it was her future, and that only if she were fortunate enough to attract a mate.

Love is possible, even in an arranged marriage, even after a fall from grace, whispered a traitorous inner voice.

But in her heart of hearts Elizabeth feared it was for her only a hope and not a real possibility. She no longer believed she could marry and then learn to love. She would have to love the man before the ceremony, she knew, or she would never love him. Tolerance and patience could be learned, but love? She did not think so.

For the first time in her life she understood how it was that some women became old maids, as they were so unkindly called. They may have chosen their path, a world without men and without babies, because they could not bear the price that it would cost them to travel the usual course set out for womankind. They would rather be alone, without a growing family at their feet, than live beside a man they could not cherish.

Elizabeth sighed, already learning to loathe this bed on which she spent too much of her day, and now there was a long evening looming ahead. It was a wide bed, built for two, which thought only made her musings turn more sour yet.

At least her door was open, having been left so by the footmen, presumably so they could hear her call out if she required anything. She felt a little less alone in the world with the door open, with bustling servants passing by on their various errands.

At that moment, Lord Greyleigh strode past her door, once again dressed for an outing. Elizabeth bit her lip in vexation at the instantaneous response she experienced, a turning-over sensation somewhere in the vicinity of her navel, that reminded her once more that he was male and she female. Yet more proof that she had no sensibility when it came to matters of men. Heaven help her, she was strung as tight as a violin, and longing for someone, anyone, to play her. It was humiliating—ridiculous. She could almost giggle—it was preferable to crying—at her warmth of feeling, at the absurdity of the awakened, passionate nature she could well have done without.

However, any giggle was instantly stifled, for Lord Greyleigh retread his steps, stopping to lean nonchalantly into her doorway. He removed his hat, and she wondered how many people upon first meeting him thought he powdered his hair in the old fashion. She wondered, too, how many women had stood close enough to him to know that his eyes were the very lightest blue, not grey as one might think.

"Do you require anything?" he inquired politely, the perfect host.

"Nothing, thank you."

"Do you wish your door closed?"

"No, thank you, I like to see people moving about. If it does not disturb you?"

"I should hardly think it could." He stood away from the doorjamb, juggling his hat in preparation of returning it to his head. "I am going to my club in Bristol," he said.

"I hope it makes for a pleasant evening," she said with a smile, faintly surprised that he should bother to tell her his destination.

He pointed at her propped foot with his hat. "Do you think you might be able to get about some with the use of canes?"

Ah, so that was why he had stopped, to inquire if there were some way to hurry her recovery. She could not really fault him for wanting her out of his house.

"Yes, I should think canes would help," she said, again with a smile.

"I am sure there are some about. My walking stick would never do, the head is too decorative for comfort, but I am certain the servants can find something about the house that could be of service."

"That would be most helpful." She could not quite keep an acerbic tone from entering her voice.

He gave a little scowl, but then he nodded, bowed, and resumed his way.

Elizabeth listened to the sound of his boot heels until she could no longer hear them, then lay back against the bed's pillows and sighed.

"She who has never lov'd, has never liv'd," she again quoted from John Gay, and the notion made her smile ever so slightly. Perhaps she smiled from the consoling truth of the saying, or perhaps from remembering the scene in the library, she was not entirely sure. On any account, her spirits lifted, and she began to wonder how one used canes to get about.

Chapter 10

A half hour later, with the sun just setting for the night, Gideon sat next to a silver-haired man already gaming at a faro table. They both sat within the slightly shabby but comfortable confines of their mutual and unsuitably named club, the Elegance, a gaming club more familiarly known as the Elly. The silver-haired gentleman nodded a greeting. "Greyleigh."

Gideon nodded in return. "Rowbotham."

"You have just arrived, but, alas, I am just prepared to leave," Rowbotham said. "The play's too deep for my pockets tonight. No luck, y'see. And I warn you, the beef is dry as dust tonight as well."

"Seems I could have chosen a better evening to attend," Gideon said with a slight smile, although it was an effort to make the comment sound light and carefree. He did not feel particularly carefree. He liked Lord Rowbotham well enough, but the man was thirty years older and not the sort of acquaintance to chase shadows from one's thoughts, not the right companion for tonight at all.

"'Fraid so, my lad." Rowbotham reached for his small pile of remaining markers even as Gideon laid his purse on the green baize of the game table. The older man slid the markers into his vest pocket, turned to signal for his hat and cane, then offered Gideon his regrets. "Hope my lack of luck runs the opposite with you, Greyleigh," he said with the absent pleasantness of a fellow club member.

Gideon murmured a farewell, saying he'd do his best, even though he already sensed the evening would not accomplish his goal of diversion, for he now sat alone at the faro table. The liveried servant behind the table inquired if my lord was ready to play, but Gideon shook his head. "A drink," he said instead, leaving his purse where it lay as he stood and crossed to where several other club members sat over glasses of port.

He was invited to join them, and ordered brandy from the waiter who appeared at once to take his request. The group was not a chatty one, and it quickly became evident that good luck at the gaming tables had been elusive this night for all but one of their number. Even he, Grant by name, was not particularly thrilled by his winnings, for the stakes had never climbed high enough in his estimation. The conversation turned to other evenings of ill luck at the cards, and Gideon soon found his attention wandering.

He had come to Elly's for the specific purpose of being with people—but people who could not, would not demand much of him. He need not engage in the light conversation, and would be allowed to sip quietly at his snifter, and no one would find him odd for doing so. Elly's was not a place for wild gaming, but sensible risks of expendable funds, a level of play of which Gideon approved.

But tonight he could have used some of the harmless chaos of a place such as Brooks's in London, where extraordinary sums were won or lost in an hour's gaming. He could have used the usual babble around the large betting book at White's—for Gideon wanted to be distracted. He wanted to be reminded that some people were in the world for the simple purpose of entertainment, and that there was something other than duty, somewhere.

Serious people with serious problems he already had aplenty at home. At a noisy, frivolous place like White's, people would speak with him, but it would be small talk, desultory. It would demand no real decisions, no judgments that affected the course of entire lives.

At home, Gideon had three men in varying stages of mental confusion, albeit two of them were due to leave tomorrow. Their families had been found and had agreed to come and retrieve their members burned out by the asylum fire. His staff would be gratified to see the men go, as they had been put to work in the kitchens and had nearly driven Cook to distraction.

But what of the one called Alfred Thompson, the one they

had been forced to tie by the ankle to the big kitchen table so
he would not wander away? The man had babbled that his family lived in Salisbury, but he had yet to produce a coherent direction for them. Gideon had sent a footman by horse to
Salisbury, hoping there was a Thompson family to be found
there. With any luck, the man would be a problem soon solved,
before Cook quit, as he threatened to do daily.

And if Thompson wasn't trouble enough, there were a dozen
others to nag at Gideon's conscience. Simons, for instance. Despite the man's missing fingers, he was competent enough as a
footman—but he'd requested that Gideon interview and possibly hire a colleague he'd met in the war, another physically injured man now out of work. Apparently the man was missing a
leg, but thought that despite the need for crutches, his service
once as a batman qualified him to do well as a valet.

A valet, on crutches? Gideon shook his head, but as much at
himself as at Simons, because Gideon had been soft-headed
enough to agree to see the man.

Then there was the maid who was in a family way; and
young Jamie in the stables who kept the other stable lads awake
with his nightly screams since his entire family had perished in
a coaching accident; and there was Elizabeth of course—the
mystery woman with the polish and poise of a queen, but the
inconsistent ways and words of a madwoman. Truth be told,
Elizabeth was the least of his problems, because she meant to
leave, she wanted to go, but only must wait upon some healing.
His biggest problem lay with those who had come to his home
to stay.

But how could he turn any of them away? If he had not been
born, would his brothers have cared for their mother? Was caring for others his fate? And how could he call it "caring" when
all he wanted to do was escape every last one of them?

Gideon sipped his brandy, not surprised when his thoughts
shifted to again linger on Elizabeth. That was only to be expected since Mr. Arbuckle had made his report on her this afternoon.

"Nary a word on a missing Miss B," the hired investigator
had said with a puzzled shake of his head. "Got a lad in London what reports to me, and I been to every city within fifty

miles o' Severn's Well, and I tell you there's nary a word. Course, folks wouldn't be looking for a missing gel from an asylum, says I, unless they has reason to know she ain't there no more. I spread that word, too, but that'll take time to work up any news, o' course. I ain't heard from Nottingham yet, but word is the post is late 'cause of heavy rain up that way, so I'll have word in a day or two. And o' course I got someone watchin' the post for letters to the asylum."

"Perhaps we're going about this all wrong," Gideon had said, cupping his chin in his hand as he gazed at Mr. Arbuckle.

"Your meaning, sir?" Arbuckle had said with no sign that he had taken affront.

"Perhaps we're wrong to concentrate on the ring, on the 'B.' She could have stolen it for all we know. Better to follow up on the news you spread of the fire. Only the coldest clan would not wonder what had become of their pretty young family member after she was burned out of her, er, residence, even if she was not right in her mind. I like that you are watching the post, but perhaps you ought to be inquiring, too, after missing heiresses, that manner of thing. Miss Elizabeth is not entirely dicked in the nob. She strikes me as the sort who might have been encouraged to go to the asylum for 'rest,' but also possibly to get her away from an unfortunate connection."

"Like wantin' to run off with her dancin' master, that manner o' thing?"

"Exactly. It is time to listen to gossip. That's where we'll most likely find something of Miss Elizabeth's origins."

"Right-o," Mr Arbuckle had said, touching a finger to his forehead in a gesture of agreement. "Right-o!" he had said again with appreciation when Gideon tossed him a payment purse. "I'll be back soon as I know somethin', m'lord."

Of course, Gideon considered now as he gazed into the amber liquid in his glass, Elizabeth's identity might never be determined. Certainly she did not wish it to be. And Gideon had other, more pressing concerns, such as why there were seemingly increasing cases of the ghost appearing in his house. He was not entirely convinced that Elizabeth had seen the ghost; she might have seen what she wished to see, what the servants told her to expect to see. Still, there was certainly something, or someone, in his house—someone who liked to tilt pictures, move branches of candles from one room to another, and someone who liked to hide his stickpins in odd places about the house.

Oh, yes, he believed someone—or something—was doing these things, despite how he had downplayed the suggestion of a ghost to Elizabeth. He would not feed any such rumor, especially not to a woman whose clarity of mind he mistrusted. That was all he needed—a hysterical guest, who in turn would make his already skitterish servants hysterical, too.

Perhaps that should be the primary question Gideon asked of this possible valet Simons wished him to interview. *Would you be willing to remain in my employ even if the house is haunted?*

Gideon's mouth twisted into a sour smile, and he set aside the brandy, which was not suiting tonight. In fact, Elly's was not suiting him either. He nodded to his associates, murmured his farewells, and waited only long enough for his hat, gloves, and purse to be brought to him before he departed into the night.

"Might as well ponder my problems at home," he muttered to himself as he signaled his driver, since there was no escape from thoughts of his problems at his club tonight. He wondered briefly if he were running out of places where he *could* escape his burdens, however temporarily. He pushed the thought aside, for in that direction lay the madness he already too often feared may have been handed down from his mama.

The next morning Gideon tucked under his arm the two stout wooden canes that Simons had discovered in the attics, and walked softly down his own hallway. He walked with care because he meant, most deliberately, to catch his temporary resident all but unaware in her room.

Sneaking into a room was a procedure he had adopted in order to monitor his mother's behavior. In her later years, when her hold on reality had become weaker and her actions less comprehensible, she had also become secretive. She would dart about for hours on end, hiding little things in her clothing, like bits of ribbon or full spools of thread or inkpots, creating havoc for the maids on wash day.

Near the end she had taken to saving bits of food in her napkin, but she had never consumed them in her room later. She had kept the food bits in her jewelry case, among her diamonds and rubies and sapphires. She had not liked it when the food bits were taken away, and so Gideon had learned to sneak in and clean them out when her maid was bathing her. He had never concluded why Mama had hoarded rinds of ham and broken biscuits and spoonfuls of butter, nor why they had been prized along with her jewels, but Mama had clearly had some unfathomable and persistent intent in mind.

He had learned to quietly follow her, since he was, what, only eight or nine? At first it had been to shield her from Papa's unkindnesses, his blustering and roaring and condemning words. Later it had been to shield her from doing harm to herself or the household.

In her last year of life, he had shadowed her frequently, in utter silence, hidden from her sight lest she howl her outrage at being "followed by fools and sycophants" or some other unjustified accusation.

Especially in those increasingly rare times when she left her room, he had learned to observe her at her odd and covert little tasks. He could not count the number of times he had restored keys to their hooks, caps to their owners, and asked the maids to re-sew buttons to garments that had been plucked clean by Mama's busy, nervous fingers.

He had been careful never to startle her, for that only brought on hours of shrieks, but to silently follow and observe what difficulty she was currently engaged in creating.

He could almost smile at some of his memories, such as the time he had discovered her painting every inch of unclothed skin, using the contents of her rouge pot. She had laughed and called herself a red Indian, and then an hour later demanded to know who had left her out in the sun so long as to burn. And once he had found her in the attics, wearing so many layers of old, stored clothes that she could hardly move, let alone don more as she was attempting to do when he had caught up to her.

"Ah, Gideon," she had greeted him cheerfully. "You are just

in time to help me with my presentation gown. I am off today to be presented to the queen, you know."

"Yes, Mama," he had answered, also with a smile, a sadder, wiser smile than hers. He had taken off the layers one by one, down to her night rail, and had somehow persuaded her that he was removing fine ermine robes, that she not be prettier or dressed more exquisitely than the queen, for that would never do, she had agreed.

Mama had not been "right" for years, and each encroaching year had taken her further from her sons. Gideon's youngest brother, Sebastian, did not remember a time when Mama had been well enough to sit at the family table. Sebastian remembered only a woman who spent a great deal of time in her room when she wasn't wandering aimlessly, and a great deal of time weeping inconsolably. Poor Mama. At least her growing infirmity had taken her further from the reach of her intolerant husband's scorn and loathing.

Despite its being a pattern revisited, and in his experience necessary, when Gideon put his hand to Elizabeth's door, he felt a flurry of qualms. He squashed them ruthlessly and knocked once upon the door, quickly pushing it open. Well-oiled hinges scarcely made a sound, even while he considered that it was one thing to make free with the privacy of his poor, addled mother, and another to enter virtually unannounced the room of a guest, howsoever reluctant a one. And a female at that. What if he interrupted a private moment, for pity's sake?

But, then again, that was what he had hoped to do: to catch her at a natural moment, just as he had hoped to do the other morning. And so he had, for she had been sleeping at the end of her bed. He still wondered why . . . but the wondering took no thought, no energy, for he had long since realized that there were some questions that would never receive a rational answer.

Elizabeth had her back to the door, which he had not expected. He had only anticipated a moment to observe her before she chastised him for entering still too abruptly. She sat on the opposite edge of the bed in her night rail, her feet presumably on the floor before her. She had obviously mistaken his knock for that of a maid, for she was not quick to turn about. "Enter,"

she said over her shoulder, her attention focused on her feet.
Her feet?

"It is Greyleigh."

Elizabeth twisted at the waist, shooting him a quick glance.
She twisted the other way, snagging up the dressing gown she
had worn just yesterday to meet with the parish ladies. "Did
you require something?" she asked from over her shoulder.

He took the canes from where they were tucked under his
arm. "I have brought you these."

She faced him once more as she belted the dressing gown
around her waist. "Oh," she said, and had the grace to blush at
her less than gracious greeting. "Thank you." She did not stand,
but she stretched out a receiving hand in his direction.

Gideon crossed the distance between them, but he did not
hand over the canes at once. "You probably should not use them
much, if at all. It seems clear your foot would heal sooner if you
did not disturb it by trying to get about."

"Two weeks in bed would drive me mad," she said, and then
her gaze met his directly as it must have occurred to her what
she had said.

He merely smiled in return, a general, pleasant sort of smile.
"We cannot have that then, can we, since your nerves are so recently restored?"

She made a small derisive noise. "I know you do not believe
my claims of mental well-being," she said, taking the canes as
he handed them to her. She gripped one in each hand, and tested
their stoutness by leaning onto them. She looked up at him.
"But I assure you yet again that I possess all my wits and am
not of a nervous sort."

He nodded reassuringly, even if he could not quite verbally
agree, but she missed the nod as she attempted to stand, using
the canes.

A smile broke across her face as she took a hop forward then
steadied herself with the canes. "Oh yes, these will suit nicely."

"Good. It was clear you were not one to lie abed, and would
need some manner of getting about. It might be possible to locate a bath chair as well, should you want—"

"These will do," she cut him off, shaking her head, clearly
not wishing to be any more of a bother to him.

"You really must not try the stairs." He spoke softly, but he allowed an edge of command into his voice.

She made a face. "No, I suppose not. I had hopes of utterly escaping the mortification of being carried about in a chair, but I suppose the stairs are beyond my limited abilities just yet."

As though to prove the point, she overbalanced, lunging forward into several quick hops on her left foot. Gideon put out his hands, grasping her upper arms. Between them they managed to keep her from falling onto her nose. He helped to right her, his hands still on her arms.

"Thank you. I suppose this only goes to show that I ought not take the stairs," she said with a shy smile and the beginnings of a blush.

"I suppose it does," he said, feeling a responding smile tug at his lips. His hands lingered a moment longer on her arms, then he thought to release her, and took a step back.

"My lord," she said, changing the subject, "am I allowed to request paper and ink?" She executed a smooth pivot that turned her back toward the bed, half facing away from him.

"Certainly. Is there someone to whom you wish to write?"

She gave a small laugh that dismissed his unsubtle attempt to extract further information from or about her. Or perhaps, as he had ascertained, she truly did not know her own surname or where she lived, such details lost in a clever but confused mind. She might have given the small laugh as a mask. Mama had done that sometimes: laughing to hide that she did not really comprehend the events going on around her.

Although, admittedly, it was becoming increasingly difficult to recall that Elizabeth must suffer from at least some form of dementia, or at least nerves. She seemed rather accomplished in her conversation, at least when it was one-to-one. It was mostly in groups that she became vague. But, perhaps like many people, groups were intimidating for her. Perhaps it was a profusion of persons or voices that overwhelmed or confused Elizabeth.

"Yes, I wish to write a letter," she answered his question, "but not for myself. One of your maids has asked if I would write a missive for her, to send to her mama."

Gideon frowned very briefly. "You need not be hesitant to

ask for such simple things as paper while you are here in my home. I would have hoped you know that such commonalties are at your beckoning."

"One hates to presume."

"Please, presume you are my guest, Elizabeth."

There was something in his voice, something inviting, that made her shiver, as if unseen fingers had trailed along her nape. To cover the gesture, she charged into the first thing she could think to ask. "Is there common paper for the servants to use, and where would I find it?"

He waved away the first part of the question. "I care not if my servants wish to use my foolscap. It is all cast in a drawer in the table in the front hall. I will tell my butler, Frick, and he will have some sent up to you."

"That is not very cost-accounting of you," she teased gently, but he thought there was no real censure in her words. "And this after I saw you poring over your account books."

"I do like to know where my money is spent," he said with a deliberately prim tone, "but it does not follow that I do not therefore care to spend it."

He had made her laugh, as he had meant to do. He almost chuckled with her, but something in her laughter stopped him, or rather he stopped to hear the something in her laughter. It was not musical or unique or anything else, but just fine, good laughter that did something unexpected in the vicinity of his breastbone, so sharp and pleasant that he almost gasped aloud from the sensation. He had made her laugh. And it had felt good, marvelous even, and it made his ears ring just a bit now, as if they strained to hear the sound again.

"I should go. I must go," he said, sounding a bit breathless, much to his further surprise. He backed up, nearly to the door of her room.

"Do you go again to your club? So early in the day?"

"Yes. Er, no. I was going to return Lady Sees's call. Do the polite thing, you see. Keep up the neighborly connections and all."

"I see," Elizabeth said. She tilted her head a little on one side, obviously perplexed by his sudden retreat. "Well, give her my best, please."

"I will." Gideon bowed and turned, all in one motion, and was out of her door and closing it almost before the words were out of his mouth.

Whatever had got into him, he wondered with a sense of consternation as he turned to find the stairs. He had acted like a moonling in there, and although he had been accused of as much a thousand times, he still could not make sense of his own sudden need to be quit of Elizabeth's company . . . well, not her company, not really. Quit of her room then, her nearness, the strange effect she'd had on him.

"Damn me!" Gideon said on a hearty sigh, not sure why he ought to be damned, but feeling as though he'd just escaped the fire all the same.

Elizabeth stared at the door Lord Greyleigh had just exited, and experienced a shiver that shook her all the way down to her injured heel. She sucked in her breath in response, and only then realized she'd been living on half breaths since he had touched her arms.

What had happened? Nothing had happened. And yet . . . she'd felt a tingle start in her arms, and it had traveled to her nether regions, to all the little curves and corners that she had until only recently scarcely known her body possessed.

She put a hand to her cheek, not surprised to find it warm. *That* was the problem, of course. She had moved too much while coming down with a fever. She had noticed she felt too warm earlier, upon awakening, and when she had swung her feet over the side of the bed, it had been painful to do so. One quick glance had told her that her right heel was swollen and red.

It was to be expected, this inflammation. It happened with most deep wounds, of course. She would have to ask a maid to help her change the bandage frequently, and if the swelling did not reverse soon, she would have to have lint dipped in vinegar placed on the rankled wound.

But all that would have to wait, especially now she had the canes Lord Greyleigh had so kindly brought her. First she needed to write that letter for the maid, Jeannie, and in return she would ask Jeannie if there was a place in Severn's Well where one might sell one's jewels. Elizabeth would ask Lord Greyleigh the same, if it came to that, but she would rather he not know the nature or extent of her finances, since he had never given any evidence that he even knew her jewels existed. Some maid had no doubt found them and put them in the drawer, and must have neglected to report their existence to the master. Which circumstance suited Elizabeth well enough.

She sat back on the bed and reached for the bellpull.

As Gideon tossed his driving gloves atop the front hall table, he noted the folded letter beside Frick's salver, the latter of which was used only for letters that were incoming. The new letter sat atop two of his own outgoing ones. The topmost letter was facedown, so that he could note the wafer sealing it rather than his own usual dollop of stamped wax.

He picked up the missive and quickly took in the direction written on it: "Mrs. Henry Powter, Shaftesbury, Dorsetshire." The hand was decidedly feminine, and unfamiliar, but it was no great work to realize that Elizabeth had indeed penned a letter for one of his maids.

It was kind of her to do so, Gideon thought absently as he tossed the letter once more beside the salver, atop the two he had placed there before going to call on Lady Sees. Powter, he thought, Jeannie Powter. Gideon knew the name from the accounts he kept, knew she was the maid nearing her time, almost ready to be delivered of her child. He wondered what she had told her family . . . but there was no need to wonder, for Elizabeth would know, since she had penned the letter.

He headed for the stairs and toward Elizabeth's room, but stopped when he caught movement from the corner of his eye. To his surprise, the object of his search was in the connecting gallery, the one that formed the center line of an H between his room's hallway and that of Elizabeth's room. She stood, dressed once again in his mama's ill-fitting gown and with the two canes under her hands, staring up at the family portraits that lined the length of the gallery.

"Lord Greyleigh," she called upon spying him, sounding a little breathless. She lifted one cane, to make a kind of shrugging motion upward toward the painting. "I recognize your portrait, although you were younger when it was made. But are these two other portraits your brothers?"

"They are." He moved to her side, loosely clasping his hands behind his back. "That is Sebastian there under the tree, and Benjamin on horseback. I would have painted them exactly the opposite were I the artist, but no one asked my opinion at the time."

"Why opposite?"

"Because Benjamin cares more about the land and all that comes with it, and Sebastian is the wilder of the two. I would have had Benjamin spreading his arms wide to invite the viewer to see all that his name owns, and I would have had Sebastian's horse foaming and wild-eyed from a hard, unnecessary gallop across that very same holding."

Elizabeth gave him a sideways glance. "You sound caustic, but I think perhaps there is a hint of affection in your voice as well."

"Truly? I am surprised you think you hear any such thing."

She merely smiled, a soft, doubting smile meant only for herself, and turned back to admire the portraits. "How was Lady Sees this morning?"

"Well enough. We had tea and old gossip, and I left after a very correct fifteen minutes. She asked after you."

"Did she? How did you answer her?"

"I said your health improved, but not your memory."

"True enough," she said. "Frick told me two other letters were going out, along with one I wrote for one of the maids."

"Yes, I saw your letter."

"I presume you wrote back to your brother? He did not send ill news, I hope?"

It was none of her business, of course, and he could not think why she would care, except for being bored by confinement. He shook his head. "No bad news. No news, in fact. We play chess by correspondence. In fact, both my brothers transact games through the post with me. Benjamin had written with his latest move."

"Ah!" Enlightenment dawned across her features, making her brown eyes shine. Oddly enough, it was only then that he realized her eyes had been lacking their usual sparkle.

"That would explain," she went on, "why there were two chessboards set up in your library. I am very glad I could not cross over and move a piece as I thought to do, for I should have disrupted the game's play."

"No great harm would have come of it," he assured her as he unclasped his hands. "May I escort you back to your room? You appear fatigued."

"That is not very gallant of you," she said on a sniff, but it was all pretense at being offended, for her outburst was followed by a weary sigh. "But you are correct, I am tired. It is a great measure more work limping about on canes than I ever should have guessed, and I had long since begun to regret giving in to the sense of boredom that drove me from my chamber."

He watched her slow progress down the hall, keenly aware he could not offer her his arm because she must make use of the canes. "I could—"

"Carry me?" she interrupted with a sharp shake of her head. "I think not. I have had more than my share of being carried about of late. Just be at hand so that you can call for help should I take a tumble, thank you."

Gideon was used to giving in on small requests, even if they did not make much sense. He walked slowly beside Elizabeth, taking the occasional one long step versus her plant-canes-then-take-three-hops advancement.

"I came seeking you to ask you about *your* letter," he said, resisting an urge to put his hand under her elbow, the better to steady her uneven progression. "Well, the letter you wrote anyway."

"We are a rude pair, wanting to know the contents of each other's letters," she said. The smile she added came with effort, he guessed, for a sheen of perspiration had broken out across her upper lip. "What did you want to know?"

"The contents."

"Ah. I cannot tell you, of course, since it is not my letter. You will have to ask the maid, Jeannie."

"I told you the contents of *my* letter," he pointed out.

"*Your* letter," she countered breathily. "Exactly my point."

"Well then, I *will* ask Jeannie." He did not like the petulant tone he heard in his own voice. "I only wanted to know if she is content. Frick tells me she means to stay on after the birth of her child."

Elizabeth had come to the doorway to her room. She gave him a speaking glance, startling him.

"What is that for?" he demanded. "That . . . disapproval I see on your face?"

"It is not my place to approve or disapprove anything regarding yourself, my lord," she said with a cool politeness that was just as speaking as her glance had been. "I would merely suggest that if you have a situation you must settle with your servants, you do so directly," she said with all the censure of a headmaster.

"My dear lady, you could follow your own advice! Frick tells me you have been asking my maids if there is a place in Severn's Well in which one might sell jewelry. You could, allow me to point out, have asked *me* such a question."

Elizabeth blushed a deep red, and it was a moment before she found her voice. "My question is the sort that could be asked of anyone. Yours was not."

He gave her a skeptical look. "So what is all this about jewels?" he asked. "If you require some pin money, I will gladly supply you with a sum."

She went stiff and tilted her head back far enough to be able to look down her nose at him. "Indeed not. I will supply my own funds. Not pin money, my lord. Funds."

"I could—"

"You will *not,*" she insisted. "I would not accept it. Please," she went on, her tone softening, "all I require is the name of a place where such a transaction may occur, and perhaps the use of a footman to conduct the business for me."

"Wendell's," Gideon said reluctantly. "There is a shop owned by Mr. Wendell. He might be in the market to purchase jewelry."

"Excellent," she said with a shadow of a smile, and then she went into her chamber and practically shut the door in his face.

He turned from her door, shaking his head, because he was well aware what Elizabeth had brought with her into his home: her person; her cloak, clothing, and shift (all now burned); her kid leather slippers; her ring marked with a B; and nothing else. There had been no jewels. The maid who had changed an unconscious Elizabeth into a night rail had listed for Gideon this woman's pitiful few belongings, for they had been searching for a clue as to her identity.

"Poor, misguided thing," Gideon said aloud, shaking his head again. He wondered briefly if Mr. Arbuckle would ever discover who the woman was. But her identity was not Gideon's problem, for she was determined to be gone as soon as possible, regardless of what he knew. That suited him perfectly, Gideon reminded himself.

Chapter 11

Ten minutes later, Elizabeth crossed her arms and, almost pouting, thought that she wanted to pace. She could not, of course, but the impulse was strong. She had done her best to put her disgruntlement with Lord Greyleigh out of her thoughts, but lying here atop her bedclothes with her eyes closed had only made her feel her pique all the more sharply.

For pity's sake, did this man not know what agreement had been made with the servant girl who was undoubtedly bearing his child? Had he left the settling of his illegitimate infant and its mother's welfare up to some intermediary—this butler of his, perhaps?

Well, no, not by way of Frick, not logically, because then Lord Greyleigh would simply ask the butler what conditions had been established for the girl and her child. Maybe Greyleigh had proposed a plan for the future to the maid, and yet awaited her response? That could be. But that made of the man a coward: asking Elizabeth about a letter's contents instead of asking the girl directly!

Not that it mattered to Elizabeth that Lord Greyleigh was as odd and intemperate as his mother had surely been. Even in far London Elizabeth had heard that Lady Greyleigh had spent all her married life in a mental decline—was it any wonder that her son inherited her affliction? Still, it was . . . disturbing to have his behavior with a servant cast into Elizabeth's own lap. It was almost as disturbing as trying to reconcile the word "coward" with the little she knew of Lord Greyleigh's disposition.

And his constant offers to help, to carry her about or settle funds upon her! The former was disagreeable—emotionally if not physically—and the latter was simply unacceptable. He had no notion of her financial needs and would be shocked should he somehow learn she meant to establish a household by herself. He was . . . intrusive, that was the word! He kept thrusting his nose into business that did not concern him, and worse yet, making her feel guilty that she would not confide that business to him.

He was her host, and only that—and only for eleven more days. She owed him nothing, except her thanks. However, she had promised him an eventual explanation—but the word "eventual" was the key. He was boorish to insist on anything else. They had an agreement, and she would remind him of that if he could not remember it for himself.

She sat up in bed, sighing heavily as she put the back of her hand to her forehead. Yes, she was still too warm. And her heel was beyond warm now, feeling puffy and throbbing anytime she moved it at all.

Elizabeth bit her lip. She hated the thought of calling a surgeon in once more, for it only meant more cost for Lord Greyleigh, more debt she owed him, but it was becoming clear that the wound would not improve without some intervention.

Although . . . perhaps she could repay Lord Greyleigh more immediately than she had thought, by leaving one of her jewels for him? She scowled, for each jewel had a value that equaled so many days of survival.

She looked down at the signet ring, with its distinctive sweeping B engraved on its surface and roses engraved on the thick band on either side of the signet letter, and realized she wore it yet on her left hand. She ought to put it in her jewel purse, but until she had the opportunity, at least she would no longer wear it on her left.

It was the work of a moment to move it to her right hand. Perhaps this very ring was the one item she could repay Lord Greyleigh with . . . but, no, it would serve her best as a ring to wear when she lived on her own. She would pretend to be a widow, and must have a wedding band to support that claim, and of her rings, this one most looked the part. In any event, what would an unmarried man such as Lord Greyleigh do with a ring marked with a B?

He probably had a mistress that he kept somewhere; he could

give it to her if the initial would serve. The thought of Gideon
giving this ring to a Barbara or a Beatrice or a Miss Brown
made Elizabeth's scowl grow deeper.

Deciding now was as good a time as any to put the ring
away, Elizabeth leaned back on the bed and slid a hand inside
one of the pillowcases. She sought the jewel purse she had hidden there. Finding nothing, she made an exasperated sound,
and tried the remaining three pillows. Nothing.

Her heart hammering, she reached back, intending to grasp
the bellpull, but then she glimpsed the leather purse just poking
out from under the coverlet's edge. She snatched it up with relief, only to gasp at its ominous lack of weight, its flat profile.
Her fingers, frantically pulling open the already loosened drawstrings, told her what her eyes had to see to believe: her jewels
were gone. Every one of them, gone.

"My lord?" One of the maids bobbed a curtsy where she
stood at the library door she had just opened.

"What is it?" Gideon asked, glancing up. Within two heartbeats he was already standing up behind his desk because of the
uneasy look on the maid's face. "What has happened?" he demanded.

"It's Miss Elizabeth, sir," the maid said, twisting the hem of
her apron with both hands. "She's tearing her room apart and
shouting at the maid what cleaned the room while Miss Elizabeth were walking about this morning."

Gideon closed his eyes for a moment, filled instantly with an
old, familiar sinking feeling. "Very well. I will take care of the
matter. Have coffee and a bottle of whiskey sent up to Miss
Elizabeth's room, please, as soon as may be."

The maid bobbed her head and a curtsy all at once, and
quickly ran off to do as she was bid.

Gideon forced himself to take the stairs one at a time, with
outward calm. Calm was best in these situations. It could sometimes be communicated to the disturbed person, averting any
further scenes.

He knocked at Elizabeth's door, but let himself in at once,
still moving calmly, smoothly. She was on her knees, her in-

jured foot leveled off the floor, while she searched with a sweeping arm under the bed.

"Elizabeth," he said a bit loudly, hoping she was not too far lost to reality to hear him despite the state her mind was in, and that he was not so loud that he conversely startled her into yet more hysterics.

She jerked upward, hitting her shoulder on the bed frame. "Oof!" She scooted backward awkwardly and turned to glare at him. "Did you take my jewels, or order them taken?"

"What jewels, Elizabeth?" he said quietly, striding with an outwardly unruffled gait toward her. He stooped down next to her, bringing his face closer to her eye level. When she did not cringe or retreat, he dared to reach slowly and touch her shoulder.

She pulled back, so that his fingers could no longer touch the fabric of her green gown's sleeve. "I believe your staff failed to inform you, at least originally, but I had a leather purse. It contained my jewels. It is now empty. I want my jewels returned." Her eyes burned with an avid intensity as she held aloft a small upended purse, which was clearly devoid of contents.

"What do they look like?" he said, daring to inch forward and reach out his other hand. He placed it slowly on her other shoulder. "These jewels of yours?"

"I have five rings, three pairs of earbobs, a very fine choker, and two hair combs. Oh, and an ivory cameo. Your maid must have taken them this morning while I was out." Elizabeth threw a furious glance at red-eyed and snuffling Jeannie. "But she will not admit to it."

"I didn't take nothing!" Jeannie cried, nearly breaking into a fresh bout of tears. "I wouldn't, m'lord. I *want* to keep on working here, honest I do. I wouldn't do nothing to lose me my position here, I never would!"

"Hush now," Gideon said softly, not aiming the comment at either woman, but for the room at large. "Jeannie, I will talk with you later. Be assured you will not lose your position." Elizabeth gave him a sharp look, but he went on just as calmly, "But we can talk about all that in a while. For now, please just leave the room. Elizabeth," he said and turned his gaze down to hers, meeting her eyes ever so briefly. With relief he saw that rationality and some measure of reason resided there, and he risked putting his other hand on her shoulder once again. Whatever fit of madness had seized her, it had seemingly passed now, for although she was clearly vexed, he believed she was also lucid.

The pregnant maid scrambled out, passing Polly, who came in with a tray of coffee and a decanter of whiskey. Gideon nodded at her to leave the tray, and Polly hastened to comply and also to make a quick exit.

"Now, this fussing about does no one any good," he said in what he called his "tranquil" voice.

Elizabeth narrowed her gaze at him.

He ran his hands down to where the sleeves ended halfway along her upper arms, applying a light pressure, a comforting pressure. She felt warm, but that was understandable given the effort she had been exerting in looking for these "jewels" of hers. "If I help you, do you think you could stand?"

"Yes," she said curtly.

He helped her to rise, until she teetered on the one good foot that, presumably unlike its wounded mate, was adorned with one of her slippers. "If you can stand so a moment, I will bring you a chair."

In short order he had her ensconced in one of her bedchamber chairs. "Coffee?" he offered, moving to pour a cup.

"I do not want coffee. I want my jewels returned."

His hand hovered over the decanter, but he turned away instead. Sometimes alcohol had calmed his mama, but other times it had aggravated her distress. Elizabeth was clearly still angry, though she was calm enough.

He brought her the coffee. "Try some. Please."

She accepted it with ill grace, then quickly set it aside without sipping at it. "I think it would behoove you to get that maid in here once more," she said, still clearly agitated, "so we can question what she has done with my things. She left my purse under my sheets, which points toward the maid if nothing else does, I should think."

"Hmmm" was his only reply.

Her shoulders heaved, and for a sinking moment he thought

it was the beginning of a keening sob, but she only offered a large sigh.

"It is evident, my lord, that you do not believe I ever possessed any jewelry," she said.

He wondered if speaking clearly and concisely, as one does to children or dunces, was the way to go on.

"It is equally evident you have no plans to search for my missing goods," she went on. She pursed her lips and drummed her fingers on the chair arm. "Very well, then. But I tell you, *I* shall! You will be the most help to me by not interfering with my search."

"How do you propose to conduct this, uh, search?" he looked pointedly at her skirt, beneath which the injured foot was held aloft awkwardly.

"The same way I saw the portrait gallery, by using the canes. I will crawl if I have to, but I *must* have my jewelry back. That is, if it is even still within the confines of the house. Your maid could be burying my belongings in the garden at this very moment, for all I know, or having them traded for money in hand at this Wendell's you spoke of."

She was calm, and she gave no signs of striking out or tumbling into hysteria—she was plainly intent on believing in her own fantasy. There would be no talking her out of it, not if his own personal history had proved anything to Gideon.

He picked up her discarded coffee cup and put it on the tray—he would not leave hot liquids where they could hurt her or anyone else who came into the room. "Do what you must," he said quietly, resigned that she would do whatever her bemused disposition dictated she must do. So one small female would turn the house topsy-turvy toward no good purpose; it would not be the first time. "Only please do not disturb my library. I give you my word there are no jewels there, yours or anyone's."

She gave him a level look, then nodded.

"I will deliver this tray to the kitchen, and then return." He did not want to ring for a servant, for who knew what or who might touch off some volatile spark in Elizabeth's mind and start this whole sorry scene all over again.

That was all he wanted, of course—peace. Some measure of

serenity in the house, this cursed house that echoed yet with his mother's cries and his heartless father's insensitive shouts. All he wanted from Elizabeth was that she become well enough to leave, to go and take all these reminders of his mournful past with her.

He owed her nothing, Gideon reminded himself as he quietly closed her door—nothing but simple courtesy, and time to heal her physical wound. Once she was well enough to travel, she was his problem no longer. As disturbing as it was to have her here now, their mutual confinement would be mercifully short-lived.

Soon he would be free of her and her disquieting presence. He ran that thought over and over through his mind, and only vaguely wondered why the thought was less satisfying than it ought to be.

Later, Elizabeth moved forward through the house in hops that were so small she scarcely seemed to advance at all, yet no matter how small she made the hops, they jarred her infected foot so that she had to grit her teeth against the pain.

It was bad enough that her body did not want to cooperate with the excrutiatingly slow search she attempted, but neither did her thoughts. While her hands opened every drawer and cupboard she came to, her thoughts kept drifting back to how Lord Greyleigh had treated her. It did not matter one whit that as of late she had been as honest as possible with him; he clearly still thought her a lunatic.

Of course, whispered her conscience, did she not think the same of him? And on what evidence? From gossip she had heard in the past? That he appeared different in his coloring?

What evidence did he have of *her* sanity? Her claims, her word? But what person, mad or sane, would embrace the claim of lunacy? Words were meaningless in this matter; it was actions that spoke so that others might see. How could he believe her to be in her right mind when he had just found her on her bedchamber floor, scrambling around for missing jewels that he had no reason to believe existed? Really, she could laugh at how absurd she must have appeared. That is, she would laugh were it not for the flaming pain that burned up her leg.

She closed her eyes in weariness, but that just made her dizzy, so she opened them again.

There were voices ahead, in the dining room. Tiny hop by tiny painful hop, Elizabeth made her way to the open doorway. Lord Greyleigh was there, and at his side stood a common-looking fellow who had neglected to doff his hat. Or perhaps he had just donned it anew, for he shook his head and said to Lord Greyleigh, "Yer cook already seen I was taken care of. I'll leave yer to yer own meal then, m'lord."

Beside a spread of news sheets that Lord Greyleigh had obviously been reading before he was interrupted by his caller, the table was set with plates and utensils ready for luncheon. Footmen were just starting to scuttle in and out from the opposite doorway, bearing trays of cold carved beef, cheeses, fruit, and fragrant buns. At least, Elizabeth assumed they were fragrant, but the overall scent of food only served to turn her stomach.

There was no possibility she could eat, she realized at once. This roiling effect in her stomach was a sure sign that the infection in her heel did not bode well. A chair, she just wanted a chair, to sit for a while, then she would ask some of the footmen to carry her away from all the unwelcome sights and scents that filled the room.

Lord Greyleigh turned and spied her. "Ah, Elizabeth. Come to join me for luncheon?"

She nodded, because it was easier than correcting his misassumption that she meant to eat. She was grateful when he pulled out a chair for her. He frowned as she made her slow progress to the table, each effort oddly more difficult than the one before it. As she reached the chair and sat down, her ears began to ring. Suddenly there were bright lights dancing before her eyes, and she couldn't see or hear anything for several very long moments.

"Elizabeth? Elizabeth?" Gideon picked up one of her hands, chafing it between his own. She had gone quite pale of a sudden, and he thought with dawning alarm that perhaps she was going to faint. Again he noticed that she felt warm, too warm.

She blinked several times, and then slowly focused on his face as her color came rushing back. "I am sorry," she mur-

mured. "I became light-headed for a moment." She gave a little shake of her head, as if to dismiss the moment, then looked
as though she wished she had not. She took her hand from his
and gave him a peaked smile. "You had a caller?"

"Mr. Arbuckle. He . . . works for me," Gideon said, but he
was not about to share what news Mr. Arbuckle had brought
him: that the investigator had compiled a list of six young
ladies who had suddenly "disappeared" from Society, one from
Bath and the rest from London. It was suspected, naturally
enough, that they had been sent to the country, either to avoid
an unsuitable connection or else to be delivered of any infant
that resulted from such an unsuitable connection. None of the
six had a surname that began with B, but Arbuckle was delving
deeper into their supposed and their actual whereabouts and
would soon have a more complete report to make.

"My lord," Elizabeth said. He thought she now looked bright
of eye, too bright, and her face was flushed. "Have you hired
that man . . . ?" She looked embarrassed, and for a moment her
voice faltered, but then she rallied. "Is it possible you mean to
protect me, or this household, from the return of the man who
tried to steal my ring? Do you think it possible he came back
and stole my jewels?"

Gideon looked into her earnest gaze and just managed to sti-
fle a sigh. It was sad, so very sad, that she was so deeply deluded. "My dear girl," he said, taking a chair next to hers. He
reached out and took up one of her hands again, noting that she
had moved the signet ring from her left hand to her right. Interesting.

"Can you tell me how such a man would get into my home
unnoticed?" he asked her. "And why would he steal nothing but
your jewels? I assure you, everything else in the house is in
place."

This was not strictly the truth, for little things went missing
all the time, but he would not feed Elizabeth's fancies with that
information. "Missing" was not the right word, for they were
simply moved to new places where they were eventually discovered. He suspected he had a servant bent on amusing him-
or herself, even if Gideon was at a loss to say who among his
staff was so inclined.

"Oh." She acknowledged the reasoning in his argument with a stark look. "I suppose you must be right. Although"——her too bright gaze narrowed—"it could be a matter of revenge. Against me. That would explain why he only took *my* belongings."

How to argue logic with an illogical mind? He only smiled briefly and patted her hand. That hand was very warm to the touch. . . . He grimaced and reached to touch the back of his own hand to her forehead.

"My dear woman, you are burning up!"

"I am afraid so." She gave a weak smile. "I hate to ask, but I think we must call for the surgeon once more."

He frowned, belatedly taking in the dark circles under her eyes. "Your heel, it does not do well?" He glanced down toward her feet, but they were lost from sight beneath the hem of her gown.

"It has become tender and swollen. Nothing too alarming, I am sure—"

He did not wait to hear more, but scooped her into his arms. The canes fell aside with a clatter, startling one of the footmen who had arrived to see if aught else was required for the meal— a meal that would now go uneaten.

Chapter 12

O h! You could warn a body," Elizabeth said faintly as her hands spread over his shoulders in a weak-fingered grip.

"You should never have been up and about, aggravating the wound," he said crossly as he resettled her in his arms.

Gideon rushed up the stairs, carrying Elizabeth to her room and setting her on the bed. He rang immediately for the maid.

Polly came promptly, bandages in hand. "Time fer a dressing change already?" she clucked with concern as she hurried in the door. There was surprise evident in her unpatched eye upon finding Gideon in the room.

"I do not know," he answered her, "but the lady requires water to drink. And tea, not too hot, with honey."

"Honey? I haven't a cold. Such a to-do about a little touch of infection," Elizabeth mumbled.

"Infection and a fever," Gideon said gruffly, feeling her forehead again even though he knew quite well from carrying her that she was completely flush with fever.

"Well, yes," Elizabeth conceded, "I do feel a bit warm." She sounded groggy, not herself.

"Get that water, girl!" Gideon said sharply to Polly, taking the bandages from the maid's hands. "Cool water. Then tell Frick to send for the surgeon at once. And have Cook send up that tincture he makes, that black foul-smelling stuff."

Elizabeth said nothing, an unusual circumstance that only made Gideon frown all the more. She did not even object, only gasping once in consternation when he sat gingerly on the bed and pulled her skirt above her ankle to examine the bandage on her heel.

He sucked in his breath at the sight of the limp and sodden bandage. "It's as well you removed the sticking plaster," he

said, only just remembering to try to sound unruffled, calm, un-
alarmed.

"It fell off this morning. We had to switch to the plain cotton
bandages," Elizabeth muttered.

The wound was weeping. Some doctors called it *purifying
infection* and others *the laudable pus,* because such weeping of
the wound was to be expected and preceded the forming of new
scar tissue. All Gideon knew was that the infection could
spread, could turn into a poisoning of the blood. Tinctures,
drawing poultices, hot and cold water dips, lancing—there
were things that could be done, and it was best to do them
sooner rather than later.

He removed the old linen, the simple movements causing
Elizabeth to bite her lip, presumably to keep from crying out.
The wound was not any prettier than its bandage had been, and
Gideon did not like its puffy appearance. Nor did he like the
way Elizabeth gritted her teeth as he gently probed around the
wound's edges. Her breathing became ragged.

She was visibly relieved when he ceased his examination. He
wrapped new cloth around her foot in a twisting figure eight,
being as gentle as he could.

"Tell me about the letter you wrote for Jeannie," he said,
wanting to distract her attention.

"Jeannie?" She sounded a little vague, but then she rallied.
"Oh, yes. She told me I could tell you anything you'd like. I
wrote a letter to her mama. Jeannie wanted her to know that a
midwife has agreed to deliver the child." She fell silent as he
tucked the end of the bandage under a fold, securing it. He carefully moved her foot from his lap to rest atop the covers of the
bed, noting that the skin around her mouth had grown white.

"Jeannie tells me her mama lives with someone who can
read," Elizabeth said, the kind of comment one makes when
one is attempting to disguise pain.

Gideon made an encouraging noise.

Elizabeth lifted her head, and he could feel the full weight of
her gaze upon him. Whereas a moment earlier all her energy
had been focused on her foot, now it was focused on him, a
scowling gaze that could have started timber on fire. He turned

his head, mouth parted in surprise, to face the fullness of this sudden wrath.

"She is going to work here still, she told her mama," Elizabeth said. "The child will be with a woman whom Jeannie lives with at night, who has six of her own, but Jeannie says she will be allowed to go twice a day to nurse her own child."

Why was Elizabeth so upset by this news? Surely since Jeannie was too far from her mama to reside there, this was the best arrangement? And why was *he* the recipient of Elizabeth's upset? He closed his mouth, only to open his lips again to inquire as much, but she went on. "She is very happy not to be losing her position."

That sounded like an accusation, but Gideon was used to those, and often as nonsensical as was this one. "Hush," he said, not gently. "You are flush with fever. You need to rest until the surgeon arrives."

Elizabeth narrowed her gaze at him, then settled back against the pillows. "I daresay maintaining Jeannie's employment is the least you could do for the poor girl."

Gideon reached with one hand to rub his chin, perplexed by her comment. "Most people would say I was being far too tolerant in having a, er, propagating female about the house at all," he explained.

"Most people do not know what it is to be alone, friendless and female," Elizabeth snapped back at him.

Since this was hardly the first time a woman had been unreasonably aggravated at him, Gideon shrugged inwardly. Instead of attempting to maintain conversation, he smiled and patted her hand, which she withdrew at once with a disgusted sigh.

Either her affliction or her fever had put some twisted notion in her head, which would no doubt be erased by a night's sleep or the surgeon's draughts.

As to doctoring, what was taking the dratted surgeon so long? He lived not five minutes away, directly off the High Street of Severn's Well. Gideon hoped the man was not making rounds, or miles away at some confinement or sickroom.

"Close your eyes," Gideon said to the still scowling Elizabeth, who stared hard at him for another two seconds before giving in to his command.

Gideon continued to sit on the edge of the bed, not wanting to move and disturb either her foot or her rest. In short order, Elizabeth slipped into a fitful doze, and then Gideon was even more loathe to disturb her.

He had nothing to do but sit and wonder why he did not just leave this strange woman to the care of a maid . . . but finding no answer that satisfied him, he remained where he was.

Two hours later, Gideon sat in his library, having been banished from the sickroom by the surgeon.

The sun was high in the sky, flooding the room with light, but there was no warmth at Gideon's core. He stared at his account books, not even pretending to work at them.

Elizabeth was ill. Gideon had not needed the surgeon's concerned expression to tell him that. He had felt her fever for himself and seen the wound.

Forcing his mind away from the grim realities of physical illness, Gideon tried instead to concentrate on whether or not this infection would mean Elizabeth would have to stay longer. The last of the male asylum patients, Thompson, had gone today. The man's brother had belatedly heard about the asylum fire and had made his way from Salisbury to retrieve Thompson. That matter was cleanly settled . . . but Elizabeth's exit would almost certainly be delayed now.

Of course, what was the hurry? Even when she was gone, he had other concerns yet to be settled. Gideon's dream of leaving this place, perhaps making some manner of a Grand Tour, of seeing the world, to follow in his brothers' retreating footsteps, it would all have to wait.

Just as it had always waited. Just as he had long since begun to fear it always would wait.

Gideon wanted escape, he longed for it, he chafed under the burdens that kept him from it.

Run away—forget duty and obligation. But this was an old chorus, begun in childhood. He knew better. He knew himself. Without duty, what was there? That which choked him was also the very thing that shaped him. If he ran, left, abandoned—what would he be then?

He was no hero, because heroes made choices. There was no

choice for Gideon. He was the eldest. He had siblings to support; two households—this meandering pile in Severn's Well and the home farm in Kent—both with servants to employ and feed; and there were horses and dogs and beef cattle to be maintained. Yet these obligations were small compared with the number of farm-workers he employed—those who worked his land in Kent, raised his crops and his cattle, and who made his profit for him. How could Gideon cease to watch over their needs, when his la-borers were the very glue that held all else together?

He could flee it all, he sometimes thought . . . only to ask himself to do what? Watch from afar as it all fell apart? Watch as people lost their holdings, as they went hungry and homeless?

He could hire a steward, then. A steward could oversee everything, could be sure that the estate made a profit, that the cogs of its machinery moved forward.

But a steward could not be generous, not with his master's money. He could be prudent, he could be thoughtful, he could even be kindhearted—but he could not use his own initiative to go beyond the norm. He would have to consult with his master, and that would mean Gideon was not really free of his obliga-tions anyway, just further removed—a step away. Gideon knew taking that one step away was what would kill the very center, the exact heart of him.

The day his papa had expired, the brand-new Lord Greyleigh had raised a prayer of thanks that the old lord could no longer threaten or bully anyone, especially Mama, who had become exceedingly fragile in her health and her mind. Gideon's second thought had been that now, at long last, this faded bloodred pile of stones they must call home would now be made to harbor only good will, soft voices, and compassion. Storms and alarms had ruled too long; during Gideon's reign as the marquess, his house would become a haven to all who resided here. It was his vow. And, God save him, it was also his entrapment.

A knock startled Gideon from his morose thoughts. Frick en-tered the library with a short but courteous bow and announced, "Mr. Clifton."

The grey-haired surgeon entered, not smiling. "My lord," he said.

Gideon murmured a greeting as he came from behind his

desk. The two men moved by silent consent to an arrangement of chairs before the fireplace, and Gideon asked the surgeon to sit. "May I offer you refreshments?"

"Tea would not go amiss," Mr. Clifton said on a nod and a wearied sigh.

Gideon rang for a servant and ordered both tea and a light repast, in case the surgeon's duties had not given the man an opportunity to consume a meal recently. He sat back in his chair and looked the man directly in the eyes. "I collect that the wound is infected."

The doctor inclined his head once more. "It is, my lord. There are two ways to treat it. One is to bleed the patient. However, I am a student of the experiments carried out by the well-known physician John Hunter, and others who have expanded on his work with the vessels for the blood, and am of the belief that bleeding is not always of benefit, particularly in cases of inflammation. I do not, therefore, recommend it in this case."

Gideon digested the information, not as alarmed as he might have been were it not for his own experience with medical men and the guesswork they were forced to, particularly when it came to the human mind. "But is there not a danger of the blood being poisoned?"

"There is a true danger of that, my lord. And Erysipelas, a febrile disease that moves very rapidly, is a very real possibility as well. You would probably know it better as St. Anthony's Fire. Short of God's bounty, it is fatal."

Gideon felt the blood recede from his face. "Then what is to be done?"

"I am inclined to believe the wound has not degraded to gangrene," the surgeon said, just as the maid returned with a tray of tea and fruit with cheese. Mr. Clifton took up a small plate from the tray and placed a few items on it as he spoke. "I have ordered fresh bandages four times a day, or more as needed, to encourage the drainage, with a pulling poultice applied prior to the bandaging," he said around a mouthful of grapes. "Food should be light. Broth, sops, that sort of thing only."

"She is still conscious?"

"Barely, my lord."

Gideon frowned, then signaled for the doctor to go on.

"For relief of swelling, it is sometimes advantageous to soak the wound in first very warm salted water, almost untouchably warm, and then do the same in chilled water. I have instructed the maid in attendance to do that daily if the patient is sensible and not consumed by fever."

"I will order ice delivered from Bristol," Gideon stated.

"Excellent." The surgeon popped a hunk of cheese in his mouth. When he had swallowed, he said, "Is it true what she told me? That her family has not yet been reached?"

"More than that, they have yet to be identified."

"Too bad. I could wish someone she knew were here. It can be soothing to the fever patient to have a family member at the bedside, especially with a woman who is prone to hysteria or dementia."

Gideon parted his lips to protest the term "hysteria"—he had never seen so much as a hint of hysteria in Elizabeth, not even when she had been searching for her "jewels" under her bed. She had been angry and upset, but not hysterical. "Dementia," however . . . now, that was not a term he could so lightly dismiss.

Mr Clifton put aside his plate and stood. "I will return tomorrow. Good day, my lord."

Gideon stood also, wanting to ask if there was not more to be done, but knowing there was not. For all that Mr. Clifton was a surgeon and not a university-trained physician, his practical experience held more sway with Gideon than all the potions a physician could dispense.

Thank God there was not yet any sign of gangrene! That was a slow and painful death, but the surgeon's words left reason yet to hope for a recovery. Although why should he care one whit about a deliberately mysterious woman's future or health? He scowled at his own turn of thought, and knew the answer without even having to think it through. He had been caring for people all his life. It was in his blood. The care of others was what defined him, what made him the opposite of his boorish father.

But did it? he thought. Once that had been true. But Gideon's growing need to leave this place, to thrust off dependability and all the constraints of his position, had begun to consume him of late.

He had often thought about riding away late in the night,

never looking back. He thought about joining the Coast Guard, as his brother Benjamin had done. He read books about foreign lands where being an English lord would mean little or nothing to the natives. When his blood was up, as all men's was at times, he dreamed of sultry, dark-skinned women who whispered in his ear in tongues that he could not understand, that could not make demands of him.

He pondered these fantasies . . . but duty's call had a stronger hold on him than even did longing and desire. Like Mama, he must be mad. Either he had been insane for a long time, to live within this narrow cage that both he and fate had built, or else he had once been sane and the pressures of his yearnings now drove him into this feeling of madness.

He did not know. He did not remember anymore. Had he once been relatively content? If so, it had been a long, long time ago, long before Mama breathed her last.

He only knew that now each dawn was a trial, and each sunset a sentence. He was locked in a prison, and it was a dark, lonely, solitary place despite being surrounded by dozens of people: servants, underlings, and dependents. That was all he had surrounding him. No family. No brothers to relieve the tedium of this place, the tedium of Gideon's position. No peer, no equal. Not even sycophants. His reputation as a madman had taken care of any toad-eaters, even if his own inclination for avoiding fools had not proved sufficient in that regard.

And perhaps that was why the thought of the mysterious Elizabeth sickening unto death caused his breath to catch in his throat. They had made some manner of . . . call it a connection. They were peers—if persons of opposite genders could be called peers—Elizabeth's clothing, her accent, even her very carriage gave her away. She was not of the common class; she had been born to money, or at least to privilege.

It was more than that, however. Gideon had his club and his interactions with the aldermen of Severn's Well. He also had the occasional social invitation, even if the things were issued with the hope they would be declined. Had he wished to put himself out just a little, do the pretty and offer the occasional invitation in return, he could have had more time in the company of those of his own station in life. Once Mama was passed away and there was no one left to protect, Gideon could have become a sociable creature.

He had even made a few feeble attempts, mostly for his brothers' sake, before they were wise enough to flee this house filled with painful memories. But it had not taken Gideon long to realize that the shallowness of gossip stemmed from the meanness of people's hearts, and what had not been tolerable when his mother was alive, was no more tolerable now that she was dead.

Conversation consisted of rumormongering and inanities. Dancing should have been entertaining, but he had soon realized it was really all about courtship. Gideon had no need of a wife, just another burden on shoulders that had already absorbed the weight of the Greyleigh estate. Even when it came to card playing, Gideon had deliberately chosen Elly's because the play was serious if light, because it was not the venue for political posturing as was found in some men's clubs.

No, Society had little to offer him. Would going abroad prove different? There would always be shallow people, that was the curse of mankind, but perhaps in places of learning or great beauty, some semblance of the peace and veracity Gideon craved could be found. His brothers had thought there was some to be found, and they had only ventured as far as London and Brighton respectively, so perhaps Gideon was not too far wrong to hunger for the world beyond Severn's Well.

Yet, now the world had come to him, in the form of Elizabeth. She was, after a fashion, the perfect mirror of what Gideon sought: newness, mystery, intrigue. Most important, she was a woman who demanded nothing of him, because she meant to keep her peace within herself. The strain of having a madwoman once again in his home had proved no real strain at all. Perhaps that was because he knew she would leave.

And I have called others shallow, Gideon thought with a wry sniff, as if he scented his own hypocrisy.

He realized he had forgot to ask the surgeon how much longer Elizabeth would need to recuperate, were she to come away well and hale from this fever.

Gideon found he was frowning again, and he gave a brief shake of his head as if to cast off dark thoughts. But perhaps here was just yet another sign of madness, that the gesture was meaningless and the dark thoughts uppermost in his mind as he made his way up the stairs, toward her room.

It is that woman, Elizabeth thought with vague surprise, the red-haired woman, the supposed ghost. The figure was turning, turning, as if she danced one of those newfangled waltzes, except her arms were empty of a partner. Elizabeth blinked and turned her head against the pillow, the better to see the woman, who moved and dipped to some music Elizabeth could not hear.

Elizabeth knew she ought to call out. Not so much to the woman, but to someone else to come and see the red-haired stranger as well. But her teeth knocked together so that she could hardly hold her head still, let alone force her mouth to shape words. She was dimly aware there were layers of blankets atop her, but the chills had a hold of her and no amount of covers would chase the shaking from her limbs. If only someone would build up the fire on the grate, then she might be warm enough.

She forced her head to turn, with the jerky movements of a marionette, and saw that a large fire already roared in the fireplace. The snaps and pops of fresh wood giving up its sap were clearly audible. To build the fire any higher was to invite a conflagration too large for the space. God help her, that meant there was no hope of getting warm.

When she turned her head once more to look at the red-haired dancing woman, no one was there. The creature had disappeared. Or had she ever really been there?

One part of Elizabeth understood she was caught in the grip of fever, the kind that roasts you one minute, and freezes you the next. But that understanding was detached, like something she had read in a book.

Mostly she just *felt*. Pain in her heel, ice in her veins, her teeth grinding together.

When next she was aware of being in her room, night had fallen. A branch of candles burned on the table, the one that had once held her jewels. My jewels! she thought in panic. Where are they? I must find them. She struggled to sit up, but something hard and firm pushed her back down to the mattress.

Elizabeth focused outward and found the something that was hard and firm—Lord Greyleigh's hand on her shoulder. "What are you doing here?" she asked, amazed by the reed-thin squeak that was her voice.

"Jeannie's time has come, and Polly is helping the midwife. You are quite ill. Would you rather Frick or Cook attended you?" he answered.

"No," she whispered.

It was difficult to tell in the half-light of candles, but she thought he smiled ever so slightly. "Good," he said. "Sleep."

His voice was deep, deeper than she had remembered. It had a reassuring quality to it, a resonance that could warm bones. Warmth! Ah, praise God, she was warm at last.

"I am burning alive!" she cried, and some tiny corner of her mind knew that hours had passed since she had last spoken. She threw back the blankets and would have peeled off her night rail if the movement to shed the covers had not exhausted her utterly. She could not lift her head. Why was that? Why was it so horribly, torturously hot in here? Why did her head ache and feel as if it would burst with every pulse of blood that beat through her veins?

"Hold her while I pour water in her mouth," a male voice said, and then she was drowning, but it was a good drowning, one that quenched a terrible thirst. Had she drunk salt water? Was that why she was so thirsty? Why would she do that? She knew better.

She was swimming . . . but in a warm bath, too warm. Was she in a bathing pool, such as she had read the ancient Romans built? What were they called? Scauldoriums? Something like that, something too hot. Where was the way out? She had to get out of these horribly hot, wet clothes that threatened to drag her to the bottom of the pool.

Someone loomed nearby, a girl, a Roman girl who put a cool cloth to Elizabeth's forehead.

"Thank you," she said to the young Roman girl. "What is your name? I would like to hire your services again when I come back to the baths."

The girl looked startled . . . but then Elizabeth saw a ghost-like figure shake its head, even as it slowly dawned on her she was looking at Lord Greyleigh, at the unbound length of his flaxen hair. She liked the look of it, down around his shoulders as it was now.

"She does not understand," Greyleigh said, his voice sounding to Elizabeth's ears as if he spoke through cotton wool . . . or perhaps it was her own hearing that muffled his words. Certainly, her head was pounding. Greyleigh had spoken to the girl, not to her, and Elizabeth felt a behindhand jolt of indignation at the idea that he could mean that she did not understand. She understood perfectly, even if everyone insisted on mumbling.

"'Tis the fever. Ignore anything she says," Greyleigh said in that strange, thick voice. How odd that Greyleigh should be here . . . at a Roman bath. . . .

It was too much, too confusing. Elizabeth let the warmth overtake her, let oblivion reach out and claim her and make her its own.

"'Tis the fever. Ignore anything she says," Gideon instructed firmly. The maid nodded—he was fairly sure her name was Meg—and was clearly out of her element.

But who else was there to help? Jeannie was having her child, Polly attending her, and the only other females in his bachelor's home were laundry maids who seldom set foot above the kitchen stairs. He should have long since hired a housekeeper . . . but "should have" was of no value at the moment.

"Her bed is soaked with sweat," Meg said, round-eyed with concern. "Her night things, too."

Gideon wondered if he blanched, for he certainly felt as if all the blood raced out of his head. "You could pile fresh linen on top of the old."

"Well, that's as may be." Meg looked doubtful. "If you like, m'lord." She chewed her lip, then burst out, "But m'mum used to say that's how folk take ill unto death, lying atop wet linens, sir."

"And in wet bedclothes," Gideon could only agree. He gave the maid a stern look. "Are you absolutely certain no other maids are about tonight?"

She shook her head. "There's a dance—"

"At Llewellyn's barn, so you said." He had been vaguely aware he'd granted permission for his servants to go off to dances; even more dimly aware that Vicar Llewellyn encour-

aged the occasional dance as "healthful recreation for the la-
boring classes."

Gideon looked down at the soaked linens and shook his head
as if to shake off indecision. "Well," he said in that same firm
tone, "we must change her things then."

"*We,* m'lord?" Meg said on a gasp, surprised into questioning him. "I mean, d'you think it seemly?"

"Are you strong enough to change her clothing and all this
bedding by yourself, while moving Miss Elizabeth with a min-
imum of fuss? I will not have her disturbed overmuch." He
sounded short-tempered even to himself. "No? Then I shall
have to assist you."

"As you say, sir," the maid murmured, her eyes wider than ever.

She moved past him to the linen cupboard to fetch fresh
sheets and blankets, and a dry night rail from the wardrobe.

"I will hold her, and you will do the, er, actual changing,"
Gideon ordered. He sat on the bed, sliding an arm under Elizabeth and lifting her into a sitting position. He slid in behind her,
propping her against his own chest.

She muttered on a half sob, "I hate you!"

"I am sorry—" he began to apologize, but then he saw her
eyes were open, but unfocused. She was not speaking to him,
but to someone inside her own mind.

"Ignore her," Gideon reminded the maid, who reached to un-
button Elizabeth's night rail. The gown was soon pulled over
Elizabeth's head, leaving her naked from the waist up and her
lower extremities covered only by a blanket. Gideon could not
think where to put his hands, especially when Elizabeth threatened to teeter to one side. He caught her arms, steadying her
against his chest. "The clean night rail!" he growled at the maid
from between gritted teeth.

The fresh gown was quickly pulled over Elizabeth's head,
but getting her arms through the long sleeves took more time.
Gideon was too aware of the warm, naked back pressing into
his chest, the curve of a breast that slipped into view. He ought
to avert his gaze, but he was afraid he might not catch Elizabeth
should she tilt again under Meg's ministrations.

Even though he told himself not to be foolish, that this was a
sickroom and gender was meaningless here, it *did* have mean-

ing. The woman in his arms was not related to him, and she was ill, and he was concerned for her. Yet even under the circumstances she was comely, lovely, soft. Devil take him! He could not detach awareness of her femininity any more than he could smother the embarrassment he experienced for her sake.

At last she was dressed and buttoned, and Gideon slid out from under her, even as he kept her balanced against his arm, to keep her from the damp sheets. It was the work of a minute to hoist her into his arms.

"I will hold her while you change the bedclothes," he said to the maid, and nodded at the pile of blankets. "Put one of those over her so she does not take a chill." The maid complied, and Gideon crossed to the nearest chair, where he sat carefully. He settled Elizabeth across his lap, freeing one hand, with which he adjusted the blanket so as to block out errant breezes. She stirred once, then resettled, her head tucked against his chest, as if she sought warmth and security from him. Were she conscious, she would no doubt be able to detect the beating of his heart beneath her cheek.

Finding no more adjustments needed to be made to the covering, his hand hovered over the blanket, and then slowly rose to touch her cheek. She was flushed from the fever, and her long black hair only half held in its plait. She did not stir when he allowed the backs of his fingers to brush her cheek, nor when he wiped away a tear trail that had run down into her hairline. He had not realized how much he had wanted to touch this face, to feel its contours under his fingertips, until the opportunity was irresistibly presented.

Then his hand froze, his fingers trembling against her cheek as he recalled the very words that had run through his mind: he was concerned for her.

Another man might think nothing of those five simple words, but Gideon knew them for what they were, what they represented in his life.

God help him, he cared about what became of her.

Chapter 13

Gideon had not cared, he knew, about anyone for too long a time. All he thought of, all he had craved for months, was escape.

His yearning to be free had started before his mother had died. Once she was gone, the need had trebled and had begun to consume him, had chased all Gideon's noble intentions from his head.

He had planned to be the benevolent Lord Greyleigh, taker in of strays, employer of the crippled, judge of none, restorer of happiness. And for a while, he had succeeded. For that matter, he succeeded in that aim even now . . . except for himself. Gideon made everyone around him happy, but not himself. He'd even made his brothers content—buying a commission for Benjamin and handing a hedonistically large sum of the ready to Sebastian, who had desired to game and wench and try to discover all of Brighton's other iniquities.

Still, it all *could* have been good. Gideon could have gone on playing Lord Bountiful . . . if only he had not seen through his own intentions to the hollow truth beneath: he had begun to "do good" out of rote.

His heart was no longer automatically squeezed at once by the sight of a twisted leg or a starving face. He had begun to wonder if some people did not invite their fates. He had started to pick and choose who should know his munificence. He looked for those who might blossom under his care. His charity was not freely given. It came with a price: he expected those he selected to prosper, to change, to grow, to become what he wanted them to be.

To Gideon's horror, he began to wonder if what he was doing

could even be labeled "charity." He did not freely give to one and all. He had expectations. He was like one of those money-lenders in the temple whom Jesus had condemned. He was the rich man who loudly cried out his prayers instead of humbly begging God's forgiveness, a man made of bluff and blow, all artificial goodness, a fraud.

He had searched their faces, this motley staff of his, and he had seen their contentment, but it was too late to delude himself any longer. If he had somehow managed to bring some happiness to these poor, benighted people, then he had bought it at the cost of his own soul. They did not know they had been "rescued" by a scoundrel, but their lack of knowledge did not mitigate Gideon's sin, his pride, his folly.

His father had been a shallow, unkind man, who had tortured his wife with critical words and unkind looks because she could not be the helpmeet he desired her to be. He had never tried to see into her confused eyes, never forgave her for being imperfect. He had been harsh with his sons as well, although Gideon had never been able to figure exactly why, except perhaps they'd had the gall to not be exactly like Papa.

Gideon had desired to be entirely *unlike* him. But, despite his best intentions, he had only managed to shadow his father's path. The soured Greyleigh blood had run true. Gideon had become a monster cloaked in fine clothes, no better than his father, picking and choosing those who could change in such a way as to make Gideon feel superior to his dead parent. He may not have shouted, he may not have struck out with his hands and a sharp tongue, but he had learned to manipulate others. Gideon's manner of manipulation was simply more subtle, even allowing Gideon to fool himself for a long time.

The irony was, the charity charade continued to play on. Gideon still did his good deeds, still found employment for the weak and the wounded—but within he was hollow—hollow and deranged, surely. He did not know how else to act, and so even though each new face that sought his help, his support, dragged him deeper into the quagmire of empty charity, still he went doggedly on.

He could just be a landowner, like a thousand other men. He could order the aldermen of Severn's Well never to send an-

other charity case his way. He could build fences around his
property, could refuse to see the needy just outside that
fence. . . . But his only hope, his only redemption, was that
even if his heart was empty, perhaps the acts themselves were
not. Perhaps God or fate or that something otherworldly that
surely looked into men's souls, would think acts were enough,
even without faith, or truth, or love.

Only now . . . now he had touched this woman's face, and an
old, old emotion had laced through him, had pierced that hollow organ he called his heart.

She was still a burden. She was still a stranger. But somehow
this unconscious, fever-racked, helpless creature in his arms
had moved past Gideon's rigid sense of duty, into something
that could only be called caring. Something in her, in the smiles
she had given him, or the promise to one day be completely
honest with him, something had caused her touch to reach
down to his very soul.

He sat, cradling Elizabeth, feeling shattered, but, too, feeling
suddenly and keenly alive.

"My lord?" A voice penetrated the seething fog of his
thoughts. He looked up at the maid, dimly aware she had been
repeating the words several times.

"Yes?" he said, his voice a croak, as though he held back
tears.

"The bed is ready, my lord."

Gideon stood, surprised to find his legs would hold him even
though he trembled all over. He took several deep breaths, re-
gaining a measure of control, and crossed to the bed. He and the
maid tucked Elizabeth in, then he sat once more in the chair as
the maid changed the dressing on Elizabeth's foot. Elizabeth
grimaced as the maid worked, but did not truly rise to a conscious state.

When she was done, the maid offered to stay with Elizabeth.
"Someone should return from the dance in the next few hours,
my lord. I can stay with her until then."

Gideon nodded, but he did not rise to leave.

"My lord?"

"I will stay, too," he said, and there must have been determination in his voice, for the maid gave him a curious look, then retreated to a chair of her own.

He stayed where he was, all night, all through the worst of Elizabeth's fever, even though by midnight there were other females who could have taken his place. He allowed them to change Elizabeth's clothing and bedding while he waited in the hall, but then he returned to the bedside, to watch and to wait.

Hours later, Gideon glanced at the maid on the other side of Elizabeth's bed. What was this girl's name? Janet? Meg had long since been replaced. Whatever this girl's name, she had finally succumbed to the lateness of the early morning hour and fallen asleep in her chair. Let the girl sleep, especially since Gideon could not. He had passed beyond exhaustion into that wakeful state that makes for either terribly muddled or else terribly clear thoughts.

He remembered her, the laundry maid, if not her name. She had been starving on the streets of Bristol until he had seen her plight and brought her back here to his home.

Daughter to a cruel man, a farmer on a small holding who beat her most days of her life, this young woman had run away, seeking some kindness in the world. She had found only more cruelty and indifference, and with no references, also no chances for employment. She had finally taken to prostitution to feed herself, but the horror of her new, degraded station in life had been too much.

She had tried to cut her wrists with a stolen barber's knife, but had not realized how deep and terrible such a wound must be to accomplish its goal. Gideon had found her on the High Street in Bristol, where dozens of other passersby had already stepped gingerly around the prone figure and its small pool of blood. He had calmly told her she was not dying, or at least not physically, but he had known her soul was in terrible jeopardy of expiring upon that street in Bristol.

He had listened to her story and had found what he always looked for in a waif or a drunkard or a pauper's eyes—vestiges of hope. Gideon had searched for the same in his own reflection and not found it, but he knew what hope looked like. He had brought the girl to Greyleigh Manor and had given her the decent employment she had sought. As usually happened, there had not been a murmur of trouble about or from her since.

Looking at the girl now, Gideon saw rosy cheeks and meat on bones that had been stick-thin only this past winter. He flattered himself the girl was content enough, that he had done some small good in this grim world. Surely that counted for something, even if his heart was empty of true compassion— even if he longed with every fiber of his being to leave Janet and all her ilk behind, tending only to his own needs?

He could not save the world, Gideon knew that. One man could only do so much. Until last night, he'd had a far deeper fear: that he could not save himself.

From Janet, Gideon's attention drifted to the figure on the bed. At last, about an hour before, Elizabeth's fever had broken. Now she slept a true sleep, not the terrible stupor of fever. Gideon did not need the surgeon to tell him the infection had run the worst of its course, that its quick and sharp strike was far less dangerous than the long, slow onset of gangrene. Barring further complications, such as pneumonia, Elizabeth would live. He knew more of her now, for she had cried out in her delirium.

He knew she was afraid, fearing the future—just as he did. However, her future sounded more directly devastating; whereas he feared the starvation of his soul, she feared the more immediate starvation of the body. In that, she was not unlike Janet the laundry maid.

And, like Janet, apparently Elizabeth had known a reason to fear pregnancy.

"Baby? How will I . . . ? Go home!" Elizabeth had cried out disjointed phrases, her imploring hand on Gideon's arm and her gaze fixed on his, but her mind lost to the realm of fever. And later she had said, with tears streaking down her flushed cheeks, "Papa . . . ! No baby! God, thank you, God. God . . . baby . . ."

Now, how could it be that a young woman feared having a child since she had sworn she was not married? The "wedding ring" she had worn on her left hand was now on her right, moved, presumably, by her. A woman did not move a ring from the left hand to the right if she wished to appear married, so

Elizabeth's claim she had no husband seemed borne out by her own actions.

The answers were all obvious enough, especially to a man who took in members of downtrodden humanity as a regular course: Elizabeth had been with a man, had lain in his bed. She feared she was ruined. She may have eloped with him, or otherwise secretly or quietly wed. She may have run off without benefit of clergy. This man of hers may have died, or he may have abandoned her. He may have belatedly discovered his new wife was of an infirm mind. This last seemed likely, as someone had surely placed Elizabeth in the asylum.

The specifics did not matter so much as the news that she had plainly left the protection of her family to be with her lover. Whoever he had been, her family would not have approved, that much was clear from the rambling comments she had made from her sickbed.

The only part Gideon did not understand was *why*. Elizabeth hated this man, whose name she never uttered in her delirium. What she did mumble were words of contempt and rejection, laid firmly upon this unnamed man's shoulders. It was near impossible to believe she had ever cared for the man's company, let alone could have loved him.

Then why run off with him? Gideon wondered. This question required a higher level of conjecture, but it was easy enough to imagine. Perhaps, again like Janet, Elizabeth's home life had been unbearable. Marriage could have been used as an escape.

Or perhaps Elizabeth was older than she appeared, and had begun to fear the status of old maid? Gideon looked at her now calmly sleeping face and rejected that thought. Elizabeth did not seem like the type of woman who feared such labels.

It was possible she had no dowry, and had leaped at the first man who did not care about the lack. That was a reasonable explanation. Or perhaps she had acted with a complete deficiency of forethought, as was to be expected in someone who was addlepated.

Her reasons were still her own, however, for she had said nothing to answer this part of the riddle, nothing beyond calling for someone named "Lorraine," of whom it was patently obvious she was fond.

She had not called for a man, other than to heap coals on the head of the deceiver, the one who had left her with naught but a ring with a B on it. Gideon knew a moment's satisfaction that no other man's name had come from Elizabeth's fevered lips, willing to believe his satisfaction came from supposing this meant she had not given herself to a series of men. There was something in the way she carried herself, or perhaps in the depths of her brown eyes, that stated she could not have prostituted herself. He guessed she would rather choose the asylum than she would the bordello.

Perhaps she had chosen to go there, to the asylum . . . perhaps he now knew the reason why she had been of a "nervous disposition." She would not be the first female whose stability of mind had been overturned by a miscalculated love affair.

There had been a dozen times she'd seemed so aware, so present in the moment, so sane. Those moments far overshadowed the few that had given Gideon pause. Perhaps she really had been helped by her stay in the asylum, and the trauma of the fire that night had caused her to slip back into old ways temporarily?

In her lucid moments—and he knew she had many—she no doubt intended to use the ring on her hand as a shield, most probably as a symbol of a past marriage, no matter if real or imagined. With the war with France still waging, many an abruptly appearing "widow" had a tale that was easily believed in some far, tiny corner of the nation, or at least accepted without too many questions. It was the way of war to disrupt lives, and the way of the world to swallow a plausibly told tale.

Gideon sighed, saddened at the thought that Elizabeth was yet another wounded soul, wounded by a man's deed as well as her own unfortunate constitution. She did not look fragile, but looks had nothing to do with the unrest of the mind. If he knew nothing else from his mother's illness, he knew that mental instability was never invited, never welcomed. Elizabeth could not help if she was "nervous" or given to "womanly vapors," as some doctors so kindly phrased it.

Mostly Gideon sighed because now she was no longer a nameless, faceless problem—she was Elizabeth. This woman, who had touched him, who had a certain charm and, in her rational moments, an undeniable intelligence. She was not a nobody, as she had once called herself. She had become visible to his world-weary heart as well as his eyes.

Elizabeth. Never mind her surname. Some rare occasions took virtual strangers rapidly beyond surnames, and this was one of them. Despite all his prior intentions, he knew he must do something to help her.

That was when Gideon decided she must have some new gowns before she left his home. The gowns would be his parting gift to her, even if he could not think of any good reason why she should accept a gift of any kind from him, other than the intimate connection she had made while lying in his arms, a connection he could hardly explain to her.

He would ask her if she wished the gowns to be made up in half-mourning colors, to help her perpetuate whatever tale she needed to be supported. A dead husband, a father lost at sea—whatever tale she told would surely be better believed if she could wear somberly cut dresses in mourning colors. So, she would have dresses, howsoever she wished them, because it was all he could do for her, the only way he could extend a circle of protection around her once she was quit of his home.

The idea of her leaving made him flinch, but the truth was only the truth and could not be denied. Of course she would leave. What else was there for her to do? Stay and marry him? That was not even laughable. Elizabeth could not marry a hollow man; it would be a crime against all that was good in this world. And only ponder, he thought with his mouth crooking sarcastically to one side, what manner of mooncalf children would such a union produce? No, marriage was beyond impossible.

Slowly he realized his gaze had turned inward, that he had been staring at Elizabeth's face without seeing it, and that she was now staring back at him.

"You are awake!" he said. His outcry was loud enough to wake the maid, who startled and blinked, then stretched with a yawn.

"Your hair," Elizabeth said on a hoarse whisper.

"My hair?" he repeated, standing to reach for the ewer of water on the nearby table. She would be thirsty.

"I dreamt about your hair. That it was unbound, as it is now."

He poured her a glass of water, then turned back to her, tingling quietly at the sight of Elizabeth with coherent, open eyes. "Unbound?" he echoed.

"I dreamt I had become your valet, and you wanted me to cut your hair," she said, licking dry lips.

"That is an odd sort of dream," he said with a small, encouraging smile. He sat down on the bed, sliding an arm under her to help her sit up as he had done once before. A shock ran up his arm, reminding him of another time he had held her very close like this.

The maid tried to assist from the other side, but it was too far a stretch. Gideon mildly shook his head. "Tell Cook we will be wanting beef broth soon," he told the girl, who curtsied and left at once.

He helped Elizabeth take several sips of water from the glass, then she licked her lips again.

"I think . . . you helped take care of me," Elizabeth said, the words more question than statement.

"I did."

She frowned, perhaps from trying to remember. "Did Jeannie have her baby, or did I dream that?"

"She did. A girl. Alice is the name."

"Ah. After Jeannie's mother."

He could move away now, to put down the glass because it was clear she did not want more water at present, but Gideon stayed where he was. Elizabeth's back was warm where she lay cradled upon his arm, no longer from fever but from the normal heat of a body at rest. He hated to disturb her when she seemed content; he hated to move away from touching her.

A knock came at the door, and suddenly Gideon wished he had moved, that they not be found in such an intimate posture, but to retire abruptly seemed churlish. Instead he transferred the glass to his other hand, that his innocent gesture of caretaking might be all the more obvious to whoever came in. "Enter," he said.

The maid had returned. "Mr. Clifton is here, my lord," she announced, stepping aside to admit the surgeon.

"Ah! Our patient is awake! This is excellent news, truly excellent," Mr. Clifton cried with genuine pleasure.

"She was having some water," Gideon said, not quite meeting the surgeon's gaze, afraid there was color rising in his face.

"Fine, fine!" Mr. Clifton beamed at Elizabeth. "I can see the fever has broken," he said, even before he put a hand to her forehead.

"I feel very weak," Elizabeth said.

"Well, you will. That's to be expected." The surgeon patted his vest pockets and frowned lightly. He set down the black bag he had brought with him, opened it, and cast about inside for some object or other. "Did you know you've had quite the sick-room nurse in Lord Greyleigh, my girl?" he asked as he finally found the pocket watch he had been searching for. "The fellow watched over you when things became a wee bit busy around here with babies arriving and all, or so the servants tell me."

"I dimly remember his help," Elizabeth said, returning the surgeon's smile with a tired one of her own. Gideon startled, but if Elizabeth noticed, she gave no sign.

Mr. Clifton picked up her wrist, settled his fingers over her pulse, and consulted the watch. "Well, you're better, but not well, eh? I can see you need more rest. But let us have a look at the wound first, shall we?"

Gideon took this as a cue, slipping his arm from beneath Elizabeth after he lowered her to the pillow. He stepped back, and the surgeon stepped forward, displacing him.

It seemed an abrupt ending to a long night. He wanted to say something, but what?

Gideon turned and strode to the maid, whom he thanked for her help. He gave her a handful of coins, and asked that she divide them with the other maid, Meg, who had helped. Janet blushed happily, and Gideon was reminded why he had once thought it the grandest plan in all the world to make this house a haven for those unwanted and friendless. Elizabeth had done that for him.

"My lord." Elizabeth's weakened voice still was strong enough to stop him at the door.

"Yes?" He turned back to face her, feeling oddly elated that she had called out to him.

"Were I your valet," she said on a tremulous smile, "I would not cut your hair. I would leave it just as it is."

He smiled and made a little blowing sound that implied light amusement, then nodded farewell. He slipped out the door, closing it quietly, and immediately leaned against the wall, aware his heart hammered hard inside his chest. It pounded as if he had run a mile, for no more reason than Elizabeth had implied she liked his hair.

Such a reaction was silly, adolescent even, and he felt a little dizzy with it. Worst of all, he liked the dizzy feeling and did not even try to do anything that might stop the giddiness that bubbled throughout his entire bloodstream.

Chapter 14

Are you a fairy?"

Elizabeth opened her eyes, instantly aware that a whole day of nothing but broth and sleep since the surgeon had last come had done much to restore a sensation of health. By the slanting of the light across her ceiling, it was clearly late afternoon.

She was also abruptly aware that someone stood near her bed. She turned her head, hoping to find it was Lord Greyleigh standing there, and was shocked when she saw instead the strange red-haired woman. In her arms, the woman held an infant swaddled in shawls.

"Are you a fairy?" the woman asked again.

Elizabeth stared, and shook her head ever so slightly.

The woman sighed. "I need to find the fairies," she complained. "I need to give them this." She opened her hand, revealing a ring that lay upon her palm.

Elizabeth gasped when she glimpsed the distinctive mother-of-pearl and rubies arrangement, a ring brought back from India by Mama's brother, Uncle Frederick. "That is *my* ring!"

The woman scowled, looking very young in her disapproval. She closed her hand around the ring, and shouted, "It is *mine*! For the fairies!"

"Who are you?" Elizabeth demanded, sitting up and swinging her legs over the side of the bed.

The woman's flare of anger died down in an instant. "Lily," she answered with a soft, even shy, half smile.

What a strange, mercurial creature, Elizabeth thought, even as she realized she had sat up too suddenly, too soon; a wave of dizziness swept over her. Elizabeth gripped the bedclothes, try-

ing not to teeter forward, trying to find her way out of the
downward spiraling blackness before her eyes.

When Elizabeth could focus her gaze again, gasping at the
effort, she was not surprised to find the red-haired woman was
gone. Even in her distress, Elizabeth had heard the girl moving
away, soft, padded steps that told of shoeless feet. A door had
opened behind her; not the door to the hallway. It had to have
been the door behind the tapestry.

Glancing down at her foot, Elizabeth decided she would not
try her luck at standing. What would she learn, even should she
be able to open the hidden door this time? Where it led, yes, but
anything else of value?

She had already learned some important things, because she
had at last seen the red-haired woman well. The woman went
about barefoot, and that explained how a person could quietly slip
in and out of rooms, unnoticed except when she wished to be. The
woman—she had called herself Lily—had seemed to have a
youthful manner. Lily acted more childlike than even her young
face implied; she had all but thrown a tantrum over the ring.

Could this Lily be someone who had escaped the asylum and
who had gone unreported as missing?

She had carried an infant in her arms, cradling the babe with
a surety and tenderness that implied devotion. Was this the
woman's child—or a younger sibling? Yet, if Lily were indeed
feeble in her mind, who would allow her the care of an infant,
even if that infant was her own?

What if the child were not Lily's after all . . . Jeannie had recently borne a child. Granted, Jeannie was recovering away
from Greyleigh Manor, but just down in the village. . . . Most
curious of all, the child had not made a sound, not even when
Lily had yelled.

Elizabeth shuddered as a second, more gruesome thought
crossed her mind: what if the infant were dead? Was that why
this Lily had asked for fairies, somehow thinking the mythical
creatures might consider such a ghastly offering fair, and as
fairies were wont to do, exchange one of their own changeling
infants for this too-quiet one?

Elizabeth shuddered, hoping she was wholly wrong as to the
girl's reasoning, and that the child was well enough.

One thing was certain: this being calling herself Lily had to be the thief who had taken Elizabeth's jewels. The ring in her possession was proof enough of that.

Lily must be found, and she must be made to return Elizabeth's jewelry. Those jewels were the very key to Elizabeth's future. If she did not have them, Elizabeth had no way to live on her own, away from Papa and his new wife. She had no way to keep scandal at bay for Lorraine's sake.

And, Elizabeth admitted, it would be rewarding to prove the "ghost" did indeed yet haunt Lord Greyleigh's halls.

That afternoon, having been pronounced "much improved" by Mr. Clifton, Elizabeth was convinced of it herself because no dizziness had returned. Indeed, she had even asked to dress.

She was glad she had, because Lord Greyleigh had come to call upon her in her room, bringing with him a pair of new crutches.

Elizabeth took them, knowing she would be grateful for the velvet fabric that padded the top of the crutches where they fit under her arms, and made a few awkward attempts. In a few moments, though, they were quickly mastered. "They will work admirably to help me move about," she said as she beamed at Gideon.

He nodded his approval. "I had them sent from Bristol."

Elizabeth sat in the nearest chair, and wondered if, during her fever, she had felt as warm as she did now. It was not effort, nor the fever that had raced across her skin however, but a glow brought on by Gideon's proximity. Elizabeth recalled only scattered moments from her time in the sickbed, but she did remember that every time she had opened her eyes, Gideon had been sitting at hand.

She sneaked a look at him as he bent at the waist, checking some facet of one of the crutches. She turned her gaze away, so that he not catch her with a look of admiration on her face.

How could she find him handsome? Others would not, she knew. Yes, he had fine features, but they were difficult to note. One had to look closer, had to get past the shock of pale blond hair, and those uncanny light eyes of his. But . . . once one became accustomed to his coloring, other factors came under notice.

His jawline, for instance. Lord Greyleigh had a faultless jawline. One might call it squared, giving his features authority, but
his jaw was not prominent and did not dominate the rest of his
face. It was perfectly proportionate to the rise of his cheekbones.
Also, he had well-arched brows, giving him perhaps a faintly
sinister air. She might have accused him of applying kohl to give
his brows their darker color, but when he had held her in his
arms, she had seen for herself they were naturally darker than
the hair atop his head, as were his lashes. At present he sported
one day's growth of beard, and it showed promise of also being
darker. Extraordinary, that nature should lend his face color and
drama, and even more drama by kissing the hair atop his head
with only the merest trace of gold, like sunlight on linen.

Add to that, he was a well-made man, with good shoulders
and a flat stomach that complemented his tailor's efforts. Yes,
there was little complaint to be made against Lord Greyleigh's
appearance.

But it was not his mere appearance that made Elizabeth feel
flushed with heat, but rather the memory of what she had said
to him, what she had dreamt of him.

True, in one part of her dream she had been his valet, but
then, as happens in dreams, Elizabeth was no longer some faceless servant but herself again, in long skirts and upswept hair.
Though now a female, she had still stood beside Gideon in this
dream, as he sat in a chair, she still had possessed a pair of scissors, and he had still been bidding her to trim his hair. In her
dream she had let the strands play through her fingers and had
taken a step nearer him. She had reached with one hand to tilt
his face up to hers where she had stood above him. Her dream
self had suddenly and strongly rejected the thought of changing
this look, so distinctive on him. It had seemed a crime. She had
thrown down the scissors and had told him no. He had smiled
and nodded, then removed the cloth draped about his shoulders,
and her dream self had been vastly relieved.

Silly, that dream. Nonsensical even. But, worse yet, whyever
had she told Lord Greyleigh about it?

It was difficult to look casually at him now, with that flaxen
hair of his pulled back, loosely held by a black ribbon. She had
a burning longing to stand, cross to him, and unbind his hair.

Her fingers itched to run through the strands, to see if they felt as she had imagined them in her dream.

She was a wicked, carnal woman, there was no doubt of that. She knew whence this impulse came, for she remembered being undressed by the maid ... while lying against Lord Greyleigh's chest, supported by his arms. The memory had been jumbled at first, but it had all cemented into logic and memory when the maid had blushed and answered truthfully upon being asked.

It meant nothing, of course, that Elizabeth's naked flesh had lain against him. He had been fully clothed, at least she remembered cloth beneath her, and he had been aiding a sick woman, not coming to a lover's bed. Elizabeth had not been in her right mind, and if she had, he never would have been in the room, let alone assisting in her disrobing. He had been there merely because there was no one else, not because he had wished to look upon her.

Still, knowing he had held her, had helped her, had sat here in this chamber, at her bedside for hours on end ... she shuddered, struggling to meet Lord Greyleigh's gaze.

Now he had brought her crutches. He had troubled himself to send inquiries if they might be obtained, and he had sent for them all the way from Bristol, at least five miles away. "These will be less effort, and easier on your heel," he had said as he'd presented the crutches.

There was nothing seductive in a pair of crutches, nor in what he had said, but in that moment Elizabeth had felt something that went beyond mere sensual regard in any event. Blinking back appreciative tears, she had felt something inside her flip, as if her heart had begun to pump her blood in reverse. It was more than desire, far more, this feeling trapped deep within her, this feeling she wanted to call friendship but which she knew went much, much deeper. She was changed, fundamentally, but she could never have said how or in what way, but only by whom.

She was still ruined, still could not go home, and her jewelry had yet to be recovered, but in that moment Elizabeth did not feel as poor or as desperate as she had just a few days earlier. Lord Greyleigh had sent for crutches when he had not needed to, and that simple act had been enough to restore her ability to hope for happier moments ahead. Peagoose! she scolded herself, and stared down at her primly folded hands in her lap.

"I inquired into the matter of Jeannie's baby," he said.

Elizabeth brought her gaze up, glad for a neutral topic. "I hope all was well? That the baby never went missing?"

"Quite well, according to Polly. She assures me the child has been with its mother the entire time, and all are healthy and happy."

"Polly has seen the baby? That it remains with its mother?"

Lord Greyleigh gave her a puzzled look. "Of course."

Elizabeth let out a relieved sigh. Maybe there had been no baby after all, merely an impression given by a swaddled bundle of cloth. That was much more pleasant a thought than others Elizabeth had pondered. Yes, that must have been what she saw, as it would explain the "child's" unusual silence.

"Still," said Lord Greyleigh, pulling Elizabeth's attention back to the moment as he came to stand before her, "I do not like the idea of your using these crutches on the stairs. I will carry you when you need to go up or down. Are you ready now for luncheon?" He made a general lifting motion, to indicate he was ready.

"The servants and the chair would serve," Elizabeth murmured, feeling a deeper flush steal across her cheeks.

"Nonsense. You said yourself it was mortifying to be carried thusly. I promise I will not drop you, if that is what concerns you."

"I never thought you would," she replied. There was no gracious way to refuse, so Elizabeth indicated her acquiescence by lifting her arms, which then slid around his neck as he lifted her from her chair.

"You are still a bit flushed," he commented, glancing at her face as he strode from her room.

His comment only caused her to flush all the deeper red, she knew. "The aftereffect of fever," she murmured, fixing her gaze on his cravat.

By the time he had carried her down the stairs and to the dining table, she wondered if she was flushed on every inch of her skin. Being held so near him had flustered her tongue into silence and made every one of her senses tingle with an awareness of where their bodies had pressed together. His scent—

clean linen and shaving soap—had made her feel light-headed, and his mouth had been near enough to hers that it had crossed her mind that she might kiss him, did she but dare to do so. When he lowered her into a dining chair, she was aware how reluctantly slow her arms were to slide free of his neck.

Were other women so keenly aware of men? What was wrong with her, to be so responsive to a man's mere touch? Although, she admitted as she gazed at the plate a servant filled before her, while Radford had awakened her to the mysteries of his gender, it was not just every man who made Elizabeth's heart pound as it did now. She sneaked a glance from under her lashes at Lord Greyleigh, and knew that Mr. Clifton could never inspire such a rapid tattoo inside her breast as did this man.

That was the way of the world, was it not? To know attraction, to aid in one's duty to pair off, to couple? While marriage was a contract, a thing of the mind, attraction was designed by its very nature to be physical. The only control one had over attraction was the ability to refute it once it was felt, but one could not keep from feeling it in the first place.

Control of one's emotions was the key. And control was not something Elizabeth could ever let go of again, she knew. The last time she had, she had ruined her life. So it did not matter that a pair of strong arms and piercing, palest blue eyes stirred her blood, for she could hardly act on the strange, strong impulses that pulled at her.

"I want to do something for you," Lord Greyleigh said as he waved away a servant with a dish that apparently did not interest him.

"My lord?" Elizabeth queried, glancing at him.

"I want to order dresses made for you. Now, before you protest, let us be practical. You will need gowns. You are welcome to have my mother's, but they would need to be altered if you do. I think new gowns would better suit. Either way, a modiste's services are required, so since one must be brought in, I would rather see you in gowns that befit you."

He was only being sensible, but Elizabeth lifted her chin all the same. "I agree. But only if I may make the selections myself, and if I may repay you in time. Although I must forewarn you that it may take me some months to have the funds to repay—"

"Very well. Repay me whenever." He lifted his knife and fork, dismissing her protests with the gesture. "I assure you, the cost will not be an inconvenience for me. Please, make any selections you require. I will have a modiste brought from Bristol by tomorrow."

Elizabeth almost gasped; a modiste from Bristol would naturally be more costly than some local female. When Elizabeth was once again at home with Papa—or in a cottage of her own, or employed as a governess or a companion—surely he could be counted upon to settle this repayment debt of hers? Elizabeth looked to the napkin in her lap, her mouth downturned at the thought of this expense she had not even considered. Of course she would require clothing, and she could hardly send home for her gowns there.

But what if this modiste might know her? Granted, Elizabeth's gowns had mostly been made by Madame Chandler in London, and London was a fair distance, but it was yet another concern.

"Bristol?" Elizabeth questioned. "Is there no one in Severn's Well?"

"Not of any skill, no."

"Skill is not so important as speed, in my instance." And anonymity, she added silently.

Lord Greyleigh looked up. "You make a good point. Perhaps the local woman would serve us best. I know she had produced a gown for Mama in less than three days, so she could perhaps have as many as three ready for you by the end of a week. Perhaps she would best suit after all."

"And her name . . . ?"

Gideon's brows slanted together for a moment. "Rowan. Rawson. Something like that."

Elizabeth felt her shoulders relax. "Employing the local woman sounds the best plan." She managed a smile and a nod. "Thank you."

"You are welcome." He nodded, smiled slightly, and returned to his meal.

They shared some desultory conversation, but the notion of the gowns Elizabeth would shortly be in need of somehow left her feeling crestfallen. There was also an awkwardness in sharing a meal with a man of whom she was sharply aware.

Since she could not bring herself to maintain either a gaze or a conversation of any length with her host, in the age-old manner of all guests who did not know what to do at an uncomfortable moment, Elizabeth looked about the room in which she found herself. It was pleasant not to have to eat from a tray in bed, and she was grateful to be at a table once more, and a fine table it was, indeed. The wood beneath the tablecloth was a dark, rich mahogany, with matching chairs of gold-and-blue needlepoint seats and the Greyleigh crest carved into the seat backs. The sideboards were carved to match, and the curtains at the windows were blue with gold sashes. The rug beneath the table was also of blue, with gold and green leaves and pink roses woven into the pattern. It was a charming room, with pastoral paintings that gave the eye something soothing to observe while dining.

The table was finely set with Sheffield plates and crystal goblets. Although the table was not especially large, seating perhaps as many as twelve at a time, it was fitted with four large branches of candelabra, set and ready to be lit during tonight's supper.

Elizabeth sat up straight, staring hard at one particular candle in the center of the nearest candelabra. Without begging her host's leave, she stood, hopping on one foot and clutching the table's edge for balance as she made her way to where the candelabra sat. She reached among the unlit candles, and although she knew Lord Greyleigh was staring at her as if she had proved any doubts of sanity he'd had about her, she reached among the candles and pulled upward, sliding a band from the centermost one. She turned to Lord Greyleigh, presenting on her palm what she had discovered—a ring.

"It is my ring!" she declared, hearing the excitement in her own voice. "This was my grandmama's ring, given to her on her sixteenth birthday by her father." She clutched her hand closed once more and hopped down to where Lord Greyleigh sat staring. She thrust the ring toward him, closing her eyes at the same time. "Here! I shall prove it. Without looking at it again, I will tell you what the engraving inside the band says."

She felt him take the ring from her fingers and hoped he did not see her tremble when his touch met hers.

"Very well," he said, his voice neutral, giving away nothing of his thoughts. "Go ahead."

"It says 'For Emma, My Pearl, Love Papa,'" Elizabeth quoted. She opened her eyes, finding Lord Greyleigh had slanted the ring to catch the midday light coming through the windows, so as to read the inscription.

After a long moment during which he angled the ring, he looked up and said, "Exactly so." He looked back at the ring, a gold band with a large pearl at its center, with descending smaller pearls on either side for a total count of seven. "I have to believe this is yours," he said, handing it to her, but then bewilderment crossed his features. "But how did it come to be on a candle on my dining table?" The look he cast her clearly said he believed *she* had placed it there.

Elizabeth slipped the ring on her finger, to avert her gaze from his. With his steady regard upon her, she had felt yet again that shock of awareness of him, male and powerful. But, too, she felt his uncertainty, and saw the doubting tilt of his head. She ruthlessly pushed aside the awareness of the former, concentrating on the latter.

"I know you are reluctant to believe that I once possessed a collection of jewelry," she said, affecting a haughty manner. "But I assure you, I brought a collection of items with me into this house. Someone found where I had hid my purse of jewels in my pillow, for when next I went to get my jewelry, every piece was missing. I now believe I know who took them." In fact, she thought, it must have been the same person who had first put them in the table drawer, for Lord Greyleigh had certainly not been informed they existed.

"Oh? And who is this person?" he asked, moving to sip from his wineglass.

"The red-haired woman, the 'ghost,' was in my room again. I believe she took them."

Lord Greyleigh set down his glass with an audible chink. Before he could comment, however, Elizabeth went on. "I saw her plainly this time. I can describe her well for you if you like. Again, I certainly do not think she is a ghost at all, but I am also equally sure she is not a maid in your employ."

"My dear lady—!" He stood.

"There is a hidden door on the east wall of my chamber, behind the large tapestry that hangs there. Did you know that?"

Lord Greyleigh stood still as stone for a long pause, but then he slowly nodded. "There are passages, designed into the original structure by an ancestor, I suppose. But they have long since been boarded shut. My mama took to using them, and it . . . upset my father to have her appear in various rooms at odd moments."

"Well, I propose to you that someone has taken down the boards then, because I have had a regular visitor. She claims her name is Lily, and this afternoon she seemed to be carrying an infant. She is looking for a fairy, she says, and she had one of my jewels, a ring, in her hand. One with rubies and mother-of-pearl, a decidedly foreign design as it was brought from India." She paused and took a breath. "This woman . . . a girl, really, I do not think is entirely in her right mind."

"I have brought no one into this house named Lily," Lord Greyleigh said firmly, scowling. "There is no one named that on my staff."

"Nonetheless, that is the name she claimed. She has long red hair, and every time I have seen her, it has been unplaited and unpinned, and not very tidy. She goes about barefoot, I think to be silent in her movements, and she is very young, perhaps sixteen at the most."

Lord Greyleigh scowled terribly and turned his back to Elizabeth. She parted her lips to reassert she spoke the truth, that she was not insane or delusional, but before she could say anything more he turned back to her.

"Show me this door," he demanded, moving at once to scoop her into his arms. Elizabeth clung to him, telling herself the excitement that rippled through her was the result of his abrupt movement and nothing else.

Gideon threw himself against the oblong door shape, but it did not give. Under his breath he uttered a curse. "It is blocked from the other side," he said aloud as he rubbed his newly bruised shoulder.

"I told you I was unable to find a way to open it," Elizabeth said, with perhaps a hint of triumph in her tone.

Gideon turned to her where she sat on her bed, but it was so good to see her eyes once again lit by interest rather than fever, that he refrained from answering the comment. Instead, he mo-

tioned to the two footmen he had ordered to accompany him to
Elizabeth's room. "Come with me. I know where the exterior
entry was. Is," he corrected himself. "That must be how someone is entering the passages."

"I wish I could see it, too," Elizabeth cried at once, putting
up one hand as though to summon them back.

Gideon hesitated a moment, for she was so recently come
from a sickbed, but he was not immune to the entreaty in her
gaze. He took the steps needed to cross the room and scoop
Elizabeth into his arms once more. "I had no notion of starting
on an exercise regimen," he told her tartly as he hefted her in his
arms. "But it seems you are intent on seeing that I am made fit."

If she took insult, she did not show it. If anything, she looked
content. "You could let the servants carry me," she pointed out,
her slender arms twining around his neck.

There was no answer to be made to that either, so Gideon
once more chose to say nothing. He used the effort of carrying
Elizabeth down the stairs as a cover for his lack of speech, but
really he was lost in thought.

Elizabeth had so far proven everything she had said, lacking
only the red-haired woman as proof. For that matter, Gideon
himself believed that someone had been taking things for some
while now. He had always supposed it was a servant, but it had
never occurred to him that the rascal might be using the passages. It was not necessary to do so, for it was easy enough to
pick up a stickpin or a watch fob and place it in one's pocket and
take it from the house, without making use of the old passages
Gideon had more than half forgot. A mere child could palm a
small object and easily carry it from the house, let alone any of
the servants. But the passages *would* make an excellent place in
which to hide things, to avoid being caught by the surprise in-
spections of pockets that Gideon had ordered randomly done—
and which had always failed to turn up any missing item.

And the oddest part of it all? Sometimes things were *brought
into* the house and left behind with no one to claim them. An
old night rail, looking as if it might have been taken from some
washline, or a bonnet with pink ribbons that everyone denied
seeing before let alone owning, or a leather ball, or a dog's col-
lar. The servants denied the things brought in as vehemently as

they denied taking anything out of the house . . . it had all made no sense whatsoever.

Now Elizabeth had "found" a ring on a candle. Yes, she made sense when she spoke. Yes, the tapestry in her room certainly did cover a hidden door, but there was the rub. How had the injured and bedridden Elizabeth known of the door behind the tapestry? It was not as if she could go exploring! Could she? But why would she, even if her wound had allowed it?

She had certainly known the inscription on the ring, but she could have read it long before she ever placed the ring on the candle! What proof was there that it had not been placed by her? Or proof that it had ever belonged to her? The truth was, she had possessed nothing when she had been brought into the house, or so his servants had reported to Gideon.

If Elizabeth had been in his home for the past four or five months, Gideon knew he would have to accuse her of being the one who took and left things. Since that was not the case, he did not know what to make of Elizabeth's claims, her findings, her obvious glee upon "discovering" the pearl ring. He knew what he wanted to believe, knew what his mind kept attempting to take as proof of a mind more sound than he had feared, but which reason told him was unlikely.

He walked through the open door that one of the footmen held for him, shook his head at a suggestion the man would help carry Miss Elizabeth, and stepped forward to lead the way. The weight of the woman in his arms was less than the heavy weight in his mind, no less so as he pondered what motivated him to keep Elizabeth there, against his heart, when he could hand her off to a servant.

He stopped before an overgrowth of ivy, and after circling once in place, spied a nearby bench, on which he deposited Elizabeth. She did not meet his eyes, and he wondered what that meant. Did she feel guilt or alarm that they were about to uncover the secrets of the passageway? But, if so, why had she pointed out the passageways in the first place? Gideon shook his head, realizing that he felt almost as confused by all the seeming contradictions as Mama must have felt in her last days.

Gideon and the footmen used their hands to pull at the ivy, at least until Gideon saw how the ivy had been lifted away from the wall to form a loose curtain on one side. "This is how they got in," he said with surety. Folding back the ivy curtain, it was possible to see a door beneath.

He ordered tools brought, and in short order the ivy was pulled down, revealing an ordinary door that one would think was nothing more or less than a servant's entrance.

"I never knew nothin' were here!" a footman named Sam declared, with eyes wide.

"That was the intent," Gideon assured him. He reached for the metal door handle, and the door swung open easily, revealing how simple it would be for someone to slip under the ivy curtain and through the door.

"Did you play here as a child?" Elizabeth called, shading her eyes, the better to see from her seat.

Gideon shook his head, staring into the dark maw beyond the limited reach of the day's sunlight. "Only a few times, but then of course Mama learned of the passages, and in short order she had annoyed Papa by using them at all hours. She frightened him in his bed one night, a ghostly figure coming out of the wall, and that was when the half dozen or so doors into our rooms were all boarded from the inside."

He turned back to look at Elizabeth where she sat on her bench. "Will you be all right there while we explore?" he asked.

She nodded, looking anxious.

Gideon turned to Sam, who had brought a lit lamp along with the hoes they had used to pull down the ivy. Taking the lamp, Gideon led the way in.

Chapter 15

When they reemerged some twenty minutes later, Elizabeth was visibly agitated. "What did you find?" she asked with widened eyes as Gideon crossed to her side.

"The boards nailing the doors shut were all pulled down. But the doors are crudely made, with rough cross boards, so someone has figured how to put a long board propped between the far side of the passage wall and the door boards, creating an easily removed block. A crude but rather effective block, in truth."

"In other words, it would be possible to enter the rooms by first removing the block, but if the blocks are in place they would prevent the idle discoverer from coming into the passage from the room side?" Elizabeth questioned.

"Exactly," Gideon said, and tried not to let his gaze narrow on her. What did it matter if she grasped the idea easily, and extending that idea, what did it matter if she had already been through the passages herself? Someone had, for the dust on the wooden flooring had been disturbed, and not too many cobwebs had dangled in his face as he'd made his way along. "There is nothing in the passages, nothing obvious anyway. No piles of stolen goods or pirated caches," he told her.

Elizabeth's shoulders slumped. "I was hoping you would find the rest of my jewelry there."

He shrugged, not sure how to interpret the disappointment in her tone. "I suppose only a more thorough search would prove there is no hiding spot, such as a loose floorboard. Do you wish it?"

"Yes, please," she said with shy, even hopeful, grace that had him again doubting what his own good sense told him. These

jewels might indeed exist beyond the scope of the one ring he
had seen, but the only person to "take" them could well have
been Elizabeth herself. What game could she possibly be playing at? This was mischievousness that went beyond anything
his mama had ever manifested. But then again, what was a bit
of indulgence? Gideon instructed the footmen to search the passageways again, looking for loose bricks and boards and cub-
byholes.

He sat at Elizabeth's side, and when she squinted at the sun
that was beginning to descend toward the west, only then did he
realize he had not thought to bring a shawl or a bonnet for her.
He offered to return inside the house to get them, but she declined, and then she turned down his offer to carry her back
within. "I would like to be here to identify the jewelry if it is
found," she said earnestly.

"You could do that as easily inside the house."

"I should like to see them as they are found."

Perhaps she did not trust him, or she did not trust his servants, or perhaps this was all some fancy she'd taken into her
head, but she assured him she would rather stay.

After an uncomfortably long and silent minute had passed,
Gideon rose. "I believe you require a bonnet," he said less than
graciously. The truth was, it was difficult to sit in silence next
to this woman, because apart from the promise he had made to
her, he wanted her to answer questions that she either would
refuse, or would not have enough sense to answer truthfully.

Once inside, he gave his request for a bonnet to Frick, who
lifted his eyebrows, pondering this unusual request. "We could
borrow one of your mother's bonnets, my lord?" the butler suggested.

"Very good."

"I shall have it fetched at once," Frick said with a nod, and
turned to issue his command to a footman, who dashed up the
stairs. "May I bring another matter to your attention, sir?" Frick
inquired.

Gideon nodded absently, not paying much attention until the
butler produced from his jacket pocket a woman's hair comb
bedecked with a row of small diamonds. "This was found by
Kendrick, not even an hour since." Kendrick was Gideon's

master of hounds. "Somehow one of the hounds got into the house, sir, and when Kendrick was summoned to retrieve the animal, he found this comb secured in the creature's coat."

"Could it have got there by accident?" Gideon asked, but even before the butler could shake his head, he suspected the answer.

"No, my lord. It was deeply set in the tuft of hair behind the animal's head."

Gideon pocketed the comb and sighed, not liking this new twist in his odd household, not liking its obvious link to Elizabeth. Still, there was nothing to be done about reality but to endure it; history had taught him that lesson.

"Miss Elizabeth has had some personal jewelry go missing, Frick," Gideon explained wearily to the butler. "Anything that is found ought to be brought to me, and I will return it to her."

Frick's eyes grew round. "It was poor enough when we had things being moved, but now am I to understand that we have a *thief* in the house?" he cried in horror, as if he were personally responsible.

"We do not know that, Frick. Miss Elizabeth . . . she may be confused, leaving things about. I should prefer this was handled quietly. Just tell the servants that a, er, game has gone awry, and the objects are to be returned to you when found."

"Yes, sir," Frick said, obviously disapproving of such discretion, but also understanding its need.

The footman returned with a straw bonnet with tiny red silk flowers bordering its poke brim. It had not been a favorite of his mama's, or at least not in Gideon's recent memory, but then again it had been quite some while since Mama had been well enough to leave the house. Ah well, he mused, at least now the hat went to good purpose. There really was no need for a shawl, he decided, as the day was quite fine.

When he handed the bonnet to her, Elizabeth placed it on her head, tying the ribbons while she murmured her thanks.

"Have they found anything?" Gideon asked, glancing at the open doorway, where the occasional flicker of light could be seen as the servants searched.

Elizabeth shook her head. She glanced down at the pearl ring on her hand. "At least I have this," she said wistfully.

If Gideon had not promised to refrain from questioning her about matters past, he would have done so now, but there was no point because he knew Elizabeth would not answer. She would feel shamed, if his guess as to a lover who had abandoned or cast her off were correct, and he could hardly blame her.

Certainly half the reason he was himself rumored to be odd was that he had always refused to discuss anything that had to do with his mother, or his father for that matter. It had been important to him to keep his family's concerns as private as possible, to refuse to rise to the bait that other youngsters had thrown at him.

Eventually he had demanded that he be schooled at home, for life at Eton, where he had been nicknamed Mama's Boy, had proved unbearable. The nickname had been meant to slice two ways, the obvious, and then too the implication that Gideon took after his mama, that he was as mad as she. The nickname had not followed him into adulthood, at least not to his face, but he had heard the echoing whispers behind drawing room fans all the same.

Yes, he understood what it was to protect one's self, to wish to avoid being grist for the rumor mill. Gideon had always done all he could to protect his brothers from the sting of gossip, by persuading his papa that their education at home would make best use of the tutor's wages. Still, there was no way to keep the local lads from teasing and taunting Benjamin and Sebastian, of letting his brothers know their household was perceived as odd and awful.

Just as he had tried to spare his brothers, he perceived that Elizabeth was protecting someone—a woman named Lorraine, whom she had spoken of during the fever. Whoever Lorraine was, Elizabeth sought to protect the woman, that much had been clear even through the rambling nature of her fevered cries.

Pondering such thoughts caused Gideon to cast aside his own chagrin, and to let the afternoon sun induce in him a relaxed feeling. If he could, he would erase Elizabeth's past, whatever it was, but that was not a task for any man. She would be gone soon, and they had, after a fashion, much in common, so he would be a fool not to enjoy her company while it lasted.

He sat beside her, stretching out his legs and leaning back on his elbows, and realized with a shock that he did indeed enjoy Elizabeth's company.

How long had it been since he could say the same of any person, male or female, and truly mean it? He loved his brothers, but familial love was not always a smooth and easy path, and he was not entirely sure he would say he enjoyed Benjamin's rigid sense of self and Sebastian's too carefree bearing. Love and liking were different things, and here beside him sat a person whom he had come to esteem despite all odds against that rare and wonderful circumstance called liking.

He *liked* this addlepated woman who would not tell him her last name. Well, here was proof then—if she were mad, she was no more so than he.

He laughed, and Elizabeth looked at him in surprise.

"What is it?" she asked.

He had to lift his hand to his mouth to swipe away a silly smile that threatened to paste itself there. "I . . . it is just"—he cast about for an explanation, and lamely finished—"I am used to being in the middle of estate matters, yet here I sit, letting the footmen do all the work."

Elizabeth gave him a puzzled glance. "I would not keep you from joining the search if you wish to join it, my lord," she told him.

"I do not wish to join it," he said, settling more firmly on his elbows. "And no more of this 'my lord' business. I think when a man has spent as much time in a woman's bedchamber as I have in yours, that you ought to call me Gideon." He grinned at her, receiving a shocked stare as his reward.

"My lord!"

"Do not go all missish of a sudden, my dear Elizabeth. I have been calling you by your first name since the moment you could speak it, and it is high time you returned the favor. 'Gideon,' if you please, from now on."

Elizabeth lifted an eyebrow, but even though she tried to look arch, he could see a small smile tugging at the corners of her lips. "What would Lady Sees say to that?" Elizabeth asked.

"She would collapse away in a dead faint, but I really do not care if she would."

"Neither do I," Elizabeth confided, and now she added her grin to Gideon's.

They sat in silence, only it had become a companionable silence, the kind old friends share. Gideon had possessed one close friend from his days at school, Paul Yardley, so he recognized a friendly hush now it was between him and this woman.

Ah, Paul, who had been struck down during the first assault against Bonaparte. Thinking back, Paul's loss had probably been the beginning of the end of Gideon's social attempts. Whispers could be borne with a friend at one's side, but when Paul had gone, so had Gideon's desire to tolerate the whispers for the sake of the company.

Then Mama had grown worse, and Papa had died, and Gideon had become the marquess. Then how was he to know who was his friend and who but a hanger-on? It had been easier for Gideon to reject everyone, to turn his energy to helping others in a way that no one had ever tried with him.

"You are frowning," Elizabeth said at his side.

"Am I? I suppose it is because I have had a thought that I do not think you will like."

She lifted that eyebrow again in inquiry, a pensive set to her mouth.

"That pearl ring, and your signet ring, and anything else we may find?" he began.

"Yes." She sounded doubtful.

"I think you should give them to me, to keep them for you until you are ready to have them pawned. I have a drawer in my desk that can be locked." She started to shake her head. "They have already been stolen once," he reminded her.

She gave him a sideways glance. "At least now you believe I had jewelry to begin with."

He nodded. He believed it. He just was not sure if *she* was the one who was placing them in odd places.

"To show my good will," he said, reaching into his coat pocket, "here is another piece I assume belongs to you." He handed her the hair comb.

"Oh, yes!" she cried, obviously pleased. She turned the comb over, inspecting it, then turned sparkling eyes on him. "It has a twin to match it. Did you find that?"

"No. That was found on one of my hounds, set in the scruff of his neck."

"Your hound?" Elizabeth echoed, and there was such a wealth of surprise and bewilderment in her gaze as well as her outcry, that Gideon could almost be persuaded she was blameless of the comb's having been placed upon the dog.

"My lord?" The two footmen came from the doorway, Sam holding something pinched between two fingers. "We din't find nothin', except these."

At first it looked as though he extended his hand with nothing in it, but then the sunlight glinted off the long, thin red hairs caught between his thumb and forefinger.

"The red-haired woman!" Elizabeth pronounced gleefully. "Proof!"

"These hairs were caught on a nail. Must've hurt when they was yanked out," Sam said.

"Well, well," Gideon said, scratching behind his ear, feeling curiously lighthearted. Perhaps a red-haired wanderer had indeed been in the passageways, and logically, also in the house. It would seem he owed Elizabeth an apology—certainly someone had been in his home before Elizabeth ever arrived, so adding the two facts together made for fairly convincing evidence that, at least in this matter, Elizabeth was neither delusional nor engaged in some strange sport.

Was it possible that she did not, indeed, have anything to do with placing the jewelry that was being found about the house? Indeed, how could she have walked all the way out of the house to where the hounds were kept in their pen? Gideon gazed at her, seeing triumphant satisfaction in the gaze she returned, just before she threw her arms around his neck and hugged him in obvious delight.

Almost as soon as her arms were around his neck, she went abruptly still, even catching her breath. She pushed away from him, flushing a dull, dark red. "Excuse me! I cannot imagine what came over me," she murmured, looking down to the hair comb that seemingly had become utterly fascinating.

Gideon felt an answering flush creep up his own features,

though not from embarrassment, even if the moment had taken place in front of the servants. He wanted her to hug him all over again, to leave her arms about his neck, to bring her lips to meet his. Impossible! he scolded himself, while yet another side wondered why impossible?

If nothing else, he wanted the sunny, triumphant smile to come back to her mouth, to see the happy glow of satisfaction in her eyes. He did not want to feel this sense of rejection that came the moment she had so quickly pulled away from him.

Heaven knew, it was not the first time a woman had turned away from him, flustered by the peculiarity of his hair and eyes, those features that lent themselves to rumors that his nature matched his odd appearance. But surely Elizabeth had long since grown accustomed to his looks? He did not want her withdrawal, her removal from this new thing he had discovered between them, this circle of friendship they could foster. He did not want any awkwardness between them.

The footmen were staring, obviously confused by the sudden tension in the air. Gideon stood, dusting absently at his clothing. "You two will have to secure that door," he said, covering his distress with words. "Nail it shut for now, and I will hire a man to come and put a lock on it. Our 'ghost' will haunt our halls no more, I think."

The servants looked pleased, and Gideon forced himself to turn and look again at Elizabeth, to face once more the uneasiness that had sprung up between them. "Well, my dear lady," he said, crossing his arms because he could not think what else to do, "am I to have your jewels, to protect them even though our visitor ought come to call no more?"

"Yes, I suppose it is wise. Thank you," she said, conceding the point. She removed her rings, including the signet ring, and handed them and the comb up to him. "That you also found the comb gives me hope that the rest of my things are yet to be found about the house," she said, not quite meeting his gaze.

"Will you make me up a list?" he asked as he slipped the objects in his pocket.

"Gladly, yes, my lord."

"Gideon," he reminded her, then added, "Good!" He stepped back and waved the footmen forward. "Help the lady, men," he said, then turned his back and hurried away, knowing he was fleeing the awkward moment, knowing he was being a coward. But, God save him, he did not think he could bear to carry Elizabeth in his arms and feel anew her withdrawal.

Late that night, Gideon looked around the interior of his club and shuddered. Something had changed. Something had opened his eyes.

Where once he had liked the exclusivity of Elly's, where once he had liked the serious play, now he saw that the other gamesters were serious, sober types. They ought to be here out of sport, enjoyment, the need to connect with other human beings. But they had their stiff drinks at their elbows, their cards before their eyes, their minds fixed on odds and opportunities to best the other men's cards. There was no conviviality, no stirring of camaraderie.

They were strangers, all, come together to play without playfulness, to try to win affordable amounts that could not change their lives for good or ill, to waste time with people who demanded nothing of them, not even friendship.

A cold sweat crept across Gideon's skin, and he pushed back his chair with a loud scrape. "Are you leaving, my lord?" the club employee behind the table asked, prepared to pay him or record his winnings in the club book against play on another night.

"Yes. Yes, I am leaving," Gideon said, knowing he meant forever. He stood, moving away from the table with unsteady steps.

"Your purse, my lord?" the man called after him.

"Keep it. A vail for you," Gideon said, not even bothering to turn around.

"Thank you, my lord!" the man cried in happy surprise, the words just reaching Gideon as he gathered his hat and cane. Without looking back, Gideon stepped out into the cool night air.

Gideon's head cleared a little, and he could even laugh a bit at his sudden revelation. He supposed the impression had been a long time coming, but something had finally made him cease ignoring the obvious this night.

"Something" was Elizabeth, of course. But why?

Because she had changed him, by reminding him the world held such things as friendship. That there was more to a day than duty and responsibility. There was laughing for no better reason than a need to laugh. But look how rusty he had become; it had taken him nigh on to four hours before the effects of laughter and camaraderie had revealed to him that Elly's could no longer meet his needs.

His needs! He had suppressed his own needs and desires for so long that now his head literally reeled from the effect of one tiny concession to himself. He closed his eyes, feeling a pressure in his chest that was not quite a pain, and wondered why this tiny little change left him feeling nearly ill. He was cheeky to wonder at Elizabeth's mental stability, when his own was so obviously askew. Still, the rockiness he felt, the almost pain, the light-headedness, all felt good in a weirdly enjoyable way.

He had given up his club, and got—what? Nothing, really, but all the same he felt curiously light on the horse's back as he rode toward home.

Gideon glanced at Frick's silver salver the next morning and saw as expected that not enough time had passed for him to have received a chess reply from either brother, and he walked on past. Only to come to a sudden halt and retrace his steps. He picked up the outgoing letter written in Elizabeth's hand. The letter was addressed to Lady Sees and sealed with a wafer.

Still giddy from last night's quitting of his club—perhaps irrationally, he admitted to himself with a lopsided grin—he felt boldly audacious. With almost no pang from his conscience, he carried the letter in to the breakfast table. He was disappointed not to find Elizabeth there, and retreated at once, heading for the stairs.

She had taken a morning tray in her room, he discovered when he bid him enter.

"Any callers in the night?" he asked as she set the tray aside, dabbing at her mouth with her napkin.

"None, I am pleased to report." She smiled at him, and Gideon felt his heart take an extra beat.

"How is your heel today?"

"Very good. It is beginning to itch, a healthy sign."

"Do not scratch it."

"I shan't, but the temptation is terribly strong." She pointed to the missive in his hand. "Did you receive a letter?"

"It is yours. One you are sending," he said as he took a seat next to her bed.

She lifted her eyebrows, a gesture he was coming to recognize as mild disapproval.

"I have not read it," he assured her. "But I was hoping you would tell me what it says, since you are writing to one of my neighbors."

"I have been presumptuous," Elizabeth surprised him by saying.

"How is this?"

"I evoked your name only to remind Lady Sees that I am your 'unusual' guest. And I used a wafer rather than your wax and seal, please note, but all the same I will understand if you wish me not to send this letter. I should have thought to consult with you first, my lord."

He stared at her blush, fascinated by her chagrin and wondering what she had done. "Call me Gideon. And how can I object," he said, "if I do not know the contents of the letter?"

"True." Her mouth turned up at one corner. "You know Simons, the footman who is missing several fingers?"

"Of course."

"He told me yesterday afternoon that he has a sister. She has been unable to find work, because she was released from her last employment without references. It was not her fault, Simons assured me, because the young master of the house was, well, he did not act appropriately, let us say. I agreed to recommend Simons's sister to Lady Sees, in hopes that there was a need for a new maid in her household, or if she knew of one nearby."

"Curious that Simons did not speak to me," Gideon said, even though he did not really find it curious at all. Elizabeth was . . . *approachable,* and in a way that the master of Greyleigh Manor presumably could not be. It was one thing for Gideon to offer benevolence, and another for a servant to come to him and request it.

"I suppose he considered it a matter among females," Elizabeth offered. "Do you mind too much?"

"That you sought to obtain work for the girl? Not at all. Shall I add my signature to this letter, to lend it my approval?"

"Would you?" Elizabeth said, her brown eyes lighting with pleasure. "I told Simons I would have little or no influence with Lady Sees, but I thought it better than not trying at all."

"I will gladly sign it," he said, slipping the letter in his pocket until he could obtain pen and ink. "Simons is a good man, and I have to think his sister must be, too."

"Thank you."

Gideon inclined his head, acknowledging her thanks. "I have come with news for you."

"News?" The light left her eyes, and her features took on a wary cast, startling him. What did she have to fear?

"Only that I thought about it last night and realized that we must not leave the retrieval of your jewels to happenstance. I have instructed all the servants to actively search for your jewels. Under mattresses, in flowerpots, that manner of thing."

"Oh," she said, the wariness slowly receding. "Thank you, very much."

"Were they your mother's jewels?" he asked, because that was not a question that invaded her privacy too deeply.

"Yes," she said, but as he had expected, she did not elaborate.

"I understand that you will be seeing the modiste at noon today."

"That is what the maid told me when she brought my tray."

"Good. Well, then." He stood. "I suppose I must get back to matters of the estate. I will see that your missive is delivered today."

"Thank you, my lord. *Gideon*," she corrected herself, and there was that smile again, the one that made his heart take a double beat.

He bowed and let himself out, and when he pulled a quill and ink from the drawer of the table where Frick kept the salver, Gideon noticed his hands shook ever so slightly. Just from being near her. Just from having her smile at him.

He did not break the wafer, instead signing "I concur" and

his name on the folded exterior of the missive, which he then placed next to the salver.

He stood upright and stared without quite seeing the letter Elizabeth had written. It *was* presumptuous of her to write to Lady Sees from the sanctuary of his home, in effect using his name, but that was not what bothered him. She had been doing someone a favor and had meant absolutely no harm.

What bothered him was the fact that *he* had not been approached by Simons. He, Gideon, the granter of kindnesses, the master of noblesse oblige, had been ignored in favor of a nobody, a nameless waif of a girl who would be gone in a week or so, who had no authority whatsoever.

And he was glad. Delighted, even, that someone else had been asked to sit and pen a letter, to grant a favor, to seek a boon. When had that last happened? Even when his father had been alive, it had been to Gideon that the servants had brought their concerns, because he might be expected to do something about them, whereas his father seldom could be bothered with the petty issues of running a household, except to roar and rampage.

Yet Elizabeth, in the space of a week, had somehow taken on the authority of one who could help, who brought order instead of more chaos. And this from the woman who had been put in an asylum because of a nervous disposition! Although, Gideon had to admit, short of odd shifts of emotion—such as the wariness that had come over her during their conversation five minutes ago—she was solid and sane enough in her manners that even Gideon sometimes forgot to coddle her nervous nature.

That is when it struck him, a brilliant idea. Elizabeth clearly had nowhere to go. These jewels she craved to have returned to her obviously were meant to pay her way alone in this world, now that presumably a lover had left her to fend for herself. If she had no particular place to be, why not be here?

Why not become his housekeeper? Heaven knew the house could use a woman's touch, and Elizabeth clearly possessed a way with servants. The idea of shifting the everyday, common concerns onto someone else's shoulders beckoned enticingly, and Elizabeth would have a roof over her head and meals to eat for her trouble. Pay, too—of course he would pay her a stipend.

And she would be here, stay here, be near me whispered a thought in his brain.

But what of her infirmity? came another whisper. What if, as months or years passed, her mind weakened?

Gideon frowned, knowing he could never send her, nor anyone, to an asylum. Which meant she would be yet another burden to the household. Perhaps the idea was not so suitable after all . . . it had been selfishness speaking, wanting to keep this newly found friend near him.

No, he could not have the responsibility for another madwoman on his hands, he simply could not. It would drive him over the edge into madness himself, once and in truth, to see Elizabeth become like his mama. God help him, he could not bear to see that, not with Elizabeth. This idea of making Elizabeth into his housekeeper was one best forgot.

Like all such ideas, however, it was much easier to say nay than to forget it, as Gideon discovered. All day long, he could not turn off his mind, could not find a resolution that would save both Elizabeth and his own soul.

Chapter 16

For the rest of the afternoon, Elizabeth watched out the window as clouds piled in the sky, creating a gloom that only deepened with nightfall. When at dusk rain began to fall and the shutters were closed against the wet breezes, even the usual branches of candles at the dining table did not penetrate the shadows. Elizabeth found herself squinting down the table, wondering if that dim silver lump might be the salt salver. Not that she particularly wanted to salt her meal, even though everything tasted bland for some reason tonight. A depressing effect of the weather, which was blustery and rainy, no doubt. Gideon must feel the effect, too, for he was unusually quiet at the head of the table, just to the right of where Elizabeth sat pushing her meal about her plate with her fork.

Perhaps the weather also explained why she felt disheartened tonight as well. Although, to be truthful, she knew the real reason. It was not that she'd had to stand too long on one leg as the modiste had taken her measurements and agreed to make up three gowns, one in grey and two in lavender. It was not that the gowns were to be made up in these shades of half mourning to suit Elizabeth's new life at pretending to be a widow. The real reason was that Elizabeth knew her heel was mending.

She could leave now, she realized. Even though it was a week shy of the healing time the doctor had allowed, Elizabeth knew that she could travel if she wished to.

Only she did not wish to.

She supposed she was a coward. Part of her did not want to face the future that awaited her, lonely and isolated from everyone and everything she had ever known. She knew she would spend her days waiting for the most recent news sheets, scouring the social page for the announcement of her sister's wedding. Only then could she hope to go home, or at least start anew.

Although, even when that happy day arrived, her future did not necessarily shine brightly. Radford Barnes would have no way of hurting her, not really, not once Lorraine was safely married. Yet, if so little as a whisper grew around Elizabeth's return to Society, so equally would Elizabeth's chances for a proper marriage plummet.

She supposed she must marry a Cit, a wealthy man of no social standing. It would be a comedown for a knight's daughter, but one Elizabeth would embrace so long as the fellow was a kindly man.

There were few other options open to a woman other than marriage: she could become a companion, or a governess, or perhaps she might qualify to teach at a school for girls. Papa would make sure Elizabeth did not starve or truly want despite a humble income, and a life of service might actually be a good way to keep her days from feeling stagnant and useless.

Elizabeth did not know how she would cope with being a spinster, but she feared her carnal nature would make it a long and miserable existence. Marriage to a Cit seemed more in keeping with her character, and then she would at least have the joy of children, God willing. Perhaps she could love this husband of hers . . . perhaps she would come to crave running her fingers through his hair, and want to kiss the weighty concerns of the day from his brow, and perhaps rejoice to see her children had their father's eyes. . . .

Elizabeth looked to the man at her right elbow, quietly eating his meal, and saw his pale eyes and knew with a heavy heart that she had to leave Lord Greyleigh's home.

She ought to speak to him this very moment. She ought to inform him she was well enough to travel, to remove herself as a burden from his household, to get on with living the life that was to be hers. But she wanted to stay. She longed to stay just a few days more, or perhaps so long as a week . . . ?

She had only one good excuse as to why she should stay, and that was the recovery of her jewelry. Curious then, that the very thing she had been praying for, that her jewels would all be promptly found and returned to her, she now prayed would take a while and give her a reason to linger. Already today two more pieces had been found: her other hair comb and one of her ear-bobs set with golden topaz stones.

The comb had been affixed into the bristles of a broom, and the earbob had dangled from the delicate frame of a miniature in the portrait gallery. Since Elizabeth herself had gazed at those portraits but a few days past, the earbob had obviously been recently added. Counting the earbob's twin and another set of earbobs, there were only nine pieces yet missing.

Elizabeth glanced at Lord Greyleigh—Gideon, he'd bid her call him—and knew with a heart that grew even heavier that it was not her future she feared to face, but a future that would never bring her again in contact with Gideon.

Could she bear never to see him again? What manner of fool was she, to have attached such importance to a connection that now existed only half as long as her ill-fated "marriage" ever had?

Despite her inner remonstrances, she knew she would not tell him she could leave, not yet. She convinced herself more of her jewels needed to be found first.

The real question at the moment was, would she tell him not to carry her in his arms back up to her room, as he had carried her down to supper? The embrace had proved too intimate, too troubling to any peace of mind Elizabeth strove to find when she thought of leaving this house. Her fingers had itched to play with his hair, with the nape of his neck, and she'd had to bite her lip to keep the impulse at bay.

"You do not eat," Gideon observed now, the right side of his face half lost in the night's gloom. She shook her head, and he pushed his own plate away. "The meal is not very good tonight. I think Cook has difficulty with drafts in his oven on these stormy nights."

"I am sure he is not to blame. I believe my appetite is at fault," Elizabeth said, also pushing her plate away. Servants moved in at once to retrieve the unwanted plates and utensils.

Gideon leaned forward, his crossed arms resting on the table, a little more of the candlelight now illuminating his features. Candlelight was kind to him, softening his startling coloring, picking out the handsome lines of his face, making his eyes appear more silver than blue.

"When I mentioned I play chess by mail with my brothers, you indicated you know how to play," he said. "Shall we indulge in a game?"

"That would be lovely," Elizabeth said on a sigh, relieved not to have to return to her room, where she had already spent too much time in too much thought about the future. With the wind pushing at the windows and rain dashing down the chimneys to hiss as it struck the fire on the grate, the storms, both internal and external, could make for a long, fretful night. Better to spend an hour or two in the simple contemplation of a game.

One of the footmen was sent to fetch a chessboard, bringing it back to the dining table. "Will this suit?" Gideon asked Elizabeth. Since the table sat before a massive fireplace and its cheerily hissing and popping fire, and Elizabeth had borrowed a shawl to match the dress she also borrowed, she agreed the corner of the dining table would suit quite well. Gideon stood to half turn her chair for her, then did the same to his own, and they faced one another over the board.

"I hope we did not disturb one of the games you play with your brothers," she said as she helped set up the pieces.

"I keep their letters to study the flow of the play, so I can easily reconstruct the game," he assured her.

"Ah, good. I would not wish to disrupt something that two brothers had between them."

He nodded, and even in the dim light Elizabeth could not miss the faint upturning of his lips, as though at some fond memory.

"I think you must miss them, your brothers, living here all alone as you do," she said.

When a long silence ensued, she looked up from the board, intrigued to see his jaw working.

"I do miss them," he said after a long pause. "Although I am happy they have a place in the bigger world."

That struck her as a curious thing to say, but he brushed past the moment by declaring her pieces were white and thus must move first.

They played for a while in silence, concentrating on the flow of the game. Elizabeth glanced occasionally at Gideon's face as he considered his moves, and wondered how she could have

ever found his appearance alarming. Startling perhaps, yes, but
his mouth lacked a tightness and his eyes a mocking sarcasm
that had marked Radford's face. Of course, that could just be
hindsight speaking, for not so long ago Elizabeth had thought
Radford's smile to be a kind one. Or had it just been charming?
She was foolish to even try to judge from appearances, she
knew, for her judgment was flawed and had once led her astray.

Still, she thought, Radford Barnes and Lord Greyleigh must
surely be judged two entirely different kettles of fish. The former
had already proven his lack of worth, and the latter . . . well, it did
not matter. Elizabeth need not concern herself, for it was not likely
she would ever see Gideon again once she was quit of his home.

Perhaps it was the sound of the wind soughing outside the
windows, but Elizabeth felt a touch of melancholy steal over
her. She sighed to herself and reached for her bishop, just as
Gideon reached to straighten a knight on its square, and their
fingers brushed together. Their gazes collided next, and Elizabeth instantly forgot where she had meant to move the piece.
Her hand remained suspended in air, the chess piece caught between fingers that tingled from that accidental touch.

It was his gaze that unnerved her most, though, for she wondered if he saw a physical awareness in her eyes such as she
saw in his. They were male and female, alone in this room. The
darkness cloaked them in intimacy, as if their voices could not
reach beyond the small circle of light, nor anyone gain entrance
from outside.

They sat thus, staring wordlessly into one another's eyes,
tension tightening between them, causing Elizabeth's lips to
part as if she needed to draw more air. Was it her imagination,
or did Gideon begin, very slowly, to lean toward her?

Something gave a sudden bang, and Elizabeth startled and
dropped her bishop. "What was that?" she asked in a strained
voice, as she tore her gaze from Gideon's and turned toward the
sound. "A shutter come loose?"

A servant had already entered the room at the alarming sound
and crossed to the windows. "Yes, miss," he assured them both
after a moment. The candle he carried showed the shutter on the
other side of the glass, swinging freely in the wind. It was the
work of a moment to open the window and secure the shutter

on its hook once more, by which time Elizabeth had turned back to the board to retrieve her bishop and make her move. If her heart pounded almost painfully beneath her borrowed gown, it was no doubt because of the startle she had received.

The servant departed, and Elizabeth and Gideon were alone once more, with candles that barely managed to light the surface of the chessboard, let alone illuminate the room. All the same, that moment of intimacy had been broken, perhaps purposely, for Gideon did not again raise his gaze to fully meet hers.

After only a few more moves she gave a little squeal of surprise, seeing that the "check" move she had intended was in fact "checkmate." Gideon tipped his king, at last raising his eyes to hers, and she was relieved to see at least a hint of amusement there.

"You bested me!" he cried, as though from genuine surprise. "Best two out of three," he proposed at once, already moving the pieces back into place.

"You are smiling," Elizabeth accused. "You did not let me win, did you?"

"In chess? No, indeed, madam. There is no letting someone win in chess. You took the game all on your own. If I am smiling, it is to hide my agony at losing."

"Liar," she said, but she did not mean it, for she had played a game or two before, and she knew she played adequately despite the distractions of the weather and her own thoughts. "My sister, Lorraine, likes to play chess," she said, and it was only when he looked up once more, a startled light in his eyes, that she realized she had revealed something personal, by naming her sister.

Gideon did not say anything, though. He did not build on the moment, did not push her for an explanation or more information.

In that moment, that very moment when he granted Elizabeth her privacy and asked nothing of her, she knew she loved him.

How long had she known?

For that matter, how long had she known *him*? Seven days? A mere week, half of which she had been too ill to lift her head from her pillow. It was ludicrous to say she loved him . . . but she knew she did, with the same certainty that Elizabeth knew her own name. It might be no more than the love of one friend for another, but it was the kind of bond that unites people for life. She knew it, felt it all the way to her very marrow, and shuddered at the knowing. Her head swam with the knowledge, and to keep her lower lip from trembling, Elizabeth had to catch it between her teeth.

How could this be? But, then again, who was she to try and divine a mystery, a blessing, a joy? She could not; she could only know the instant when it was upon her, and thank God for it, and wish there was some way to keep things exactly as they were at this very moment.

But just as her heart had begun to soar, it was brought crashing back to earth by reality. To be a true friend to him, she ought to disappear from his world and never speak or write to him, promise or no promise that she would. She had nothing to offer him but an association with a fallen woman—which could hardly enhance his already forbidding reputation. Nothing had changed. Nothing but her very heart.

"Gideon," she said, glad he had granted her permission to call him by his given name. He looked up from the board, no doubt alerted by the quality of her voice that something had altered.

"Elizabeth?" he said, his voice soft and inviting.

"I just wanted to say that, as soon as my jewelry, or at least most of it is found, I am well enough to leave."

Gideon sat back in his chair, clearly taken by surprise. "But the surgeon said—"

"I am much better, truly. I think Mr. Clifton was overcautious."

"I see." His voice was of a sudden hoarse. He cleared his throat and made an offering gesture with his hand. "Naturally a carriage is at your disposal whenever you wish it."

"Thank you. The day I leave depends on the jewelry being found, of course."

"Indeed. Yes." He looked away into the deep gloom of the room's corner, but then he sat forward, leaning toward her. He hesitated a moment, as if he paused to rethink what he'd meant to say, but then he rushed on. "Elizabeth," he said, his face arranged into lines of concern. "You need not tell me where, but I would like to know that you have a place to go to—that you have a home waiting for you somewhere."

For a moment gratified tears teetered on the verge of erupting, but Elizabeth blinked them back. He was a caring sort, she already had seen that; although the world called him odd, he was a good man, and she had to tell him as much. "Gideon," she said, her voice trembling, "you are the very best of all men."

"Nonsense," he said, and she could tell the word was a reflex. He had once upbraided her for calling herself "nobody," and now she understood why he had scolded her; she could not let him get away with degrading his own worth.

"What other men do you know who take in all these wounded people? Who gives employment to those who otherwise would not find any?" she declared. "I saw your new valet in the hall just this morning, making his way about on his crutches. He looked so pleased, so thankful to be here."

Twin spots of color formed on Gideon's cheekbones. "A one-legged valet!" he grumbled. "How much help can he possibly be to me? I was a fool to hire the man."

"Not a fool, Gideon. A wonder. A marvel." Elizabeth reached out and touched his hand, wanting him to see she meant what she said. Sensation arced between his fingers and hers, and when he looked up, the light irises in his eyes were almost obscured by wide, black pupils.

"You do not know what you are saying," he said hoarsely. "If you knew how empty I am inside . . ."

"Empty? How can you say such a thing? Look at all you have done for me, a complete stranger. Look around you at everyone who is near you! At first I thought this the oddest of households, full of one-eyed girls and maimed footmen—but, Gideon! They may be maimed, but they are happy. They are not begging on the streets. They have real work to do. If this household is strange, then may it please God to make even more households like it! How can you feel empty when you do such good in the world?"

"Because it is all a fraud," Gideon said, snatching back his hand, as if her touch pained him. "I only choose the people I think who will do well, who will make me look good. I offer charity, but for all the wrong reasons."

Elizabeth stared at him, and he looked away as though shamed.

"But, Gideon," she said, speaking very softly, "of course you would choose those who would thrive. What purpose would be served by trying to help those who will not help themselves? Even the Bible says we are not to throw pearls before swine. Do you not see? Did you think you could help even those who are unwilling or unable to accept your help?"

Gideon slowly turned his head to face her once more, and there was an agonizing mix of dread and hope written across his face. Elizabeth reached for both his hands, wanting to touch him, needing to.

"You have been too strict with yourself, I think. You have forgot that charity can be given to, but never forced upon a person."

"But I do not care about anything, nor anyone," Gideon whispered, his words a confession. "I have wanted nothing more than to escape this place, these responsibilities. I have lived for months now, perhaps years, thinking of no one but myself."

"Nonsense!" she repeated his own frequently issued comment. "If you did not care, would you have hired Simons's friend from the army as your valet? Would you have taken me in, a bloodied, half-dead stranger? You may be wearied by all that sits upon your shoulders, but not because you do not care."

"I do not feel as though I care," he said very softly, but the words lacked conviction.

"A man who does not care, who has no feelings, would not miss his brothers," she told him, giving him a steady look, defying him to say otherwise. "Why do you not take a holiday?" she suggested with a tentative smile. "Even God rested on the seventh day, you know."

He gave a little laugh and hung his head, shaking it as though in denial. But when he glanced up at her again from under his lashes, she thought she saw that the dread had been chased from his eyes.

"I am sorry. I did not mean to unburden myself on you like that," he murmured.

Elizabeth took a deep breath, then let it out. "It is the sort of evening for sharing burdens, I think," she said, glancing toward the window as though she would be able to see the wind and rain they could hear, but which the shutters hid from sight. "Now it is my turn, my lord."

"Gideon," he corrected even as he lifted his head to gaze at her in surprise.

"Gideon. I would like to tell you my story, as I said I would."

"You said you would write." His eyes clouded with confusion. "Later. When you were free to—"

"You deserve to hear it from me directly. You have been very kind, my lord. Gideon. I owe you my life. I wish to repay that, albeit very poorly, with the truth. That is, if you would hear it."

He stared into her face, then nodded.

So she told him everything, about how Radford had courted her, that she had allowed herself to believe his words of love, had wanted to believe them, had wanted to love him. She told him of her new stepmama, who longed to have the stepdaughters out of her home, how if Elizabeth married it would solve so many difficulties. She reaffirmed that Lorraine was her sister, and it was for Lorraine's sake that Elizabeth could not go home, and why.

"Pardon me if I do not tell you the name of Lorraine's betrothed," she said, staring at his right boot, unable to look him in the eye and admit to the series of follies that had brought her, unconscious, into his home. "But suffice it to say the man conducts the slowest, most circumspect courtship ever known to man. Until Lorraine has wed him, I will do nothing to bring a hint of scandal near her."

"Whoever he is, the man's a fool. If a man would do a thing, best to do it quickly," Gideon said.

"From your lips to God's ear," Elizabeth said, just managing to glance up at him, to be sure he saw her small smile.

She told Gideon, too, that the B on her ring stood for the surname of the man who had convinced her that an elopement in their case was the best way to marry. Her false husband must have belatedly remembered the signet ring might identify him, that Elizabeth had it yet upon her finger, for from the description Gideon had given, Elizabeth had recognized who had approached her as she lay injured and unconscious in that ditch.

"But how did you end in the asylum? Did you put yourself there to escape the cad? Or was he so much a scoundrel that he drugged you and placed you there?" Gideon asked, silvered eyes flashing in the candlelight.

"No, my lord," she said softly. "I never resided at the asylum.

I was just a passerby caught in the devastation the night it burned."

Gideon went very still. "Then why did you act so strangely when you first came into my home? You kept gibbering on, in a childish manner, about dancing at your wedding."

"You mistook me for a patient at the asylum, naturally enough. I did not disabuse you of the notion, because it seemed the easiest way to hide." She blushed, now examining the roses in the carpet pattern as though they fascinated her.

"Hide? Why did you feel a need to hide?"

"I was running away from—from the man I thought I had married, because he had revealed to me that night that the special license he had used for our wedding was false." She sniffed back sudden tears, silently commanding them not to fall. She even managed a little laugh at her own expense. "In theory, someone could pull the same trick on me again, since I do not really know what a special license is supposed to look like, more the fool I."

She told him how Radford had revealed he had done this to other women as well, that he had blackmailed their fathers by promising to remain silent about the ruination of their daughters only in exchange for money.

"I thought he was wealthy enough not to want my dowry," Elizabeth said, shaking her head at her own gullibility. "But he wanted more, much more than one paltry dowry. I could not let him blackmail my father, nor ruin Lorraine's chances to marry well. So I left him in the dead of night."

Elizabeth glanced up, dreading to see the comprehension that indeed shone from Gideon's eyes: that she had believed herself married, that she had shared her "husband's" bed.

She went on, perhaps speaking a trifle too rapidly, to cover her humiliation. "I suppose he came after me to retrieve his horse. It was a fine horse, I grant you, well matched with the other in his team. But the horse was taken from me by a patient from the asylum, and I was injured, and Rad— *He* must have thought I was dead or dying. If you had not interrupted his taking of the ring, or pulled me from that ditch . . ." Her voice faded away, and she shivered.

"Tell me his name—the man who did this to you," Gideon

said, his voice level, but there was a high, hot flame of anger in his eyes.

"No," Elizabeth said with finality. At Gideon's astonished glance, she explained. "I do not seek to protect him, but to protect my sister and father. Any word against this man would be passed to them. The only thing that keeps him from doing my family mischief has to be the uncertainty of whether I am alive or dead, and the knowledge I still have his signet ring."

Gideon threw back his chair and began to pace, his jaw working as it had before, only now with a darker emotion. "I want to kill this man," he growled.

She surprised him with a laugh. "I know," she said. "So do I."

He scowled at her, but she began to laugh at the incredulity on his face. Then her laughter swept him up, and she could see that despite himself he was grinning with her. "You are a savage creature!" he accused.

"Only likely to grow more so with age and regrets, I should think," she agreed with a little shrug and an answering grin.

He gave a huff of a laugh, looked into the shadows, and then back at her. He crossed the room, stopping before her chair, his feet spread so that he loomed close enough for his breeches' legs to brush the silk of her borrowed gown. While the corners of his mouth turned up faintly yet, still she could feel the anger that had not completely left him, and in a curious way felt warmed by his outrage on her behalf.

"Elizabeth, why did you tell me this? Why not wait, as you proposed earlier, to state it all in a letter? Do you not realize that you have taken a risk, that I could spread your story?"

"Of course I realize it."

"Then why tell me?"

"Because . . ." she began, but she could not tell him it was because she would never see or write to him again, that she would disappear from the circle of Society in which he resided, even if at its very edges here in Severn's Well. Even if she returned to Papa's home, her life would never be the same; it would never coincide with a marquess's world.

So she told him another truth. "Because I trust that you will not cast my tale about."

"You trust me?" he echoed, as though the words scarcely made sense.

She gave a tiny laugh, little more than a breath. "It would seem I am doomed to be forever a fool for trusting people." She gave a small shrug that included a moue of her mouth. "My great flaw," she conceded.

He stared at her without blinking, so near that he blocked a little of the warmth from the fireplace, replacing it with a different kind of warmth, one that made her toes curl inside the ruined slippers that she wore beneath her gown. He stood thus for a long time, perhaps as much as a minute, and when he spoke, his voice had lost its angry edge.

"You have not answered the question I originally asked," he said to her.

"Remind me what it was."

"Do you, Elizabeth, have a home waiting for you?" His words were soft, gentle even.

"No." It was a difficult answer to give, but she was done lying to Gideon, forever.

He took a deep breath, letting it out in a rush. "Then stay here, with me. Be my housekeeper. You have a gift for managing—"

"No!" she cried, and now it was the greatest effort of her life not to allow tears to appear on her lashes. She lifted a hand, whether to reach out to take his or to fend him off, she could not say. She did neither, her hand held before her, becoming a poor shield against the pain that welled in her. "Gideon, my lord, thank you for the offer. But no." She swallowed hard. "I must go. I have to leave here." And she truly must go and soon, she knew, for those were the most difficult words she'd ever had to utter.

She stood, forgetting about her foot until a sharp pain laced up her leg.

He reached out for her at once, steadying her.

"A servant, to carry me," she said, unable to get out any more words through the thickness in her throat.

"What is it?" Gideon asked, his fingers tightening on her arms. "Why are you crying?"

She shook her head, her hands now both against his chest, pushing away from him, furious with herself for losing the battle with her own tears.

He scooped her into his arms, cradling her so close to his chest that all she could do was lean into him, letting her tears blot against his cravat and shirtfront.

"Elizabeth," he said in a distressed whisper, "I never meant to insult you. I know you deserve better than to be a mere housekeeper—"

She could only answer with fresh tears.

"What else can I do?" he lamented, and she wondered if he meant about his offer, or her tears, or something else. There was no answer to give.

She tried to swallow her tears, not very successfully, as he carried her up the stairs to her room.

He left her there, but with obvious confusion, and not until a maid had been summoned to care for her. Elizabeth had wanted to explain, had wanted to let him know she was not insulted to be asked to be his housekeeper, but how could she assure him of that without revealing the real reason for her tears? How could she tell him she could not stay, could not be in his employ, because she loved him?

To stay, to be his housekeeper, would be the sweetest torture, to be near him, to see him daily—but it would be torture all the same.

Gideon lifted his head from where he had buried it in his hands and stared at the chessboard on the dining table before him. What had he said? Had his offer of employment been such a terrible blow against Elizabeth's expectations?

What was a man to make of a woman's tears when she has just been offered a solution to all her difficulties? They had not been tears of joy, or relief, but rejection and denial.

Why had she told him about her past when she would not do so before? What had changed? Why not merely write as she had promised?

At least now he understood why some part of her had worried about being with child. Such was the legacy of a scoundrel. But that concern was behind her, as he had learned during her fever. Other things she had said made sense now. Indeed, many things at last were made clear . . . except for why she had been reduced to tears.

Granted, his offer had not been a prime one for a cultured young lady, but it would have provided an income, shelter, food, and a place to belong. In fact, all the things she would have to find out in the cruel world by herself. Why was she so intent on leaving? Had there not already been enough change in her life?—the false marriage, the escape from her pretend husband, the events of the night of the asylum fire. . . .

Gideon suddenly went very still, slowly lifting his head as the obvious at last occurred to him, as her words at last reached his dazed and confused brain: Elizabeth had not come from the asylum. She was not, nor ever had been, placed in the asylum for a "nervous condition."

She was sane—as sane and stable and unafflicted as any other person who lived outside asylum walls. Gideon sat up straight, feeling his heart take slow, pounding thumps in his chest.

Only, wait, he thought. What of all the times he had questioned her behavior? His heart felt as though it had begun to pound at twice its normal beat. Some of the odd silences, or hidden truths, could now be explained by the tawdry tale she had not wished to confide, as indeed no right-thinking person would. She had been duped, her innocence used against her, and such deceit could not be happily admitted to. But, still, he had thought her actions, her words to be lacking. . . .

Perhaps, he thought, shaking his head as though the motion could sort out his muddled thoughts, perhaps the whole world was mad. His own mama had resided but once in a hospital for the disturbed, and yet she had been undeniably touched by lunacy. Perhaps he saw in Elizabeth what others did not yet perceive, because he had spent so many years seeing it in his mama.

Or perhaps there was nothing *to* see; perhaps Elizabeth was sane, and it was Gideon who made too much of simple human vagaries. People said Gideon himself was mad, and God knew he sometimes had trouble believing them wrong.

One thing he did know for a certainty: Elizabeth meant to leave. And, heaven help him, if anyone's sanity would be challenged by her leaving, it would be his. She had brought change, good change, to his household. She had made Gideon stop and think that perhaps he had been mistaken, too wrapped up in his own miseries to see the misery he was able to relieve for oth-

ers, that good was still possible to accomplish even after one
had grown weary.

Elizabeth! God, she *had* to stay! But all this was ridiculous,
impossible. What did he know of her? Only an unfortunate
story . . . and that she knew how to show compassion to a servant's unemployed sister; to her own, older, last-chance-for-
marriage sister who waited upon a slow-proposing beau; that
Elizabeth knew how to laugh at herself, and how to make
Gideon laugh despite himself.

She said she trusted him . . . she had made a joke of it . . . but
the words burned through his thoughts, like a brand burning
into wood, leaving its indelible mark once the smoke had
cleared. She trusted *him.*

But Mama had trusted him also. Until the very end, she had
always known Gideon even if she had not known anyone else
by name or feature. His voice, his hand on her shoulder, had always been a comforting thing for her.

It was possible, he had to admit, that Elizabeth had not spoken the truth at all. That she had made up a story, to stir his
sympathy. She might still be that deluded creature who had
somehow escaped the asylum's flames, with a glibness of
tongue that had fooled her caregivers as easily as it fooled
Gideon now.

His shoulders slumped, but more from confusion than disappointment.

He could not believe she was crazy. If Elizabeth could be so
convincing, then she was no more mad than half the world. He
would believe her . . . because she had said she trusted him.

"It does not matter," Gideon said aloud. "I do not care if
she's mad or sane. Or an actress. Or a liar." It did not matter,
because they had befriended one another.

She would leave, he understood that. And he also understood
the hollowness in her gaze meant she did not expect anything
beyond that. He was supposed to wave her a farewell, and that
would be an end of things.

But her leaving would *not* be an end of things. Gideon picked
up the white queen from the chessboard, cupping it in his hand
as he gazed at the ivory piece.

"I have too few friends to give you up so easily," he told the chess piece, replacing it then on the board, near a center square. He picked up the black king, set it next to the queen, and nodded with satisfaction.

Gideon then turned to call loudly for his coat, hat, and a saddled horse.

Within the half hour, Gideon stood before the humble home of Clyde Arbuckle, who stared out his front door at the marquess before him. "M'lord?" the investigator questioned, busily buttoning his bed jacket closed. He stepped aside, signaling for Gideon to enter.

"No, thank you," Gideon said. "My business is brief. I have come to pay you for your services, and to let you know that I no longer desire for you to investigate the matter of Miss B."

"No, m'lord? I assure you, I were makin' progress—"

"Indeed, and I was most pleased. But I am satisfied that Miss B requires no more of my time and attention in this regard. Your fee?"

Mr. Arbuckle's fee was quickly and generously settled, and he retired with a cheery "Right-o!" to the comforts of his home.

Gideon, also intent on retiring to his home, rode through the streets of Severn's Well, not caring if his whistling at night was bad luck. Tonight he did not believe in bad luck. Tonight he felt lighthearted enough to wish to whistle. Not to invite bad luck, but because he finally felt as though a stroke of good luck had come into his life, via a ditch and a pair of brown eyes.

Chapter 17

The next morning in the library, a cameo, one matching pair of amethyst earbobs, another of pearls, a single topaz earbob, a diamond and amethyst choker, and two rings were placed in Elizabeth's cupped hands.

"What is yet missing?" Gideon asked while he resumed his seat opposite hers in the library.

She looked up, hoping the stricken feeling roiling in her stomach was not reflected on her face. "Only two rings," she answered.

"That is all?" Gideon asked, looking pleased.

Elizabeth nodded. "Where were these found?" she asked bleakly, not really caring, but because it would be expected that she ask.

"According to Frick, the cameo was hanging from a string from the balustrade, and one of the rings was decorating the cap to my inkwell, here on my desk." Gideon leaned away, half twisting to indicate his desk across the room. He turned back to her. "I do not know about the rest. Frick did not say, other than to mention that the servants are searching more diligently than when we have had things go missing in the past. We all assumed one of my servants must be taking and moving the things, and one hated to accuse without any hint of proof, of course."

He laid a finger to his lip for a moment of thought and narrowed his eyes. "I could never fathom why things were brought *into* the house. But"—he gave an elegant shrug—"I daresay the red-haired woman—"

"Lily."

"Yes, Lily, had her reasons, incomprehensible though they might be to the rest of the world."

"Although much can be excused because of her youth, and I think she must not be sound of mind," Elizabeth said, feeling sorry for the poor, confused creature, whatever her story.

"I only hope that our 'ghost' hid all your jewels before she was denied entry to the house via the door behind the ivy. That is, if it was this Lily person who did the hiding to begin with."

Elizabeth lowered the jewels to her lap, arranging the folds of her skirt so that it cupped them. "Surely it was her."

"I should think so. The important thing is that everything that was taken from you ought to be found soon, perhaps even before your new gowns are ready," Gideon told her.

"Yes," she agreed, not sighing aloud as she wished to do. She was a fool to want to put off leaving, but she wanted it all the same. Fool indeed, for each day would make the wrenching of her heart all the more terrible when it came at last.

This morning Gideon had not appeared curious about her unexplained tears of last night, and seemed to have dismissed them altogether, for today he was bright and cheerful—the exact opposite of how Elizabeth felt. This morning he had even stated that the dark red bricks of his home were altogether too somber, too off-putting, and he planned to have them whitewashed. The comment had surprised her, as it had Frick when Gideon had issued his command from the breakfast table.

"Today?" Frick had asked, his voice squeaky with surprise.

"'Tis a fine day," Gideon had observed. "Why not begin today? I am sure we can manufacture some whitewash."

"Yes, my lord," Frick had said, hurrying off to consult with the head gardener, whom he claimed could be depended upon to supply the need.

And even before that Gideon had been all that was pleasant, even lighthearted, as he had arrived at Elizabeth's door, proclaiming his readiness to carry her downstairs for breakfast. She had tried to protest that she would prefer a tray in her room.

"Nonsense!" he had announced and had scooped her up in his usual abrupt manner, leaving her grateful she had dressed, for she was not entirely sure he would have refrained were she still in her nightwear.

"Have you been drinking this morning? Or up all night drinking?" she had inquired, sniffing near his face for hints of alcoholic vapors.

"I am insulted!" he had cried, smiling at her, reminding her that he had a very pleasant smile, one that made parts of her flutter that had no right to be fluttering at all. "Do I look as though I have been awake all night?"

She meekly answered, "No," because it was the truth. He had clearly been at some pains to look tidy and fashionable, plainly the results of now having a valet. He wore all grey, except for a cream-colored waistcoat shot with yellow threads, and his hair was neatly combed back and caught taut in a queue. Although she liked his hair long and unfettered, this cleanly swept-back look, too, had its advantages, making the most of his strong features.

Now breakfast, surely one of their last together, was past. Gideon had carried her into the library and then returned nearly all her jewels to her. And it was only a few days until the modiste could deliver the ordered gowns. Time was sweeping by too quickly . . . and Gideon was being all that was jovial. They sat together, supposedly selecting something to read, except Gideon was more interested in cheerful banter than selecting from the tomes surrounding them. She remembered his reluctance to have her here at all when first she had wakened from her unconsciousness, and could not help but think he must be delighted at all this proof that his guest would soon be gone.

His garrulousness now extended to rising from his chair to perch before her on one knee. "May I see these on you?" he asked, nodding toward the jewelry in the folds of her skirt. "The pearls?"

"Whyever for?" she replied, her heart fluttering painfully in her chest.

"Because I have never seen you in jewels."

"Very well," she conceded, dropping the pearl earbobs in his palm.

He affixed one to her right ear, then leaned back and tilted his head, gazing at the result. "Just as I thought. With your dark hair, pearls suit you well."

Color spread up Elizabeth's face, as much from his nearness as from the compliment.

"As does a blush." He smiled at her, reaching to affix the other earbob. He leaned back again to admire his handiwork and sighed. "I could wish you had no need to pawn your jewels, dear lady."

"I must," Elizabeth said simply, probably blushing more deeply from the endearment, but not caring overmuch that she did. What was there in her life left for her to blush about that Gideon did not know?

He reached for both her hands, cradling them between his own. "If you wish it, I will see to the task for you. I could get a better price in Bristol, if you would not mind my doing this for you." His gaze was sympathetic, but at least it was not pitying. Elizabeth did not think she could bear knowing that he pitied her; it was good of him to hide it from her.

"Thank you, yes. I am assured you could obtain a superior price than could I."

He nodded, accepting the commission. "Tell me, Elizabeth," he said quietly, still holding her hands with his left hand while he reached to tuck a strand of her hair behind her ear with his right. "Why did you blush a moment ago, when I said the pearls suited you? Was it that the pearls must be traded away, or that I gave you a compliment?"

Her color deepened as she tried to think how to answer, how to say it was both and neither, how to avoid saying that he need not speak a word, but only remain near and that would be sufficient to put her to the blush. But when she parted her lips, there were no ready or glib words. All she could think was that Gideon had become precious to her, and that he was near, near enough that she had but to lean forward and she could kiss him.

"My lord," came a voice from the open doorway.

Elizabeth gave a shaky breath and slowly slipped her hands from Gideon's, who merely turned his head. "Yes?" he inquired with casual aplomb.

Upon seeing his master on one knee before Elizabeth's chair, Frick averted his gaze to the level of the wainscoting around the library's perimeter. "Pardon me, my lord, but a coach-and-four has arrived. With baggage atop, sir."

Gideon rose, tugging his waistcoat to assure its proper lie.
"Visitors? Who are they?"

"Master Benjamin and Master Sebastian."

Elizabeth watched as first astonishment and then something
unmistakably touched with pleasure raced across Gideon's
face. "My brothers," he said in Elizabeth's general direction. To
Frick he said, "Show them in as soon as they have shaken the
dust of the road from their boots."

"Show them in at once," a man, a darker-haired version of
Gideon, said from the doorway.

"There is more, my lord—" Frick attempted to interject, but
he was cut off by a cry from the master of the house.

"Sebastian!" Gideon shouted, smiling widely and striding at
once across the room. The two men embraced, and then Elizabeth had a moment to observe that the other man was not as
much like Gideon as she had first thought. He had the same
squared jaw, but his face was longer, more narrow and sharp of
feature. He was obviously younger, and even from across the
room Elizabeth could see his eyes were a true blue, the color of
the ocean on a fair day. His hair was also worn long and loose,
brushing his shoulders, but it was decidedly brown, albeit a rich
multicolored golden brown.

Elizabeth just had time to form these thoughts when another
brother appeared. Benjamin too was embraced by Gideon. This
brother was somewhere between his siblings in hair coloring,
although it was cut very short, no doubt to accommodate the
military cap he carried under his arm. Being capless suited him,
showing off hair that was a rich wheat color with a plentitude
of sun-bleached streaks, resembling sunlight skirting shadows
across a field. From his darker skin, too tanned for fashion, he
obviously spent more time out of doors than did his siblings,
which only made sense when one observed the Naval uniform
he wore. Even from her seat, Elizabeth could see this man's
eyes were never so pale as Gideon's, but neither so rich a blue
as were the youngest brother's.

Elizabeth saw that nature had used a different palette for
each: the eldest as pale as a creature of the spirit world; the next
painted with the colors of the heavens; and the youngest with
the tones of the earth. She glanced among the three of them,

marveling at the likenesses and the differences, but when her gaze rested on Gideon, she thought to herself that he was the most striking of the three.

Gideon turned, obviously intending to make introductions, but Frick cleared his throat, looking with emphasis at the uniformed brother.

"Ah yes, the girl," Benjamin said, tossing his cap onto the nearest table. "Bring her in."

"Her?" Gideon questioned.

"'Her,' indeed," Sebastian said. "We found the creature just outside the house, sitting among some recently destroyed ivy. She was moaning and mewling against a door Benjamin claims he knew was there, but which I surely did not."

Frick and a footman brought a wild-eyed girl into the room, each of them holding one of her arms. Beneath the hem of the white night rail she wore showed two bare feet. Her long red hair was unbound as always, and had not been recently washed or combed.

Elizabeth rose, the jewels in her lap dropping to the carpet to scatter at her feet. "Lily!"

"This is Lily?" Gideon echoed, looking from one woman to the other.

"She had this," said the footman Simons, holding forth the shawl-wrapped bundle Elizabeth had seen the girl carry, only now the pink skin of a scalp could be seen peeking out of the arrangement of shawls. Elizabeth began to move forward, despite her heel, noting the odd way Simons held the child, but at that moment he lost his grip, and the infant tumbled to the carpet. Lily screamed and lunged, almost breaking free of the restraining hands on her, even as Elizabeth cried out, and Gideon leaped forward, hands outstretched, but already too late.

Amid a terrible silence Gideon reached down to the motionless child, but then he hesitated. A moment later everyone stared as he pushed aside the shawls and revealed upward-staring painted eyes.

"It is but a doll!" Sebastian declared.

Gideon stood upright, looking both shaken and annoyed, as Benjamin demanded, "Who *is* this girl?"

Lily fought still against the restraining hands, a terrible gib-

bering sound of anguish issuing from her clenched teeth. A gesture from Gideon indicated the servants ought free her, and the
moment they released her arms she lunged for the doll, scoop-
ing it up. Her moans instantly turned into a croon, a little comforting song against the doll's composite head.

"Poor creature!" Elizabeth breathed. "She did not know what
to do once the door in the ivy was locked to her. She must have
felt utterly distraught." Elizabeth looked at Gideon. "Do you recall I said Lily was searching for fairies? I think that is why she
has been leaving my jewels about, hoping to entice them to
come. I feared the worst . . . but if this is her child . . . ?" She
shuddered, remembering the terrible thought she'd had that
perhaps the girl had longed to trade a dead infant for a fairy's
changeling.

Lily ceased crooning, looking up, intensely staring at Elizabeth. "I want the fairies to come," the girl said in a small voice.
She looked into all the faces in the room, and whatever she saw,
her distress left her features. "I want the fairies to come," she
said again. "I want them to make my baby alive, like it was."

"You have a very nice baby there—" Elizabeth began.

"But it needs to be alive again," Lily said, and she looked
down into the painted face, her expression shifting once more,
this time to terrible sadness. "Wake up, baby!" she cried on a
rising note. She rocked the child with one arm, even as she covered her face with her other hand and began to sob. "Wake up,
baby. I want the fairies to wake her up," she said between sobs.

"Gideon!" Elizabeth cried, casting him a helpless look.

"We must find her family. She will require comforting and
care," he said at once, and his look confirmed Elizabeth's own
feelings that the girl was harmless, but clearly out of her right-
ful mind. "Frick, until such time as we can locate someone to
be responsible for her, take, er, Miss Lily to the kitchens and assign a couple of the maids to care for her. See if she'll eat or
drink something. Something warm would be well. Simons, you
and I will ride into the village. Perhaps Alderman Wallace will
know who she is."

"Very good, my lord," Frick said, taking the girl's arm firmly
but not unkindly, and leading her from the room. Simons nod-

ded at the instructions Gideon gave him, while Elizabeth bent
to retrieve her fallen jewelry.

When Gideon turned back to the occupants of the library, he
moved at once to assist her. Elizabeth became aware of the silence that had fallen as Gideon's brothers stared at her, the jewels, and their brother working to hand the jewelry to this
stranger among them.

Gideon stood, dusting his hands and giving a small smile as
Elizabeth placed her jewelry on the nearest table. His smile was
meant to dispel the odd moment. "That girl, gentlemen," he
said, "is our resident ghost, the very one who has taken our bits
and pieces and left others for us to find these months past." He
noted the comprehension that dawned in his brothers' faces and
shook his head. "I cannot think why the girl ever decided the
fairies live in *my* house."

"By Jove!" Sebastian gave a lopsided grin, crossing to put a
hand on Benjamin's uniformed shoulder. "It would seem the
house has turned to Bedlam since we left it!" he declared.

Any sign of amusement vanished from Gideon's features.

"I mean to say, brother dearest," Sebastian went on with a
laugh, "first we find the old bricks are being painted over in a
cheerful white, which was enough to startle our horses in their
traces, I vow. They did not know the place! Next we see that
our sober and serious brother has donned a waistcoat with some
actual dash about it! If these are not oddities enough, we discovered a simple-minded female gathering wool amid the
ivy—"

"And have had no time for introductions to our present company," Benjamin interrupted with a shade of impatience, looking pointedly at Elizabeth.

"The most charming surprise of all," Sebastian agreed.

The scowl dissipated from Gideon's features, and he turned
slightly to glance at Elizabeth. "Elizabeth, these two rogues are
my brothers, Benjamin and Sebastian."

"We already make free with our Christian names?" Benjamin
asked, not smiling. Sebastian, on the other hand, made his eyebrows dance over his sea blue eyes, and Elizabeth thought
Gideon's title of "rogue" suited this fellow admirably.

"Christian names are all we have, in this instance," Gideon

said glibly. "Benjamin, Sebastian, this is Miss Elizabeth. Her surname is unknown. She has been injured recently and has been unable to supply us with a surname. She has been convalescing here this past week or so."

"Miss Elizabeth." Sebastian greeted her with a little bow, as did Benjamin.

Upon straightening, Sebastian slipped with negligent grace onto a settee, but his eyes were wide as though with fascination. "There you are, Brother Ben! I told you something was astir. I told you Gideon's letters were peculiar."

"Peculiar?" Gideon frowned again.

"'Chatty' is the word I should use," Sebastian said, grinning at Elizabeth when she gave him a quizzical look. "Perhaps there is a better word, but since I have never before received a chatty letter from you, Gideon"—he belatedly looked toward the object of discussion—"I am new to the experience and do not know what to call it."

"I can see you are in a mood for sport," Gideon said, grimacing. "But I, alas, at present do not have the time for it. I have an alderman to call upon, who I hope can afford me some answers. I am anxious to know why you two have come from afar, but my curiosity will have to wait." Gideon turned to Elizabeth. "May I carry you to your room before I leave?"

"No, thank you. I would like to hear what you have to say when you return," Elizabeth said, looking up at him from under her lashes, feeling abashed by the startled look Benjamin had thrown his brother upon hearing the word "carry."

Gideon either missed the look, or else did not consider any need to explain, because he bowed to Elizabeth and moved to the library door. There he turned. "Elizabeth is my guest, gentlemen. Please mind your manners." With a scalding glance at his brothers, Gideon exited.

Elizabeth looked to the two other occupants of the room. Benjamin lifted an eyebrow in disapproval, and Sebastian grinned widely.

"So, you are 'Elizabeth the house guest,' of whom Gideon wrote."

"House guest?" Elizabeth repeated, unsure why Sebastian found her role so amusing.

"Come now," Benjamin said, rotating in a crisp military turn to face Elizabeth. "Tell us what happens here? That is to say, what are you to Gideon?"

"He means," Sebastian said with a wicked gleam in his eyes, "are you the cause of our brother's sudden aberrant behavior?"

"Aberrant?" Elizabeth began to sputter out a confused protest, but Sebastian interrupted her.

"Let me see if I can put it more politely. How about, what magic have you worked to change Gideon so?"

"Magic?"

"We will get nowhere if you repeat everything I say," Sebastian quipped.

"Come, come, Miss Elizabeth," Benjamin said, taking the chair opposite hers and running a hand down his uniform front to rid it of any subsequent creases. "We tell you freely, we came home because Gideon had sent each of us a letter—"

"A letter about the chess games?" Elizabeth inquired.

"Yes, only these were different. It was evident that something was altered—significantly."

"You have to understand," Sebastian explained, "Gideon's letters are usually three sentences long. They read: 'Queen's Rook to Rook Four. Lost the wheat crop on the lower twenty acres. Frick has the toothache.' And that is all they say, Miss Elizabeth. But these letters we each just received were suddenly three pages long, full of bits and pieces of news, such as some maid or other had a girl child—"

"I still cannot approve of Gideon taking in a servant who is in the family way," Benjamin interrupted. "It is one thing to see to one's own, er, discrepancies, but taking in a girl already in a family way from another household, without references . . . ! It is undignified. Not to mention the mother will no doubt expect Gideon to grant the brat employment when he is old enough to hold a horse."

"She. The baby is a girl," Elizabeth corrected, her lips threatening to tilt upward in happy surprise to learn the child was not Gideon's. It was silly of her to feel so blithe of a sudden, but Elizabeth had to bite back a smile.

"Never mind that. I was talking about Gideon's letter," Sebastian said, angling his head as he recomposed his thoughts.

"Ah, yes, Gideon also wrote of the ghost that has been active again, and how his favorite hunter has recovered from taking a stone under its shoe, and, well anyway, he just went on and on."

"And at the end of *my* letter—" Benjamin began.

"Not mine, I am piqued to say," Sebastian put in.

"At the end of *my* letter, which I felt compelled to share with Sebastian here," Benjamin went on pointedly, "there was mention of a house guest named Elizabeth. Gideon wrote of how this female, of whom he offered no proper title or surname, had had her things taken, some jewels or other."

"I ask you, who would not be intrigued?" Sebastian asked, spreading his hands as though seeking Elizabeth's affirmation.

Elizabeth gazed from one to the other, seeing the coolness in their faces, even under Sebastian's impudent manner. She sighed, knowing what they must be thinking. "I can scarce blame you for wondering if I am hunting a fortune."

Sebastian inclined his head in acknowledgment, but Benjamin just stared hard at her. "Well, are you?" he asked without polish.

"Gentlemen," she said, laying a hand atop her jewelry on the table. "This is all the fortune I have. I brought the pieces with me, and I shall leave with them and nothing else, be assured." She paused. "Well, that is not quite true, for I am to have three dresses, for which I will one day repay your brother."

She saw their doubt and put up her chin. She boldly lifted the hem of her skirt, exposing the bandages that yet wound around her foot. "My heel was badly injured. Now it is better, and I am free to leave. I promise you, I would not take anything else, not even were it offered to me."

At the satisfied look that came over Benjamin, Elizabeth fixed him with a look of her own. "Your brother has been very kind, and I would not repay that kindness except with my thanks," she said pointedly. "Although, there is one thing I would do for him, to truly thank him."

Sebastian sat forward, his expression urging her on.

"I would ask that you either stay here with Gideon, or else take him with you when you leave," Elizabeth said firmly.

"What?" The two men exchanged sharp glances.

"Why?" Benjamin demanded.

"I think, because you came so promptly when his letters changed, that you know why."

Both men had the grace to look discomfited.

"He has everything, the estate, the servants, the weight of everything on his shoulders," Elizabeth continued. "It is a weight that ought to be shared, not borne alone."

"We are well aware of that," Benjamin said crossly, his shoulders moving in agitation under his uniform coat. "The only one who does not know it is Gideon."

"That is not true," Sebastian said, his mouth downturned for once. "He knows it. He just does not know how to stop being in charge, to take a breath and be free of it for a day, or a week, or a month. Imagine if Gideon could be unworried for a month! He would be a changed man."

Elizabeth sat forward in her chair, feeling growing excitement. "Take him with you, to London or Brighton. Or abroad, if you can! I can imagine Gideon in Rome or Greece. He would like the sea, I think."

"How well you seem to know him," Benjamin said drolly. "How long is it you have known him? No, do not answer, it does not signify. Let me tell you instead, that you ask us to move a mountain, Miss Elizabeth," Benjamin went on, rising from his chair and shaking his head. He crossed his hands behind his back, a habit very like Gideon's. "Do you think we have not tried to wrestle Gideon from this pile of bricks before? He is convinced the entire earth will cease to spin if he leaves here for so little as a day."

"Oh," Elizabeth said, feeling deflated.

"As to that"—Sebastian crossed one leg over the other, allowing the topmost to begin to swing in a small, insouciant arc—"perhaps Miss Elizabeth has powers of persuasion we do not?" He glanced up at his brother.

Benjamin turned to give Elizabeth another of his abrupt stares, his features marked by a curious mix of doubt and hope. "Perhaps," he conceded. "Gideon certainly thinks well of you, that much is clear." He straightened his shoulders. "Would you speak with him? Do your best to convince him of a holiday?"

"Yes," Elizabeth said at once.

Both brothers exchanged glances again, and Benjamin resumed his seat. "Perhaps we should tell you Gideon's history, that your powers of persuasion might be heightened," he said, and Sebastian nodded agreement.

They told her much she already knew, about their blustering, bullying father, a man poorly suited to affect any good in their mentally fragile mother. About how Gideon, from a tender age, had protected his mama and saw to her welfare until her death.

"Do you know about the one time Mama was a patient in the asylum?"

Elizabeth shook her head. "The one that burned?" she asked.

"Yes, we saw that as we drove past," Sebastian said. "And good riddance to it."

"That very one," Benjamin confirmed.

They told her that their mother had gone into some manner of decline when Gideon was around the age of eight. Their father, in typical response, had sent her to recover at the asylum. Gideon had insisted on visiting her, and when he came home again, Benjamin remembered his brother was white around the mouth, both from horror and rage.

"I never knew exactly what he saw there, for even in later years Gideon would not speak of it, other than to confirm our mama had been fixed to her bed with ankle chains to keep her from wandering the asylum wards. And she'd had nothing but one meager blanket wrapped around her as she'd waited for her clothes to dry following a dunking in a cold-water bath. Cold-water baths," Benjamin said, his face tight with disdain and doubt, "being frequent. They are supposed to shock the patient back into sensibility."

Sebastian took up the tale, explaining that Gideon had gone into their father's library, and although he was too young to remember it himself, Sebastian explained that raised voices had been heard. Gideon had received a caning for daring to shout at his father, and Papa had refused the boy's demands that Mama be returned home.

"Gideon stopped eating. Completely," Benjamin said, and there were echoes of those strident times in his eyes as he spoke. "Father said 'let him starve,' and he did. I tried to take food to him, sneaking it from the table in my pockets, but Gideon would not eat. 'I should rather starve than eat from a table that does not feed my mother,' he said to me, to the servants, to the doctor who was called in a week later, to our father. Over and over again. They spoke of forcing food into Gideon . . ." Benjamin's voice trailed away, and Elizabeth thought she saw a shudder course up his spine.

Sebastian took up the tale. "That is when Gideon began haunting our father. He would just stand before him, gaunt-faced, saying nothing, just staring. He received another caning, and then the doctor came and took Gideon away from the house. The doctor came again, two days later. Again there were shouts in the library. But the next day, Gideon and Mama both came home."

"And both ate at the table," Benjamin said. He gave a small, bitter laugh. "Although Gideon could only eat a half cup of broth and a single bite of bread. It took weeks for his appetite to return."

"But Mama never returned to the asylum," Sebastian said quietly.

"No, she never did," Benjamin agreed. He sighed. "Unfortunately, Gideon never lost that stubborn streak. He has it yet. It is what keeps him here, what keeps him from letting us help him."

Elizabeth looked up sharply. "You have offered to help?"

"Of course." Sebastian scowled. "But for all intents and purposes he has had the reins of this household in his hands since he was eight years old! He does not know how to apportion duty. I think he fears he is like Mama, that if he releases even a hint of control, he will begin to disintegrate."

"Gideon," Elizabeth said on a near whisper, a lump forming in her throat as she remembered the shadows she had seen in his silvered eyes.

"Yes, our stubborn, dutiful Gideon." Benjamin stared into the ashes of last night's fire on the grate. Sebastian rose to ring for a servant, murmuring about requiring something to eat after their travels.

Elizabeth lapsed into her own musing. Meeting Benjamin and Sebastian did not make her own leaving less painful, but she was glad, more than glad, that Gideon's brothers had returned. It seemed clear they would do all they could to break Gideon free of the prison this house had become for him.

Did the childhood tale, or his brothers' concern, prove Gideon was not mad like his mama? No. Certainly Society thought the man had inherited her terrible legacy. But Society had not spent any time in his company, had not looked into his compassionate gaze, had not seen the good Gideon did, that he could not seem to keep himself from doing even at a terrible cost to his own peace of mind. Elizabeth had seen these things . . . and if they were signs of madness, then let Society be entirely overrun by such madmen, for the world could use more men of Gideon's ilk.

Frick entered, rather than the servant with a luncheon tray whom Elizabeth had expected. A frown creased his face.

"What is it?" Benjamin asked, sounding as concerned as Elizabeth abruptly felt.

"A caller," Frick said, "a man who claims no acquaintance with Lord Greyleigh, but who insists he will wait in the entry for my lord, no matter how long it takes for him to return."

"His name?" Sebastian asked, also not smiling for once.

"Mr. Radford Barnes," Frick said.

Elizabeth sank back hard in her chair, black spots whirling before her eyes.

Chapter 18

Gideon pulled up his horse, realizing there was a second carriage in the drive before his home. It bore no crest, but it was a private vehicle, not one for hire. It seemed today was a day for callers.

He dismounted, lightheartedly tossing his reins to the nearest groom, who caught them with a grin. "Extra oats, m'lord?"

"Extra oats," Gideon confirmed, thinking the contentment he felt must be showing, or at least contagious. He had learned two things at the alderman's house, not just what must be done with this young woman calling herself Lily. He could not wait to tell Elizabeth what he suspected he knew.

He hurried from the stables to the rear of the house, hearing Benjamin's deep voice rumbling, then Frick's voice, sounding strained. Gideon came upon the butler just as the man announced, "Mr. Radford Barnes."

"Who?" Gideon said, stepping around Frick to follow in the wake of the dark-haired man who preceded him into the library. A quick glance proved there were equally blank faces on Sebastian and Benjamin as the dark-haired man bowed to them. They offered shallow bows in return.

"Mr. Radford Barnes," Frick repeated unhelpfully. "The . . . person insisted he must see you, my lord."

Gideon glanced at Elizabeth, and suddenly his good mood evaporated. He strode across the room, taking up her hand, alarmed by the lack of color in her face. "My dear!"

Elizabeth looked at him with horror in her eyes, in the way she held her shoulders. She was absolutely mute, her throat working without making a single sound. It was a simple thing to deduce who had just entered Gideon's library.

"Frick, please leave us and close the door," Gideon said, aware his voice had dropped to a growl.

Frick did as he was bid, collecting Radford Barnes's hat and gloves as he went out. The dark-haired, rather handsome man sauntered further into the room. "Lord Greyleigh," he said, beginning to bow, but then his vision settled on Elizabeth, and he offered her a bow as well.

"It *is* you!" Mr. Barnes said to Elizabeth. "I thought from what they said in the pubs that it had to be you, but I scarce dared hope."

"Hope?" Elizabeth rasped, her voice trembling. "You left me for dead in that ditch."

Gideon's gaze flew to take in the other man's reaction, now that it was confirmed this was the knave who had ruined and abandoned Elizabeth to her fate.

Gideon was across the room in a flash, the other man pinned against the wall next to the door, his coat caught in Gideon's two hands as Gideon shook the man like the cur Barnes was. "You have no business here," Gideon growled, even as his brothers crowded around him, their postures declaring they were prepared to support any action he chose. "Get out!"

"Not so quickly, Greyleigh," Barnes managed to get out even though there was a fist against his voice box. "That woman is my wife!"

Elizabeth made a strangled sound of protest, and Gideon pressed more firmly against the man's throat. Benjamin made a noise of disapproval, and Sebastian's face creased into lines of shock and puzzlement.

"Gideon," said Sebastian, "I do not know your quarrel with this man, but I would like to suggest he might not be worth the punishment of incarceration or hanging should you happen to kill him. I suggest you let him go, and that we escort him from the property. After a proper thrashing, if you like."

"Tell them," Gideon said to Barnes, giving him one final shake before letting the man go. "Tell them she is not your wife at all, you lying blackguard."

"Well, perhaps not in actual fact, not yet," Barnes said, putting a hand to his throat, from which issued the raspy words.

He flinched when Gideon made as if to seize him again, and quickly added, "But her stepmama wishes her to be."

"Stepmama?" Elizabeth echoed, and if color had been returning to her face, it was now gone again.

"Yes," Barnes said, straightening his cravat and the lie of his coat. "She has been visiting in Bath, and she saw me, unfortunately. I was forced to explain our, er, parting of the ways, my dear, and she was most displeased. She could not like what our . . . disassociation might mean to her consequence."

Barnes gave Gideon a long stare, then stepped to one side, where he could clearly see Elizabeth. "My dear, your stepmama has settled a handsome dowry on you. Our financial worries are past, so that now we can concentrate on cementing our bond, as she is most eager to see us do. Therefore, I now ask you to be my wife."

Gideon felt his jaw clench and his hands curl into fists, and it was all he could do not to smash Barnes's nose down his throat.

"Steady," Benjamin cautioned in his ear, a hand on Gideon's punching arm.

As awful as it was, Gideon had to admit that this offer by Barnes for Elizabeth would solve a great number of her difficulties. No one need ever know her elopement with Barnes had never ended in marriage. She would not be ruined. She could resume her position in Society. The two could lead entirely separate lives, living in different cities if they liked, taking lovers while living under the protection of the married state. Elizabeth would be foolish not to comply with her stepmama's scheme.

Do not do it, Gideon wanted to scream.

Elizabeth did not rise, but there was something in her posture, a lifting of the shoulders, a gleam in her eyes that made her seem to grow taller. It was clear she considered every word Barnes had spoken, that she realized the same advantages that Gideon had. All eyes fixed on her, awaiting her answer.

"You are lying," she said to Barnes, clearly, unemotionally.

"I assure you, I am not," Barnes protested, beginning to scowl.

"Yes, you are. As to my stepmama being humiliated by what has happened to me, that much is true. But what matters a step-daughter's foolishness? It has nothing to do with her, as she did not raise me. It is no reflection on her. She would be content enough to disown me. And Francine would never ask my father for the funds necessary to satisfy your excessive and craven needs, Radford. She does not love me well enough to be foolishly blackmailed on my account."

A hush fell over the room, a thick silence in which the clock on the mantel could be heard ticking.

"You only want your ring back," Elizabeth said, glancing down at the hand that no longer bore it. When she looked up again, there was fire in her gaze. "Once you had it from me, you would abandon me again. But that will never happen. I have the ring locked away, Radford. I will never give you the one piece of proof that you have lied to and deceived me." Her voice rose, becoming a command. "You will never speak of our association, never, or I shall take your ring to a magistrate who will force you to explain your actions in a court of law. When you have no defense against what you have done to me, you will find yourself in Newgate, where I will be happy to think of you rotting away."

"Elizabeth!" Gideon whispered in astonishment, knowing the truth when he heard it, proud of her for seeing past this man's lies and manipulations, proud of her for showing so little of the dread and aggravation she must be feeling. Many another woman would have succumbed to the hope of redemption, would have seized an offer of reputation-saving marriage, but not Elizabeth. Elizabeth's redemption would be of her own making.

Barnes glared down at her, any loverlike vestiges erased from his face. "You are exactly right, my dear. I want the ring. And I still know how to obtain it from you, how to make you hand it over to me. Have you forgot your sister?"

Elizabeth closed her eyes, as though he had struck her.

"I can still ruin her prospects with Mr. Broderick Mainworthy," Barnes said, his upper lip curling into a feral smile.

Gideon started to step forward, his hands curling as though to shape around Barnes's neck, but Benjamin grabbed him and held him back. "In war, it is best to know everything before you attack," he said, his quiet words scarcely making it through the fury fogging Gideon's brain.

"Do what you must," Elizabeth said to Barnes, rising from her chair to meet Barnes's stare, holding on to the small nearby table to maintain her balance. "To abet evil is to become evil, and not even for Lorraine can I allow myself to become like you, Radford Barnes. I must hope that Mr. Mainworthy is a more honorable and admirable man than are you, that he knows what love is."

"You are a fool to wager your future and your sister's against that flimsy hope," Barnes said angrily, preparing to depart. He crossed the room to stand before her, and before Gideon could move to intercept him, had already whispered something fiercely to her.

"Were I him," Sebastian said in his own whisper, "I would be threatening to make her father pay even more, to protect both daughters." His lip curled in distaste as he glanced again at Barnes.

"If I were such an ass as him, so would I." Benjamin said on a glower. With the hand not holding Gideon's arm, Benjamin reached to his belt, which normally would support the military sword he wore, but which he had naturally left in Frick's care upon entering the house.

Gideon glanced at Benjamin's gesture and shook his head. "Sebastian was right. This halfwit is not worth killing."

He shrugged off his brother's hand and crossed to Elizabeth's side. He stood between her and Barnes, forcing the other man to take a step back, and then another. Gideon brought up his right hand curled in a fist that he held before Barnes's face. "This scapegrace is not even worth hitting," he sneered directly into Barnes's face. "Not that I will let that stop me."

Gideon threw a short, sharp blow directly to Barnes's mouth, sending the man reeling backward, blood instantly gushing from a cut on his lip.

"You *bastard*!" Barnes lisped, blood all over the hand he pressed to his mouth.

Sebastian tossed the man his handkerchief. "Lud's sake, man, you are getting blood all over the carpet," he scolded. "Have you no manners?"

Gideon turned his back on Barnes, ignoring the stinging in his knuckles from the blow, and stepped back to Elizabeth's side. He took up both of Elizabeth's hands, gazing into her face.

"Elizabeth," he said with quiet firmness, "there is a way to thwart this cretin, if you wish it, and that is if you marry."

She shook her head emphatically. "I would never marry him, not now I know what manner of man he is."

"That is not what I meant. Will you marry *me*?"

Barnes snarled, and Benjamin stared.

"Ha!" Sebastian cried at once. "I see your logic, Gideon! If Elizabeth is married to you, she is shielded from whatever Barnes wants to claim against her. What he says only reflects poorly back on him. And if you cared to grant his rumormongering any credence by protesting it—which I would not be bothered to do myself—you could always then call him out and kill him in a duel, defending your lady's honor!" Sebastian crowed. "Although you would have to be careful not to be caught at dueling, because then you would have to flee England, of course. But it might be worth it." Sebastian gave Barnes a dark look. "Or if you did not wish to call him out, I would not mind taking ten paces with the creature myself."

"Elizabeth," Gideon said, smiling ever so slightly at his brother's words as he gazed down into her confusion-filled eyes. "You have not answered me."

"Gideon," she said, sounding poised despite hands that had begun to shake within his grasp. "You have saved too many people in your life already. I cannot allow you to throw your future away on me, for my sake."

"You cannot *allow* it?" he said, his mouth pursing to keep from giving her the fierce grin that threatened to cross his lips. "My, are we not haughty? But you misunderstand me, my dear lady. I do not want to throw my future away on you. I want to regain it." The humor faded, and he spoke in a low, urgent voice. "I want to laugh again. I want to let you run my household and manage my staff, because I am so very poor at it, despite all the years of practice. I want to keep you selfishly near me, to remind me that there is more to life than duty. You have opened my eyes to the realization that we must seek out those who need help, not those who want to take and take and give nothing back, like this churl here," Gideon said over his shoulder, to indicate Barnes.

Elizabeth looked down where his hands covered hers, blinking back tears. Or perhaps she felt his own hands trembling as though to match hers.

"There is something else you should know before you answer," Gideon went on, now able to share the news he had discovered when he had gone to call on the alderman. "I would not have you believe there is no other recourse but marriage left to you. Today, while I waited for Alderman Wallace to return to his home, I read the *London Times,* dated two days ago." He reached into his pocket and handed a folded piece of news sheet to her. "I thought this must pertain to you when I read the female's name, but I was sure of it when Barnes mentioned Mr. Mainworthy."

She unfolded the sheet with unsteady hands. "Sir Edmund and Lady Hatton," she began to read, only to look up at him, startled.

"Go on," he urged.

"Sir Edmund and Lady Hatton announced today the marriage by special license of their daughter, Miss Lorraine Hatton, to Mr. Broderick Mainworthy. The ceremony took place in St. Clement Dane's at ten in the morning. Wedding breakfast to follow, by private invitation only."

"Devil take it!" Barnes muttered, and now it was his turn for the color to leech from his face, his trump card played and defeated.

Elizabeth lowered the sheet and gave a small, incredulous laugh, tears of happiness forming in her eyes. "Lorraine? Married? I never could have imagined a hasty wedding between those two!"

"I think your sister must have been concerned for your future, my dear, ever since she would have found the note you left for her," Gideon said, ignoring Barnes completely, "and wished to clear an obstacle she knew would concern you if you were not so happy with your choice of 'groom.' Or perhaps she was inspired by your example of elopement. But come, either way," Gideon coaxed, "you still have yet to answer me, even now that you know your sister has found her happiness. Will you save yourself and stick your thumb in Barnes's eye, all in truth to save me from myself? Will you marry me?"

"You deserve someone better—"

"Who would that be?" he demanded.

"Someone . . . untainted."

Barnes snorted, but Gideon would not give him the satisfaction of looking at him, not even when there was the sound of a blow and a curse that implied one of Gideon's brothers had heard enough from Radford Barnes.

"Untainted? Do you mean someone like myself? Someone with no history of insanity in their blood?"

"You are not insane, Gideon."

"I could be, someday. We never know. But this is the sanest question I have ever asked. Elizabeth, will you have me?"

Uncertainty remained in her eyes. "You ask me to be impetuous," she said very softly. "But it is impetuosity that has brought me nothing but terrible heartache these weeks just past."

"It also brought you to this moment," Gideon pointed out. "To me."

"Yes," she said slowly. She reached to arrange the folds of his cravat, but when she raised her gaze back to his, something else had replaced the anguish that had been there. "We are both undeniably mad—"

"Then let us be mad together."

Elizabeth lifted her chin, and something in the look she gave him told him she knew what a concession he had just made, to not weigh the consequences, to let the future bring what it would, and to do this for himself. "Yes," she said. "Let us be mad together then. I will marry you, Gideon."

He let out a pent-up breath. "I hope all your decisions are not so long in coming," he complained, causing her to give a teary bubble of laughter as she leaned her forehead against his chest.

Gideon cupped her chin with a finger and lifted her face to his. He lowered his mouth to her lips and kissed her, not caring they had witnesses, caring only that she kissed him back.

"Tears?" he questioned when he lifted his mouth from hers, reaching to wipe a tear track from her cheek.

"Happy tears," she assured him, wrapping a hand around his wrist to pull it to her lips to plant a kiss there.

"Well, dear girl," Barnes interrupted, tossing the blood-stained handkerchief back at Sebastian, "I pray Greyleigh's offer of marriage is more sincere than mine ever was. Personally, I doubt it, since you are soiled goods—"

Gideon spun to face the man, and would have planted him another facer were it not for a sudden scream. The hair rose on Gideon's neck as he turned to see the red-haired girl standing in the library doorway, her mouth open, her scream turning into a name. "Radford!"

Barnes sucked in a breath sharply.

"Where the devil is Frick?" Benjamin asked in irritation, striding toward Lily. "Why is this girl unattended?"

Before Benjamin could reach her, Lily cried out again, a scream that turned into a long moaning wail, and she flew at Barnes, hands outstretched. "Where have you been?" the girl cried, almost incomprehensible in her agitation. "Please, Radford, I beg you, you have to help me with the baby!"

"Let me go, you . . . you creature!" Barnes cried, trying to pry Lily's hands from his coat.

As he loosed one hand, she grabbed him with the other, sinking down to her knees before him, her hands clutching at his breeches. She sobbed and repeated over and over, "My baby! I will give you money, all the money you want, but you must give me another baby!"

Elizabeth gasped audibly, her gaze flying from Lily to Barnes. "You cur!" she declared with loathing. "You seduced her, too, this child! She had your baby," Elizabeth accused with steely certainty.

"Nonsense!" Barnes cried, pale as chalk. "There is no proof of that!"

"There is proof that the girl had a lover, for she had his child," Gideon said.

"Not my child!" Barnes tried to squirm free of Lily's embrace, but was nearly tripped for his efforts. "Get this thing off me!"

"Yes, your child," Gideon said with certitude. "We all heard Lily call you by name! We all saw that the sight of you made her hysterical. I saw your response to her when she came in, that you knew her. These are proofs enough for court, and yet we have not even asked Lily's family for confirmation of your identity, which I highly suspect they could and will provide."

"What a farce! A fairy tale—"

"Alderman Wallace," Polly, the maid with the eyepatch, announced nervously from the library doorway.

"Ah! Here is the very man who was able to tell me a great deal about Lily. Let us see if Alderman Wallace thinks Lily's tale is to be believed," Gideon pronounced, waving the man in.

Barnes paled, still fighting against the hold Lily had on him, her moans and sobs buried against his legs. He only exceeded in tripping himself and falling to the carpet with a painful-sounding thud.

Alderman Wallace entered, spying Lily at once. "Good gad, what happens here?" he cried, looking between Lily and the sprawled man whose legs she clutched.

Gideon quickly explained that they all suspected Barnes was the man who had seduced Lily, fathered a child on her, and abandoned her.

Alderman Wallace eyed Barnes with disapprobation. "I daresay Lily's father, Mr. Tuttle of Westbury, will be able to tell us if this is true. The scoundrel who seduced his daughter also tried to blackmail him, only to discover the Tuttles are far less affluent than they appear to be. The man got not a groat for his trouble, and promptly abandoned poor Lily."

Barnes began to squirm again and got one foot free. He kicked at Lily once, but then Gideon's brothers descended on him, pinning him to the floor until Gideon could gently but firmly pry Lily from the man.

"Poor girl," Elizabeth said, sinking into her seat once more. She opened her arms, and Gideon led Lily into them, where the girl lowered her head to Elizabeth's lap, continuing to quietly sob.

Alderman Wallace went on to explain that Lily was never right, but when she took a lover who then deserted her and the child she was to have, her grasp on reality faded. When the child was born, her family took it from her in the night and fostered it out to a childless couple, telling Lily that the fairies had taken the babe. "I have heard from Mr. Tuttle myself that Lily has been seeking the infant's return from the fairies ever since."

The reason Wallace had spoken with Mr. Tuttle was simple enough. Four months earlier, Lily had wandered from her home, and no one had known where she went. Lily seemed to have disappeared, for even though her father rode from village to village for weeks, seeking word of the girl or a sighting of her, none were reported.

"As happens, sad to say, everyone began to assume the girl was dead. Her father stopped looking."

"How has she lived? Or eaten? Or slept?" Benjamin asked no one in particular. "How has she avoided being found?"

"If she lived in the hidden passages of this house, she left no sign of it. At least, not beyond her visitations," Gideon supplied. "But her presence in the passages explains a great deal about items that have been 'lost' and others that were 'found.' I know for a fact that Cook once had a wheel of cheese taken from the pantry."

"Ah! Our home's 'ghost,' " Benjamin said in comprehension.

"Exactly," Gideon said, turning his attention to Barnes, who had scrambled to his feet and was dusting his breeches and his coat with his hands. Gideon strode across the room, satisfied to see a look of alarm come over Barnes's face as Gideon raised his hand. But instead of hitting him, Gideon placed his hand in the center of Barnes's chest and shoved the man back until his knees hit a chair and he sank ungracefully to its surface.

"How dare you, sir!" Barnes cried. "I will not tolerate any more of your brutish brawling. I am leaving—"

"You go nowhere, sirrah," Gideon said in a dark voice, standing over Barnes with clenched fists. "You have to answer for what you have done to this poor creature." He pointed to Lily.

Gideon turned to Alderman Wallace. "Do you believe Mr. Tuttle would be willing to swear out a warrant for the arrest of Radford Barnes for attempted blackmail?"

Wallace looked from Gideon to Barnes, then nodded slowly. "I believe he would, my lord. His poor daughter has no reputation left to ruin. And I can only think it would not go amiss if Barnes was made to pay restitution for his acts!"

"Then I suggest you arrest Barnes today, or it is unlikely you will see his face again on English soil," Gideon warned.

"You cannot have me arrested!" Barnes shouted, sounding truly alarmed.

"Alderman Wallace can, under the law," Gideon said, turning from the man in dismissal, disgusted that anyone could use a young woman, little more than a child, so cruelly as Barnes had used Lily.

Elizabeth still held the red-haired girl, Elizabeth's expression torn between sympathy for Lily and gratification that Barnes must answer for his deeds. "He will go to prison?"

"Or be transported, if he is not hanged," Gideon assured her.

"No!" Barnes screamed, leaping up from the chair. He dashed for the library door, but Sebastian put out a foot and tripped him, sending him sprawling. Benjamin had Barnes's arm up behind his back with a military precision, pinning the howling man to the floor.

"Get him out of here," Gideon growled.

"I've a lockroom in my barn where we can keep him until he can be delivered to the Assizes," Wallace offered, and Gideon nodded his thanks.

Benjamin wrestled Barnes to his feet and out into the hall. "You there, bring rope!" Gideon heard Benjamin call out to a footman.

Confusion broke out then, for Frick entered, frantically seeking Lily. It seemed the girl had faked sleeping, and the maids assigned to watch her had been distracted by kitchen duties. Lily began to sob anew when she was lifted to her feet and led away. Alderman Wallace was thanked by Gideon, and then took his leave, just as two maids arrived at the library door with fully loaded trays filled with the luncheon Sebastian had ordered some time before.

"This room smells of knave's blood," Sebastian said, wrinkling his nose. "I would far rather eat in the dining room now," he instructed the maids.

Chaos reigned for several long moments more, but then just as suddenly as they had all filled the room, now everyone was quit of it except for Gideon and Elizabeth. They turned to one another with stunned expressions.

Elizabeth took a deep breath and gave her head a little shake, as though to clear it of cobwebs. She folded her hands together, perhaps striving to appear calm. "Now is your opportunity to recant your offer," she said to Gideon.

"Do you mean speak now or forever hold my peace?" Gideon asked, looking at her from where he stood across the room. "The same is true for you. We need not marry, I think, to protect you anymore. Barnes is done in."

"Exactly my point," Elizabeth said, rising to her feet despite her injured heel. "*I* am one of Barnes's indiscretions. I cannot imagine what your brothers must think of me, or of your pre-cipitate offer to me."

"I can. Benjamin is horrified, because he does not know you and doubtlessly thinks you an adventuress, and Sebastian is de-lighted by the idea of our marrying for the very same reason." Gideon smiled at her, to take any sting from the words, even as he slowly crossed the room and took up both her hands. "You do not have to change your mind now, not unless it is some-thing *you* wish to do."

She shook her head. "Of course I do not wish to change my mind, even though it would be the intelligent thing to do. We would be fools to plunge ahead with this demented scheme. Yet, I wish to plunge ahead. How can I like you so well, when I know you so little?"

"Because I am very charming," Gideon said, and then they both had to laugh.

Their laughter soon trailed away, however, and Gideon stepped even closer to her. He did not ask any sort of permis-sion, but pulled her into his arms. After a long, searching look at her face, he pressed his lips to hers, and both knew it was a kiss that sealed a pledge between them.

He raised his head, met her tremulous smile with one of his own, and kissed her again. When, some minutes later, he finally took half a step back, there was a different manner of smile on her mouth and a slow fire in her eyes.

"Look at them," came Sebastian's voice from the doorway, causing the occupants of the room to spin and find him casually propped against the doorjamb, Benjamin gazing over his shoulder. "Light and dark. I tell you, Benjamin, their children will be striped like skunks!"

There was no answer to that, of course, except to laugh anew, and then for Gideon to reintroduce his bride-to-be to his brothers, because she could now lay claim to a surname.

Chapter 19

Elizabeth waved and tossed an airy kiss from the phaeton toward her happily weeping sister, her new brother-in-law, Broderick, and Papa. Her stepmama remained in London, just recovering from the grippe, which occasion had suited Elizabeth at least as well as it must have suited Francine. Elizabeth tossed another kiss, then turned to find Gideon still in conversation with Benjamin.

"That bottom field will need draining," Benjamin was saying. "I was thinking of—"

"Hush, Benjamin!" Elizabeth said in mock severity as she slipped her hands over Gideon's ears. "Gideon is on his bridal journey. He does not need to hear one more word about the home farm."

"He asked!" Benjamin protested.

Gideon looked from his bride to his brother and said, "Do with the field as you see fit."

Benjamin nodded and gave a rare smile. "See you in two months. That is, if I am able to transfer my service to Bristol. Otherwise, you must call upon me in London."

"We will," Gideon assured him. "Unless we like Bath or Brighton so well that we settle and never continue our journeying."

"Come now, good fellow, you must return here. Sebastian is not nearly so clever as you, and certainly nowhere near so clever as your wife. The estate will eventually suffer at your absence. More important, you cannot deprive Severn's Well of its ghost and its madman all at once, can you?" Benjamin teased.

"I suppose not." Gideon rattled the reins and clucked to the horses, setting them in motion. "There is the family reputation to keep up, after all," he called over his shoulder as the carriage rolled away from Greyleigh Manor.

Benjamin laughed, and Elizabeth turned to wave one last time to Lorraine and Papa. She sighed happily when she turned to face forward once more, her husband of two days beside her.

Gideon glanced at her. "I am glad we found your topaz earbobs. They suit your coloring and of course the dress."

It was the same dress that Elizabeth had been married in, a sunny yellow one ordered from the Severn's Well modiste while Elizabeth had lived at Lady Sees's, awaiting Lorraine and Papa's arrival at Greyleigh Manor. Gideon had not wanted any whispers of a lack of chaperonage until they were married, which had been exceedingly amusing to Elizabeth. How many times had he held her close, carrying her, sometimes while she wore nothing more than a thin night rail? And had he not held her while a servant had stripped her of her clothing? Still, it was the thought that mattered, and Elizabeth had docilely gone to Lady Sees's, where she had happily learned that the maid she had recommended had been hired.

"We will see that you have plenty of other new dresses," Gideon told Elizabeth now.

She slipped her arm through his, laying her head against his shoulder. "I have everything I want already."

"Flatterer," he teased, but the warmth in his gaze made Elizabeth long for the night ahead, when she could lie in his arms once more and know she was not wicked as she had imagined, but only very, very lucky.

"Tell me, my dearest Elizabeth," he said, and she was glad to hear the excitement coursing through his voice, the joy he could not hide at leaving Greyleigh Manor for this tour of England together. "Is there anything you regret? Would you change our courtship, if you could?"

"Not one moment of it," she said with conviction, and when he smiled down at her, she knew he felt exactly the same.